THE CLEPSYDRA

A novel by

Derek Olsen

Aurora Books, an imprint of Eco-Justice Press, L.L.C.

Aurora Books
P.O. Box 5409 Eugene, OR 97405
www.ecojusticepress.com

The Clepsydra
by Derek Olsen

Library of Congress Control Number: 2018968500
ISBN: 978-1-945432-29-3

For my spiritual teachers.

(Isn't that everybody?)

This novel is both a work of fiction and an allegory. The author in no way intends to represent the actual views or practices of any religious organization, creed or identity. All interpretations of religious texts given are strictly imaginative and not to be taken as instructional or used to question or obscure the interpretations of those texts held by their respective religious traditions.

By the sky and the night visitor—
What will explain to you what the night visitor is?
It is the piercing star
Truly, there is a watcher over every soul

Man should reflect on what he was created from:
He is created from water pouring forth,
Then he emerges from between the backbone and the
breastbone
God is certainly able to bring him back to life

On the Day when secrets are laid bare
He will have no power and no one to help him

By the sky and its recurring rain
And by the earth that splits open—
This is truly the final word

The Quran, Surah 86

Chapter 1

Waves of love resounded through the sacred pond followed by an exuberant crocodile roar. The air was muggy and hot, but the lusty sounds of nature softened the Sub-Saharan heat like steam in a sauna. From the depths of an adjoining swamp, two amorphous, gray heads slapped vigorously upon the water's surface sending ripples in all directions.

"They are mating," the guide explained to Amara, the mysterious robed woman who had hired him. He tilted his head in admiration. "If you watch them closely, you will feel the passion in their movements. It is like beautiful poetry."

The robed Amara grimaced. She clutched a Taser concealed in the pocket of her robe.

"Do I have your word that these crocodiles are...*peaceful?*"

"I swear to it on my own life," assured the guide.

She knew that he suspected nothing. *All is going according to plan.*

"You see," the guide continued, "each time a child is born to us, a crocodile is born to its mother here. From then on, the crocodile carries the soul of that child. It is a sacred bond that all Mossi people share! Throughout our lives our crocodile watches over us, protects us and nurtures us, until one day, after many years, we die. And as we die, our crocodile also dies."

As she listened, Amara adjusted the sash around her colorful, hand-woven robe. It was the heirloom she treasured above all others. Covered with bold geometric motifs, each square and line and polychrome curve woven into the robe's fabric was a rich and textured expression of her Andalusian heritage. It was a garment that might have made one suffer who was less acquainted with the sweltering heat.

"I thought Nile crocodiles were supposed to be bigger," she sneered.

"Look around you! Are we in the Nile?" The swamp gurgled. "Hundreds of generations have passed since crocodiles first came to this pond. And after all that time they asked themselves, *why grow so large when you live in this small pond*?"

"I see."

"That is why our crocodiles have never harmed a human being."

"Never?"

"Creatures with great strength breed among the toughest elements of nature. But we have no need for that. We are peaceful. All we desire is right here in this pond."

The robed one slowly removed her Taser and pointed it at the guide's brawny torso.

"What are you doing?"

"What I desire is also right here in this pond."

The guide became stern, barely flinching.

"What is it that you want?"

"I want you to surrender these crocodiles to me and load them onto my caravan. If you do this peacefully I will cause no harm."

The guide puffed out his chest.

"Who are you to threaten me?"

She aimed the Taser at his face.

"These crocodiles will make an excellent army. The Watcher will be pleased."

"Army? Listen, outsider! Our crocodiles will not serve any army. Leave our village at once!"

The robed one gazed menacingly into the large man's eyes. In a flash she fired the Taser into the swamp, electrifying one crocodile and startling the rest. The sacred animal groaned as it turned over in the water.

"Stop! Please!"

Amara lowered her weapon.

"War is imminent, and victory is upon us. Do not get in our way."

"Where? I don't see any war!"

"Every village on earth is connected. Even yours. When one struggles to make peace, the whole earth feels it."

"No. Our village does not concern you. Go back to France."

"We are from Spain."

"France, Spain, you are all the same. Outsiders!"

A cunning smile dawned on the robed one's face.

"Your village is more important to God's plan than you realize."

"God's plan," he repeated with disdain. "What plan?"

"Just do as I say. The Watcher has God on his side, and God knows only victory. He is not someone you want to go up against."

The rainbow-striped pleats on Amara's robe shook with authority as she spoke.

"But why does your army want our crocodiles anyway? They are not fighters!"

"You assured me that these crocodiles are peaceful."

"So?"

"For an army that exists to bring peace on the Last Day, they are the perfect recruits."

The robed one concealed her weapon. The sacred pond rippled anxiously as the crocodiles scattered and the heat began to take its toll.

The struggle for peace was just beginning.

Derek Olsen

Chapter 2

A troupe of preteen prep students circled round the majestic water clock in the center of Nanaimo's Woodgrove Center Mall. It was designed like a transparent skyscraper. Inside its rectangular frame were four giant silver pendulums kept in motion by the pouring of water from four silver spinning wheels. The structure had four clock faces at the top, stylized with golden hands, and bold Roman numerals. Each face was illuminated from the inside by a faint yet effective lamp. The tower was a work of art—a tower of remarkable engineering—whose ancient ingenuity and inspired design were of unparalleled importance to human history.

"This timepiece," explained the teacher, a robust nun of indeterminable age, "is one of only two water clocks in British Columbia. Also called a *clepsydra,*"—the eager bunch quickly jotted down the word—"a water clock tells time using a series of tubes and siphons. They pour water at precise intervals, moving the hands entirely by hydraulics. In medieval Spain, clepsydras were used as timing mechanisms to regulate the channeling of water from the reservoirs. This made it possible for each place to receive an exact amount of irrigation in its time of need. Along with shadow-based clocks such as the sundial, the water clock represents one of the oldest methods of keeping time known to humankind." A breath of awe struck the group at once. They gazed up from all directions at the clock's four faces.

Close by, a slender man of thirty-two stood bedazzled by the way these children took to their teacher. He was Tariq Kamal, a linguist from the University of Washington in Seattle. Tariq had come to Vancouver Island in search of a vital informant to his research: a woman known as the Waymaker. The Waymaker was the chief elder of the elusive Quoquamish tribe, and Tariq was the linguist assigned to investigate and document the language of the Quoquamish people. The Waymaker, however, held a somewhat mythical status: no one outside the tribe had ever seen her. The academic community was not convinced she even existed! Still, the research had to be done; it was up to Tariq Kamal to prove the skeptics wrong.

Until recently, in fact, the last of the full-blooded Quoquamish were thought to have died out over a hundred years ago. Because of this, it was believed that they had carried their indigenous language to the grave. However, in recent months there was talk of the Waymaker and several other Quoquamish coming out of hiding and speaking out against inter-tribal hatred and genocide. Mysterious pamphlets and editorials appeared and circulated, all of which were credited to the Waymaker. Even photographic evidence of hidden villages located in the Canadian wilderness uncharted by any modern map or satellite began to appear.

All of these signs pointed to one of the greatest ethnographic wonders ever to come to light in the Pacific Northwest—a First Nations tribe who had hidden itself completely from the world's eye for an entire century! Naturally, the prospect of being first linguist to document the lost Quoquamish language was presently Tariq's most promising ambition. Such excitement it brought him to think of finding and meeting the Waymaker! What a journey of discovery, a journey of scholarship and challenge. However, like any journey wherein knowledge was the goal, he was sure that it would present many unexpected detours. As he stood beside the water clock observing the nun with her students, he realized that this was one such detour.

"Who can explain how a siphon works?" the nun asked.

Hands flew into the air. Then the nun pointed to a petite girl with dark, elliptical eyes, who answered:

"The water moves up because a vacuum is created inside a tube that is placed under the water's surface. Then, a change in pressure keeps the water flowing upward. It stops only when the mass of the water in the receiving container is equal to the mass of the water in the original container."

"And for us"—interjected the nun—"the key word is *when!*"

Without warning, the water clock began to chime. It startled the ring of folks who had been secretly listening to the nun's riveting lecture. Ironically, when they heard the chime they all glanced at their own watches out of reflex. Then they casually dispersed. Tariq clutched his blue fedora and lowered his head a few degrees. His hands fidgeted in his jeans' pockets, worried someone would notice him listening in. This wouldn't have been the first time he was caught eavesdropping in public. Fortunately, the intensity of the class's concentration was unyielding. Tariq the linguist was but a shadow on the wall to them, silent and unassuming.

"You see, class, the genius of the scientist is not that she can test and describe the laws of nature, but that she can orchestrate the timing of these laws and utilize their effects for a higher purpose."

The nun paused, gently rubbing a wooden necklace that rested just below her collarbone. Her eyes drifted slowly downward as she entered a state of profound contemplation.

"It is written," she continued, "that there is a time for everything and a season for each activity under the sun."

Holding her inward gaze, the nun stood impeccably still. She turned her palms face-up, as if summoning a force that could part the waters of the Strait of Juan de Fuca. Without hesitation her students likewise cast down their eyes and began to quote the scripture in unison:

A time to be born and a time to die, a time to plant and a time to uproot...

Thoughts raced around in Tariq's curious mind. He had thought about this scripture verse before. Birth and death, planting and uprooting—for the linguist these concepts had literal and metaphorical meanings. They reminded him of his departed grandfather, who had immigrated to Seattle from Pakistan during the 1960's. Tariq's grandfather was an activist and a devout Muslim who fought to preserve the legacy of his faith and culture, including the Urdu language, for as long as he lived. In the wake of war and terrorism in the early 21st century, Tariq's grandfather rose as a prominent voice in the movement to heal the world of its prejudice against Islam—not the warped and war-torn ideology that condoned violence but the peaceful, compassionate Islam, the true Islam.

...A time to kill and a time to heal, a time to tear down and a time to build up...

Tariq had learned from his grandfather to appreciate the side of history often neglected by the western perspective: throughout history, Muslim empires were among the most tolerant and respectful of human life. Under Islamic rule, people of all faiths were allowed to practice their religions openly without reprimand or scorn. Furthermore, Islamic scholars of the middle ages were more scientifically advanced than any western civilization. The early Muslims were the first to map the human circulatory system, discovered algebra and trigonometry, and built ingenious circuits of irrigation to grow the gardens of the Alhambra; indeed, this was the hydraulic technology that would lead to the creation of the time-telling water clock—the clepsydra—that stood before him.

Proudly, Tariq's grandfather had taught him to stay true to Islam's legacy of peace and tolerance even in the face of blame and misunderstanding. He taught Tariq to think critically about the words people said and to seek a deeper understanding of what they believe. "Most of what people believe is true," his grandfather would say. "We only disagree with them because we get lost in interpreting their words." Indeed, Tariq knew that words meant different things to different people. Nevertheless, language was a gateway to understanding people's beliefs. Acquiring a new language, he believed, was akin to romancing the hearts and minds of its speakers. This underlying romance that inspired Tariq to document languages, especially ones as mysterious and aloof as the Quoquamish language. "Only when you understand the beliefs of all believers," his grandfather also said, "will you see the beautiful traces of Allah in every human being."

...A time to weep and a time to laugh, a time to mourn and a time to dance...

For the most part, Tariq's upbringing was secular. In contrast with the tenacious beliefs of his grandfather, his parents had never forced religion upon him. They allowed him to pursue academia without the slightest obligation to spiritual inquiry. His parents did not even emphasize the five spiritual pillars of Islam—the recognition of the One Supreme God; the five daily prayers that make up *salat*; the giving of alms to the poor; the observance of fasting during the holy month of Ramadan; and the *hajj*, the spiritual pilgrimage to Mecca. Instead, Tariq was left to investigate these matters for himself and weigh their truth within his own heart. After all, what were these lessons but words taught from one person to another? And what was to say he could ever understand the words alone without having direct experience?

At times it seemed ironic—even tragic—that in its tolerance this soft form of Islam was left to a constant vulnerability: each new generation of Muslims would be left to discover the faith through their own reason and judgment rather than through obligatory worship. Still, Islam was growing in all corners of the world, begging to be understood for its deeper truth, crying out for its followers to demonstrate the kind peace that human history had shown to be so fragile.

...A time to scatter stones and a time to gather them, a time to embrace and a time to refrain...

For Tariq, growing up almost entirely among non-Muslims, religion had always been a somewhat uncomfortable topic. At the most subtle level, it was the looks people gave him. They didn't see him first as a scholar or a Pakistani-American but as simply a Muslim, an outsider. Nothing beyond that seemed to matter. After all, when terror struck the twin towers of New York City, where did the fingers point? When bombs and shootings swept the streets of Paris, London, and countless other cities, where was the fear directed? The victims of these unforgivable acts were left to harbor a cold, undiscerning desire for vengeance; and this desire would lead Muslims everywhere to shoulder the wrath that should have been reserved for those few shameful, guilty attackers and their leaders.

And on a deeper level, it riled his bones—as a Muslim and as a linguist—that society was unable to distinguish between the word *Islamic*, meaning related to the actual religion, and the word *Islamist*, meaning related to the kind of violent extremism that was undeniably egregious in the eyes of Islam. Perhaps the most offensive case of this was the politically deceitful name of the militant group ISIS, which the world had chosen to call an 'Islamic' state. If anything, it was an *Islamist* one. It was such a simple linguistic corruption! And yet it successfully persuaded millions of people to fear Islam, fear the Middle East, fear the language and culture of millions of peaceful Muslims. It taught people to assume that words, rather than the underlying beliefs of the heart, must define our shared reality.

But maybe, Tariq thought, *my work as a linguist will affirm what Grandfather taught. Maybe it will affirm that our aim in life is not to judge others by labels and categories but to show tolerance and seek to understand them. I wonder if the Quoquamish went into hiding for this very reason. Perhaps they long for the kind of open-hearted investigation that only a linguist can endeavor, one who can read into their language carefully enough to see the true people and not get lost in the interpretation of words.* The linguist let out a sigh. *Each language has the power to shape our beliefs, for better or for worse. If we could only find a common language, we might reconcile the differences between cultures everywhere.*

He continued listening to the recitation.

...A time to search and a time to give up, a time to keep and a time to throw away...

As the nun and her pupils continued, the liquid of the water clock seemed to trickle through Tariq's mind like a soothing mantra. Images of the nun, the wooden necklace, the clock's four faces, and the children's eyes all swirled around in front of him, stirring up a vision of the completeness of all life—it was a vision of Nature and its timeless cycles of birth and rebirth. His vision led him to contemplate these matters even further: *It all ends eventually, doesn't it? War and death eat up everything under the sun. While we are living we move the world forward as much as we can according to our ideals. And then we die, letting new life advance it farther than we could have carried it ourselves. In each of us, also, a season is measured. And when it's finished, time will cease. Like withering petals and fallen leaves, we too will someday find our place in the dust.* And yet these thoughts came to him not in despair but as a sort of awakening into eternity, into completeness, and into a timeless awareness that could not be measured.

...A time to tear and a time to mend, a time to be silent...

Tariq basked in his bittersweet awareness for as long as he could. He let the flowing water relax his senses and slow his racing mind. For a brief interval, or so he believed, the gushing sound of the water clock nearly brought time to an absolute stop. It was a complete hypnosis! *If I open my eyes, right now*, Tariq the observer wondered, *will time itself have come to a standstill?*

...And a time to speak...

The voices of an elderly man and woman interrupted his trance. They were standing behind Tariq, talking in another language. When he heard their words, the linguist's mind hurried into linguistic analysis mode. He tried to identify the language. He listened to the phonetics of its vowel and consonant sounds and tried to parse where each word began and ended. He reflected on the language's rhythmic intonation, which seemed to slide effortlessly off the tongue like waves

falling upon the shore. Based on these observations, he figured the language was probably Nanaimo or Lushootseed or
some other Coast Salish dialect native to the Pacific Northwest. But his hypothesis was tenuous—he needed more evidence. Like sand collecting the incoming waves, he continued
to take in their words.

"She doesn't know," the old woman scoffed, switching to
English. "She doesn't understand."

"She may understand enough to *slow down* time," the old
man assured her, "but not enough to *manipulate* it, let alone
reverse it."

"As if the Christians didn't have anything left to pillage
from us. Now they are after our ability to move through time!"

"You're right. We went into hiding to prevent this very
situation from happening."

"I don't know who is to be feared more: them, or the Muslims."

Tariq's heart skipped a beat. *Do they know I can hear them?*

"It's a mess, this imbalance between religions," the old man
grumbled. "And what is the value of 'religion,' eh? It leads only
to division and opposition. When people of one religion make
alliances with each other, they grow their resistance against
everyone else. And all the while it is we who end up pulling
the two worlds back into balance."

"Grumble all you like about the politics of opposition,"
the woman retorted, "it's the crisis of the heart that makes
me nervous. Under pressure the heart races like a humming-
bird's wings, but in shock it stands still like a grizzly up in
arms. Each year we see its rhythm distorted to even greater ex-
tremes. Too fast or too slow, it is all unnatural. If the human
heart can't keep a balanced beat, then—"

"Time itself will come to an end!"

"And the earth will have nothing left to do but weep."

The couple then switched back to their native tongue, and
Tariq continued to wonder. *What are they talking about?*

The recitation had ended, and the now distracted observer

carefully opened his eyes. The nun and her troupe were gone, but Tariq sensed the elderly Salish couple still behind him. The sounds of the clepsydra gushed and rippled in his awareness, echoing a slow, steady whisper in his heart.

The voices of the Salish couple began to trail off. They were leaving.

"We must track down every last nun from the Order of the Libraries," declared the old man in his subtle Salish accent. "We must stop them from abusing Nature by slowing down time."

Tariq watched them leave, listening as intently as he could to their fading voices. And then, just when they were out of range, Tariq heard a bellowing whisper:

"Go with them."

He froze. *Who is there?*

The voice reverberated in Tariq's mind like a whisper in an empty tomb; as clear and intentional as any human utterance. Yet it came from the direction of the water clock. Indeed, despite all reasonable explanation, the voice had come from the water clock itself.

Go with them.

The clepsydra had spoken.

Derek Olsen

Chapter 3

The sun was setting. Amara, the mysterious visitor with the colorful robe, escorted her army of sacred crocodiles out of the pond and into twelve queen-bed-sized cages stacked together upon her caravan's six cars. It was an elegant procession. Gentle snorts and hisses filled the air while the whole Mossi village watched in silent lament. The Watcher's army was getting its crocodiles, and there was nothing they could do to stop it.

The Watcher was clever to pick such a village for the harvest. No one among them had the slightest inclination to fight back. Outwardly the Mossi people hid their sadness and grief. Inwardly they worried. *How will we live without the sacred crocodiles as our guardians?* A little child in ragged clothing grabbed his mother by the legs. *Who will watch over this lonely soul?*

The crocodiles, likewise, bore their capture respectably. They followed the robed one back to the caravan without nooses or restraints. Not one of them protested its call to war.

Night fell. The heat was disappearing quickly. Claws inched their way across the dry, dusty landscape. Tails swayed stoically, and teeth withdrew submissively into the majesty of each scaly maw. Their wise reptilian eyes glistened with an inexplicable sense of knowing.

Naomi Rivera, the zoologist, was waiting at the caravan. She evaluated the crocodiles one by one as they entered their cages, checking for signs of disease and attrition. All was well—strangely well—for in her twenty-year career caring for reptiles she had never treated such docile creatures.

The last of the crocodiles brought into the caravan was the largest one of all, just over seven feet long and full of girth. He was the only one who would not fit in a cage with the others; instead, he would be strapped to the top of the jeep that led the caravan.

While they prepared the ropes, the old crocodile lifted his snout and heaved out a yawn like a sleepy dog.

"That one is mine," the guide told Amara, pointing at the beautiful reptile. "He has watched over my soul since I was a baby in my mother's arms. He is trying to make me look at him, but I won't. I can't look."

The guide choked with sadness while his guardian reptile was pinned down to the roof with heavy-duty chicken wire. With the help of the zoologist, Amara tied it just tightly enough to hold him in place.

"Seogo!" he cried, bending at his knees for a moment. Then he wiped his eye and stood up straight again. "His name means *rainy season*. Do you know why I call him that?"

The robed one shook her head.

"During the dry season all the lakes whither up, and the rivers and swamps vanish—all except one pond, which keeps a small amount of water year round. This is where the crocodiles live, and it is why we live here with them. Each year, at about this time, after the dry heat has scorched us all, Seogo disappears from the pond. Then, after a few days, he returns and brings flowing streams and rain with him. You see, Seogo brings us our rainy season." The guide's eyes turned scornful. "Without Seogo, we won't have enough water to survive."

"Oh, but you will have water, I assure you!"

"How can you know this? Have you lived our history? Have you suffered through our dry seasons?"

"My family has seen more of history than you would ever believe!" she blurted out. "But history itself may not move forward if the Watcher does not have his army."

The guide furrowed his brow and winced. The sun reflected off of his shiny, bare forehead. Amara let go of her concealed weapon and placed her hands on the man's shoulders in good faith.

"Listen to me," she continued. The sleeves of her colorful robe billowing in the gentle breeze. "It is said that Allah created every living creature from water pouring forth. Do you not believe this?" She looked the man in the eye and then brought her lips close to his ear without touching him. "Endure and have faith, my brother. Truly, He who made you from water shall return you to water."

The guide glared at her, grabbed her hand and placed it over his heart. She could feel the rough, frayed threads of his tattered shirt.

"This is what I believe," he told her. "The God who watches over our village will be just and merciful and compassionate. And on the Last Day He who watches over outsiders like you will also be merciful and compassionate…and just."

Derek Olsen

Chapter 4

The clepsydra's voice echoed in Tariq's mind like an invitation from another realm: *Go with them*. He tried to convince himself that it was the voice of his intuition, and yet he found it strange that it resounded so vividly, as if it had come from outside him. *Could it really have come from the water clock?* The more he considered its words, *go with them*, the greater the anxiety surged through his spine. Tariq had never been one capable of acting immediately upon his thoughts, even thoughts as intriguing as this one. He always overanalyzed things. *If I follow that elderly couple, what will I say to them? Will they care that I have been eavesdropping all this time?* He stood still for what felt like a restless eternity. His willpower was paralyzed. His journey was stalled. Eventually he mustered up the courage to turn around and obey the water clock's instruction. *Go with them.*

Tariq sensed the old Salish couple moving farther and farther away from him. He walked quickly and trailed them, all the while racking his brain for a way of introducing himself. The couple proceeded down the main corridor of the mall, continuing a conversation that the linguist could no longer overhear. He followed them through the food court, past a slough of stores, through crowds of unsuspecting consumers, and into an antique print shop at the end of the mall.

The Salish couple wandered through aisles of inks and parchments looking for something. Trying to evade their attention, Tariq picked up a book from a nearby table—a history of the antique printing press—and hid his nose behind it. After a few seconds Tariq lowered the book to find the old man and woman glaring at him. A shiver went down his spine. *They caught me. I am finished. How will I excuse myself from this shameful chase?* Not wanting to appear rude, he quickly closed the book, forged a calm composure and removed his blue fedora.

"Good day, sir, ma'am."

The two of them did not respond but stared at him. Their bodies were perfectly still, almost like holograms, except they cast shadows along the shop's tile floor.

"You're probably wondering why I am following you." His teeth all but chattering. "I admit, I was too shy to approach you at first, but I promise I am nothing more than a harmless eavesdropper."

Tariq's attempt at being playfully direct was apparently unsuccessful. His palms sweated. *Did I say the wrong thing? Did I blow my chance?* The couple just kept staring.

"I am sorry for the intrusion," he attempted again, "I only heard you talking in front of the water clock and was listening to your language. I also heard you discussing religion and nature and *slowing down time*, and I was curious—"

"You're lagging behind us," interrupted the woman, gesturing at her watch. "It's time you caught up."

"I don't understand. Lagging behind?"

Suddenly a light flashed before his eyes. All the sounds and images around him began to accelerate. People zoomed right and left and in and out of the shop, and they spun round his field of view like the swift oscillations of a fan. Their words and the sounds of their footprints were slurred together into a continuous white noise. Somehow everything he could see and hear was being fast-forwarded through time. And yet, despite the overstimulation of his senses, a breath of release blew through him. Then, before he could draw any kind of conclusion as to what was going on, it all stopped. Time resumed its normal pace.

"What happened?"

"You caught up."

"Caught up? What do you mean? Who are you?"

"I am the Windstepper," announced the woman, undulating her hands as if to still an errant breeze. "And this is Gray Fin."

"Don't answer his questions!" criticized Gray Fin.

"Why not?" asked the Windstepper, scratching her head.

"To explain would be a waste of time."

"But I need to know!" exclaimed Tariq. "How did you make time go so fast?"

"We didn't," Gray Fin answered tersely.

"What my husband means," corrected the Windstepper, "is that time was already slowed down. We didn't speed it up, we just returned it to its natural pace." She snapped her fingers for effect.

Tariq scratched his head. "What do you mean, time was already slowed down?"

"Another question!" whined Gray Fin.

"We noticed you in front of the water clock. If you recall, the nun was there too. Did you notice how you felt when you stood near her?"

"Yes," the linguist answered. "It was like I was caught in eternity and nothing could happen."

"Exactly." The Windstepper scratched her forearm. "That is the hypnosis of the Order of the Libraries."

Tariq struggled to believe what they were telling him. But, as any good linguist would do, he waited to interpret the entire explanation until he could understand how their words might correspond with his own notions of what was real and what was possible. He knew there must be some kind of underlying truth to be uncovered. It was simply a matter of clarifying the meaning.

"So, you are saying that the nuns can actually make time slow down?"

"Yes."

"How?"

"They use water clocks."

"What kind of water clocks?"

"Any kind."

"Like what?"

"The usual kind. The kind the Christians use."

Tariq realized this line of questioning was getting nowhere. To start with, he couldn't be sure he understood the semantics of the terms they were using. What was their concept of time? What was their concept of slow versus fast? Who did they include in the category of 'Christians,' and why did they presume the Christians had a 'usual' kind of water clock? Indeed, these questions were opening up too many unknowns. If Tariq was going to understand them, he would have to get at their underlying beliefs. He would have to ask a deeper question.

"Why are they doing this? Why are they slowing down time?"

"We don't know," answered Gray Fin. "Frankly, we don't understand religion. Not Christianity, not Islam, none of it."

"Islam?" he said in outburst.

"You see," the old man continued, "we catch the Christians trying to slow down time, while the Muslims try to quicken it. This puts them constantly at odds with each other. Imagine yourself being sped up and slowed down over and over again. It's a violation of the laws of Nature! But we, our tribe, must stop them all. Time is an ever-flowing, everlasting stream, and yet each religion thinks it owns the whole ocean! That is why we have come out of hiding. It's the worst our tribe has ever seen."

Tariq's eyebrows rose with intrigue. "Are you the Quoquamish?"

The elders smiled and nodded. The shining of their eyes confirmed that these were the Quoquamish people Tariq had been seeking.

"Can you help me find the Waymaker?"

"That depends on what you can give us in return," answered Gray Fin.

"You can help us!" the Windstepper interjected. She leaned in and pinched the collar on his shirt.

"How?" asked Tariq.

"You are a hero!"

Gray Fin scoffed.

"A hero?" Tariq repeated.

"You have an aura about you I can't quite explain," the Windstepper said, probing her fingers in the air in front of him as if to read his heart with her hands. "It's a kind of peace that comes from within, I think. We can see it in your body and hear it in your words."

"My words?"

"Your words are very genuine," admitted Gray Fin. "And yet I can tell that you are not attached to your words. You are not limited by your words. They flow through your brain, and yet you never let them completely define how you see the world. Because of this, you are open to understanding the world in different ways and in different terms. I don't know if this makes you a hero, but maybe the Windstepper is right that you can help us."

"But why do you think I'm a hero?" he asked the Windstepper.

"Think of it this way," she answered. "The fact that time slowed down for you proves that you are different. Not everyone can be changed so quickly by the Order of the Libraries! Maybe it is your heart, I'm not sure. But in any case it is clear that you have the ability to experience time objectively without needing to bend it to your own will. This is why we need you. That is why you are a hero!"

Gray Fin rolled his eyes.

"Okay," the linguist acceded without fully understanding its implications. And yet in spite of his habitual shyness he had always believed he was born to do something important, to bring peace between opposing worldviews perhaps, or at least help them flesh out a common language. Lofty as his academic aspirations were, Tariq's eyes were set on the even higher goal of using language to bring communities together through mutual understanding. Whether that would make him a hero was, of course, unclear. He merely thought of it as a personal quest, a destiny written into his heart to guide him on his way in life.

"So I will help you, and you will take me to meet the Way-maker?"

"Tell us," demanded Gray Fin, avoiding his question. "What are your skills?"

"Well, I'm a linguist—"

"Good! Yes! Words are your power. You will bring peace to others through your words!"

"And how will I do that?"

"You need a pen—a hero's pen!"

"A pen?" Tariq crossed his arms, unsure if she was speaking literally or metaphorically. "Why?"

Without warning, the couple grabbed his arms and thrust him down the aisle.

"Go!" The Windstepper flailed her arms in the air. "Find your pen!"

Against his worrying nature, Tariq attempted to take to the task without question. He perused the print shop's merchandise, keeping his eyes peeled for pens. The elderly couple chaperoned.

"How about this one?" He showed Gray Fin a blue, wooden ballpoint pen.

"No, that won't do. Try that shelf over there."

They made their way to the shelf on the opposite end of the aisle, where Tariq spotted a red calligraphy pen lined with fine gold engravings.

"No, no, no," chided the Windstepper as she shook her finger at him. "Find your pen! Use your head!" Swiftly she poked the linguist on the forehead, making him bump into a tree of gift items and knocking a shiny bauble onto the ground behind Gray Fin. Gray Fin turned around, and Tariq graciously went around to retrieve the object from the ground.

Tariq stood up and revealed the bauble in his hand. In it was a thin, round, intricately decorated glass ornament strung on a chain. Inside it, seaweed-green ink flowed through tiny tubes resembling a miniature pipe organ. At the center was a solid, iridescent ball bearing, which was what made the piece so heavy. And at the bottom of the round glass exterior was a pointed tip through which the ink could be let out.

Gray Fin picked up the glass piece from Tariq's hand and admired it for a moment, then folded it back into his follower's hand with a squeeze and a shake.

"You have your pen. Good. Come with us."

As they left the store, Gray Fin muttered a Quoquamish phrase and tossed a wad of money onto the counter. Tariq noticed a tattoo of a fish skeleton on his forearm.

In the distance, the chime of the water clock signaled that it had been fifteen minutes since it had made its mighty whisper. *Go with them.* The old couple proceeded down a stairwell and into a long, dark basement hallway. Tariq followed, pinching his wrists to make sure he wasn't dreaming. When they got to the end of the hallway, the Windstepper turned to Tariq and spoke:

"Now, use your pen."

He felt around in his pockets and pulled out his new trinket. "But what do I do with it?"

"Just write, and the message will come to you," the Windstepper instructed.

"Don't ask, just receive!" advised Gray Fin.

Tariq looked at the tiny bauble in his hand, and a flash of insight came to him, as if telepathically. Without thinking he turned to the concrete wall and used the tiny, round pen to etch out a message onto its surface. Light emerged from the pen's muddy, green ink as it poured out. Then the three of them stood back to read what he had written:

WAR IN SEVILLE
FIND THE CLEPSYDRA

Tariq trembled as he withdrew the pen from the wall and thought about his destiny. If the writing on the wall were an indication of where his life was headed, he would have to accept the invitation without understanding it completely. This was certainly not a detour to his journey that made sense. He turned to the Quoquamish elders and saw them nodding at him. He knew exactly what they were thinking.

You are a hero.

"But what does it mean? I haven't heard about any war in Seville."

"I don't know," answered Gray Fin. "But your words come from a place of truth. Your words have the power to bring about peace, remember! Perhaps you should follow them and find out."

"Go to Spain? Just like that?"

"Be patient," advised the Windstepper, touching her fingertips together at her heart. Then she made her two fingers walk upon the palm of her other hand. "With time, no matter where you start from, the way forward always becomes clear."

Chapter 5

Twilight engulfed the African wild. Seogo the crocodile lay perched atop the jeep with his mouth open, as if inviting the stars in the sky to fly into his mighty belly. Naomi, the curly-haired zoologist, sat sleeping in the passenger seat. Everything appeared to be in order for their departure.

Amara, the robed one, had her intentions fixed on one task alone: to take all the crocodiles back with her to Spain and deliver them to the Watcher. She got in the van and started the ignition. "We have the crocodiles," she declared. "Let's go."

She rolled down the window and shined a flashlight, signaling to the caravan it was time to pull out. Mild-mannered groans rang out from the cars as the captive crocodiles cried farewell to the Mossi village.

"Hey!" She swatted the zoologist's shoulder. "HEY!"

"What?"

"When you sleep on the job, you lose your reward."

Before the robed one could finish her reproach, Naomi maneuvered her body through the car door's open window and up to the canopy of the jeep. She pulled out her own flashlight and inspected Seogo's fastening wires one last time. Then she lit a cigarette.

"So, Amara, how far is Spain from here?" asked the zoologist, stretching her arms and twisting her limber spine. The burning cigarette lit up the night like an orange, glowing sun.

"Put that out and get down here!"

Seogo snapped his jaw closed and growled at his inharmonious captors.

"Relax, I'm almost done," Naomi whispered loudly in her

raspy voice.

"You know, that's poison you're breathing!"

"Who are you, my mom?" The zoologist climbed back into her seat and chuckled at the well-adorned Amara, who was at least a decade younger.

"Enough of this. We have no time to lose."

"Fine, fine. So, how far is it to Spain?"

"It's about a week's drive," Amara answered, as if the time were a small matter. "We should make it to Ouagadougou by nightfall and then to the Algerian border by Monday."

The zoologist figured there was a good chance that she was joking. "And then what? Just wander on through the Sahara with our whole entourage?"

"Precisely."

"Are you crazy? We'll die out there!"

"Once we get to the Moroccan coast, we can ferry across the Strait of Gibraltar."

"Oy vey, why did I agree to this?"

"Haven't you ever crossed a desert before? I thought you took this job because of your sense of adventure."

"Adventure, I like. Danger, I welcome." She took one last whiff of her cigarette and tossed the butt out into the sand. "What you're trying to do is suicide."

Amara released the brakes and adjusted her colorful robe. She had never had any reason to doubt Naomi's fearlessness or her oath of secrecy. No other zoologist had even come close to matching Naomi's qualifications. Still, Amara felt the need to keep her on a tight leash and make her understand the significance of the Watcher's army.

"You knew perfectly well when you signed up that death was a possibility."

Amara led the caravan onto a dirt road. Then she made an abrupt right turn, off of the road and into the uncharted African wilderness. The zoologist took a shallow breath and gripped the seat to stabilize herself.

"Slow down! What is your rush?"

"We are drawing near to the Last Day."

"Sorry, I'm not Muslim."

"The Last Day is the day when all believers will be reunited in paradise and peace will prevail."

"Well, if there is a Last Day, you're not going to make it come any quicker by driving fast."

"You would think that. But that is because you don't understand the nature of time. Time works like a windup clock. Once you know how to wind it, then its pace is in your hands."

"I don't believe that. Time is fixed. How can you change it? What clock are you talking about?"

"The clock that measures all of creation—*the cosmic clock*. It chimes with every human birth and ticks with every heartbeat, counting the minutes, days, years, until death overtakes all."

"So, by speeding and endangering our lives you think you can attain some kind of cosmic power?"

"This is no matter for mocking! The cosmic clock is real. It is as large as a lake and has the power to influence humanity on a global scale."

"Really? What does it look like?"

"It is a clepsydra," the robed one explained. "The largest one ever made."

"A clepsydra? You mean, a water clock?"

"How appropriate, don't you think, considering water is the key ingredient of human life on earth?"

"Can't argue with you there," the zoologist conceded, lighting up another cigarette. The jeep bumped speedily across the open earth.

"But it is lost, buried somewhere beneath the earth. Only my family knows how to find it. And once we find the Clepsydra, it will put an end to war and restore the human heart to its eternal state of peace."

The zoologist rolled her eyes. *She's a nutcase. But at least she pays well.*

"This is how civilization must advance."

"I'm not so sure. One civilization's advancement is another civilization's decline."

"Listen to me," Amara retorted. "The Last Day is for the advancement of *all* people, not just for Spain, not just for Islam, but for everybody."

"And what about you, Amara? You're young. What's in it for you to gamble with your life like this?"

"I obey the Watcher because he is my leader, and obeying my leaders is my duty to God. Do you believe in God?"

"Which god? I've told you, I'm not Muslim."

"There is only one God; Muslim or Jew, He is there."

The zoologist thought back to her childhood before she was orphaned. The God of her parents was one who tested believers, keeping them obedient, productive, and ever mindful of Him. But the Torah was filled with admonishments against false prophets trying to paint God in the likeness of human nature. How could she hope to distinguish between them? As usual, such thoughts left her uncertain, ever questioning, ever alone.

The jeep jostled them fiercely as it ran over a giant baobab nut. Amara put on the breaks and let go of the wheel, nearly sending the unbelted zoologist crashing through the windshield.

"It is written," Amara began, "that God has the power to restore life to the dead. Don't you think—"

"Look, I don't want to get into a theological argument. Life's too short for that. I just hope you're wise enough to know what you are doing."

"Fine. Sit still and stick to your own expertise. Your job is to tend to the health of our army."

Some army, she thought. *All you have are crocodiles who don't even bite!*

Amara shifted the jeep back into gear and resumed driving. The zoologist tossed her second cigarette into the vast sub-Saharan wasteland, into which it vanished like a flake of a dying ember into the ashes. *Who knows what God is stirring up now?*

"Have you heard of the *convivencia?*" Amara asked, breaking the silence.

"Of course. It was the period when the Moors ruled Spain a thousand years ago."

"In Seville, during the *convivencia*, peace between religions was a reality. Muslims, Jews, and Christians lived together in a society marked by harmony and tolerance. Our caliphates allowed people of all religions to exercise equal freedoms and even hold political office. But ever since the Christians began pushing us out of Spain in the 11th century, my family has watched peace between the religions decay like a slowly unraveling tapestry. Oh, the violence and terror we have seen—Jews and Muslims slaughtered in the streets!"

"You don't have to convince me of that. Before coming to Spain, my family fled Auschwitz."

"Then you can understand why we are here and why the Watcher is building an army: we must reclaim that peace. We must win this war for the glory of the Last Day."

"Sure," Naomi acknowledged. "But what you are saying doesn't add up. You say you want peace, and yet you are building an army. Who are you going to attack?"

"It is not about attacking, it is about sending a message. Words can heal. Words can mend. Words can bring together warring people in reconciliation. When docile crocodiles fill the streets of Seville, people will realize there is nothing to fear. And when we find the Clepsydra, we will use it to tap into the hearts of humankind and restore them to their original state of peace. Our message will resonate loud and clear."

"And what is your message, exactly? When you have the attention of all the *cosmos*, what will you say?"

The robed one hesitated. "It is not my job to create the message."

"Then whose job is it? The Watcher's?"

"The Watcher has found someone," she explained, "who may be clever enough with words to craft the message we need. He is a linguist from Seattle named Tariq Kamal."

"And what's your job, Amara? Will you operate this Clepsydra?"

"My job is to gather the army and make sure *nothing* slows down God's plan."

"I don't think any of us knows God's plan. Do you?" She had no idea what kind of Pandora's box she would open with such a question.

Amara grabbed the zoologist's head with both hands and captured her eyes. The geometric swirls on the robed one's sleeves coiled tightly around the zoologist's head like thread around a spool.

"In Seville, my family has always discerned God's plan."

The jeep charged precariously forward. The zoologist frantically attempted to grab the wheel.

"Shouldn't you keep your eyes on the road?"

"Be at peace, Naomi. By God's power, you will soon be restored."

The robed one cupped the zoologist's face with her left hand and placed her right hand on her eyebrows, slowly swiping the woman's eyes closed like a corpse.

"No more words," Amara whispered. "We will arrive in no time."

Chapter 6

That night, Tariq lay in bed with his eyes open. After such a transformative experience with the Quoquamish elders, he could scarcely hope to sleep. *War in Seville. Find the Clepsydra.* The writing on the wall was as intriguing as it was frightening. Tariq replayed his conversation with Gray Fin and the Windstepper in his head, trying to make sense of it. Thinking back, he realized that it all began with the water clock. *Go with them.* Those words had caroused yet haunted him, as did his entire discussion with the Quoquamish elders. Why did the Windstepper call him a hero? More importantly, why did they need a hero in the first place? Indeed, the whole encounter raised many more questions than he could hope to answer.

With some hesitation, he considered the possibility of some spiritual dimension to his encounter with the Quoquamish elders. The secular world of academia had nearly stamped out all traces of his faith, and yet this same scientific training opened him to the possibility of seeking answers beyond his current realm of understanding, no matter where they might lead. Indeed, the experience itself was self-defining: time had slowed down in the presence of the nun and the water clock, and then Gray Fin and the Windstepper restored time to its natural pace. And to be sure the encounter had really happened, there, in his hand, was that ink-bearing trinket that had written the message on the wall and, by the same stroke, etched in his mind an invitation into what was to be an inexplicable realm of human experience.

Early the next morning, Tariq drove from his hotel in Nanaimo to a vantage point not far past Fort Rupert. According to Gray Fin and the Windstepper, he could find the Waymaker's village by walking northwest from there and not stopping. He would have welcomed more specific directions, but at the time he was too shy to speak up and press the elders for more information. Besides, Gray Fin had a tendency to avoid answering his questions anyway. But Tariq decided it was for the best. He had looked forward to the mystery of the search from the very start.

He parked his car and unloaded his waterproof sack containing a few notebooks, a GoPro camera for audiovisual documentation, a compass, a compact rain poncho, and rations that he could stretch to last a few days if needed. He kept the mysterious, round glass pen in his pocket. With silent enthusiasm, he strapped on his heavy-duty hiking boots and took off into the wilderness. He brushed through mossy corridors and climbed over lush, emerald nurse logs.

He persisted for hours, circumnavigating the trees and tramping through ferns and low bushes. The anticipation of reaching the hidden village stirred in him vivid memories of early childhood, the only other time he had ever felt so excited about arriving somewhere. Young Tariq was barely five years old, and his grandfather decided it was time for his *hajj*, the pilgrimage to Mecca that every believer must make at least once during his or her lifetime. Not knowing exactly what it would entail, young Tariq jumped at the chance to join in the *hajj* with his elder.

In Mecca, the young boy saw incredible sights: sheiks in white cotton robes, weary globetrotters with parched faces, and hoards of men of all ages and races being drawn in like magnets to the holy site. Some rode in on camels and others on donkeys. But most of them, like Tariq and his grandfather, came on foot. From what he remembered, the *hajj* was an arduous journey that seemed to take forever. With every tired step his legs ached and the soles of his feet burned. But when they arrived at the gate enclosing the sacred mosque known as the *Kaaba*, all the pain vanished and Tariq became wholly elated.

Tariq's grandfather took him around the *Kaaba* and taught him to chant the holy words. He led his grandson and joined in with strangers as they circled the sacred mosque. It was the first time Tariq remembered feeling like he truly belonged somewhere. And the first time he could feel his soul's thirst quenched like the sipping of sweet water under the desert sun. However, the memory was incomplete. For the life of him, he could not remember what happened next or how he ended up at home in bed the next day. Had they cut their trip short? It was an inexplicable lapse in awareness. But nevertheless, he could still remember the feelings leading up to his *hajj*.

While trekking through the misty, green forests of Vancouver Island, Tariq reminisced about the *hajj* and about his grandfather. The water clock's play with time had invited him to awaken those dormant feelings and observe the contrasts between his past and present journeys: long ago, it was hot sand and deserts, and now it was moist dirt and vegetation. On the *hajj* it was religious duty, and now it was scientific vocation. With his grandfather it was a strange new world of crowded masses orbiting the *Kaaba*; now, it was an even stranger world of dense wilderness and isolation, not knowing exactly where this elusive Quoquamish village would be.

Yet somehow, as if a gravitational force of destiny guided his sense of direction, Tariq knew exactly which steps to take. He recalled the words of the Windstepper again: *You are a hero.* Even as his legs grew tired, he continued walking, wondering what his future had in store. And even while rain tumbled down upon him from the unforgiving clouds, he persisted, thinking only of arriving, completely devoted to the mystery of his quest.

Grandfather would be proud.

After the rain cleared, Tariq encountered a babbling brook pouring westward toward a row of cottage-sized, thatched-roof huts. The walls were made of wood and seemed to glisten on the outside as if coated with an invisible protective enamel.

And yet, he could see the knotted graininess of the wood's uneven design. Upon closer inspection, each house was markedly distinct from the others. Each imperfection of the lumber's edges suggested a personality, a living presence somehow not fully uprooted from the ground that grew it.

It was late in the afternoon. From the leftmost hut a woman emerged and walked toward Tariq. Her slow, mindful gait, her unpretentious smile, and her large, inviting eyes all radiated wisdom and grace. Like the wooden huts, her stoic face suggested the same kind of uniqueness, a kind of personality that was firmly rooted in the presence of Nature that surrounded her. There was no mistaking it; this was the chief elder. She was the Waymaker.

"Good day," Tariq attempted to say with his rudimentary grasp of Nanaimo. He figured it was probably related to the Quoquamish language, and that common phrases and greetings would be somewhat similar. "I am a friendly visitor."

"Please," she answered. "Don't strain yourself with that foreign tongue. Use English."

"Okay."

"Now, who are you?"

"I am a field researcher—a linguist to be precise—and I have come to meet with the tribe's elder. In fact, I have already met with the Windstepper and Gray Fin. They helped me find your village."

The woman gazed into Tariq's eyes for a long moment without speaking, and then she inhaled as if being rushed out of a sleeping state.

"You may call me the Waymaker. I am the elder you seek." She extended her hand in front of him with the grace of flowing water.

"I am Tariq Kamal." They shook hands. "May I sit with you?"

"Yes, yes, by all means. Come in!"

"Thank you."

The two of them entered the wooden hut and sat down

on identical mounds of wedge-shaped rocks. Between them was an unlevelled stone table covered in pamphlets. Breathing loudly, the Waymaker swept up all of the pamphlets into a single pile and removed them from the table. These were the pamphlets, Tariq noted, that had proven the Quoquamish were still alive. As more of the table became visible, Tariq marveled at the peculiar unevenness of each stone as it joined together with the whole, reflecting shades of gray, tan, red, and sky-blue in a singular design.

From his seat at the table he could see into the rest of the lodge . In front of him was the kitchen, which housed even more rustic furniture pieces. Plates and cutlery rested upon shelves made of smoothed alder branches strung together and mounted to the wall. Next to them were baskets woven from cedar bark, each with a unique size and design. Behind him was a living room, in the center of which was a round, stone fire pit. Around the fire pit were four masterfully carved wooden rocking chairs. A newly treated animal hide was stretched upon the smallest chair to dry. On the other side of the fire pit were the largest of the rocking chairs, presumably for the chief elder herself, with a hand drum and mallet placed as if to add character to the room.

"Can I pour you some hot tea?" the elder offered with a grin.

"Yes, please. What do you have?"

"You would never believe me," she answered.

Tariq watched admiringly as the Waymaker lifted her pot of boiling water and poured it dexterously into an oddly shaped ceramic cup. The clear water filled the cup and gradually turned a dark, earthy green.

The Waymaker poured a second and a third cup, and in sauntered a short, slouching, round-faced man. The floor creaked as he dragged his feet.

"This is my companion, the Silent One."

The Silent One's clothes were so dirty that under the room's dim light Tariq could not even tell their color. And yet, his face was impeccably clean-shaven and his long, dark-gray hair nicely combed back. His huge, callused feet barely fit in his sandals.

"Good to meet you," Tariq greeted him. He held out his hand, but the Silent One only scowled and took his tea to a smaller table in the corner of the room with a newspaper.

"Please, take a drink," invited the Waymaker.

For the first few minutes they sipped their tea in silence. As Tariq continued to look around, the ambiance of the room revealed itself more and more with each new detail noticed. Small wooden carved figurines stood in a line on a shelf opposite the front door. Below their feet was a dirt-colored rug that would have been comfortable to walk on without shoes. Above, in the highest corner of the ceiling, there was an open channel to let out the smoke from the fire. Presumably, this could be closed in the case of rain or snow. On the drum on the chair was a green and red painted design with two fish and a canoe. One could only imagine the hearty sound that could fill the room if that drum were played.

After a few minutes, Tariq realized he needed to begin his interview. Suddenly his stomach churned as he wrestled with what question to ask first. *Should I ask about her language? Her activism? Reasons for coming out of hiding? Or, should I ask something else in order to gain her trust first? I didn't even plan out my questions! How could I be so unprepared?*

As soon as he could manage, Tariq took the risk and broke the silence.

"Tell me, Waymaker, how is it you speak English when your tribe hasn't been in contact with anyone for a hundred years?"

"What do you call my pamphlets? Doesn't that count as contact? Isn't that how you found out about me? "

"Yes, of course. I meant that before you wrote them, you were completely in hiding."

"Being in hiding doesn't mean you don't have contact," she answered. "Each of us lives a kind of double life, you could say, sometimes in the village and sometimes out there."

The linguist listened intently. The Waymaker's answer begged so many questions he had not anticipated needing to ask. His mind raced, hesitant to ask anything too intrusive too soon.

"Who all lives in your village? How many people are here?"

"How many, you ask? Why, we are like the salmon in the rivers, numerous when swimming together and yet very few when caught in the hand."

"I see." Tariq jotted down the Waymaker's words in his notebook. "What is life like for you here?"

"What is life like for us? Haven't you read my pamphlets? It's like living on Nature's deathbed! The earth is suffering, Tariq. All First Nations people feel it. So many millions of us have fallen at the guns of western civilization in defense of Nature, and for what? They think we are fighting to save our own identity, and partly that may be true. But what they don't understand is that all of our identities are interconnected. They are connected to the earth from which they are born. But who is there to save our shared identity, eh? These are the arrows and slings of western advancement—we adapt and accept the ways of those who force 'progress' and 'religion' upon us, but inside we tremble in fear of losing the land and all that has existed in Nature throughout all time. In fact, we are afraid of losing time itself."

From across the room, the Silent One let out a deep, loud snarl.

"This is a great truth that spans all human events," she continued. "Our people are the warriors and defenders of Nature. Our narrative is like all those who have fought for the land and against the oppressions of the west. Our story of woe and loss is the source of history and of time. After all, who was it who was pushed into reservations on all sides of the continent? Who was made to tread the trail of tears and fall upon wounded knees? My friend, we are one of many nations pushed forth along the river of time, gasping for air at the water's surface, made to sever their connection with Nature for the sake of modern technology and convenience." She paused and made a loud, breathy sigh. "But you can learn that from anyone on our side of history. I think you are interested in learning what makes the Quoquamish unique."

Tariq nodded his head and smiled as the Waymaker continued.

"We are like starlight from the stars, luminous beyond measure and yet scarce to reach you from such a distant place." The Waymaker paused and squinted at her interviewer. "The Quoquamish have a word that is used for the people in our village. We use this word because we respect and trust each other. I don't know you, Tariq Kamal, and yet there is something about you that I trust." She stilled her brow and relaxed her jaw. "You are one of us. You are a *Mahatma*."

The Silent One slammed his teacup down upon the table and let out a raspy, monosyllabic laugh. His wife turned and scolded him with her eyes.

"Mahatma?" Tariq knew this word meant *great soul* in his native Urdu. The same name that even Gandhi was known by! But the Waymaker pronounced it with such fluidity and command that it appeared perfectly native to the Quoquamish language.

The Waymaker stood up. "I have something to show you. Follow me, Mahatma. And bring your teacup!"

Without delay, they exited the wooden hut. The crisp air welcomed Tariq into its sobering embrace. From outside, Tariq could see the Silent One through the window stirring his tea with his index finger. The Silent One fixed his eyes like arrows upon Tariq for a moment, and then he looked down and closed his eyes. The tea was a precious gift from Nature. The Silent One sloshed the tea around in his mouth and swallowed it, beaming a pleasant, blissful smile. Then he took his finger out of the tea and licked it forcefully as if the tea were a sticky, sweet maple syrup. For the Silent One, it was clear: Nature tasted divine.

"Follow me," the Waymaker commanded.

The Waymaker treaded lightly and gracefully through the shrubs, and her follower did the same, using his GoPro to document their conversation. Fortunately, the linguist's lack of prepared questions had turned into an advantage, as this allowed the otherwise academic interview to take twists and turns into philosophical matters. Over the next few hours of hiking, they discussed everything from the history of the Quoquamish people to the meaning and origin of human life. The linguist hung on her every word, imbibing her knowledge like a wide-eyed child.

"Where are we going?" Tariq finally asked.

"We aren't going anywhere, Mahatma."

"Aren't we?"

"Your question assumes that what I am showing you is a matter of *where*."

"Humph."

Tariq raised his near-empty teacup and shook out a few drops onto his tongue. He found it strange that no matter how certain he was that he had drunk the last drop there was always a little more to be shaken from the cup.

With every few steps, it seemed, the ecosystem shifted revealing a new species of plant or fungus that Tariq had never seen before. Large, curly ferns cloaked the rotting stumps. Gray, spiny mushrooms shot up from the moistened earth. *Where are we?*

Without warning, the Waymaker stopped in her tracks. They had reached a waterfall five meters high, terraced with countless intricate beds of dark green algae. It was one of the most breathtaking waterfalls Tariq had ever seen. And yet, seeing it was only part of the experience. Streams of trickling water poured out a mellifluous symphony of splashes, drops and ripples, to which the algae appeared to dance. Robins and stellar jays sang lullabies to the stream, and in its own way the stream sang back. All was in harmony. As the evening sun shown through the treetops, the water scintillated like a bed of precious sapphires, captivating the newcomer beyond all hope of release. Tariq gazed into the waterfall bedazzled, listening to it, feeling it, taking it all in.

"Take a look," instructed the Waymaker. She pointed down at the base of the waterfall and traced her finger down to the stream ebbing and flowing at their feet. "The movement of these waves is timed very precisely, like a highly sophisticated clock."

"How can that be? Doesn't the water level change with the seasons?"

"Of course. But you see, it is the algae. The algae meter the water. They hoard it in times of downpour and release it when there is a lack. They manage the ebb and flow so that all is in perfect rhythm, never overflowing, never changing. These algae are the greatest timekeepers in Nature."

"But if nothing overflows, then where does the water go?"

"Again, your question presumes that it is a matter of *where*."

Tariq rolled his eyes. "Then what *is* it a question of?"

"First, put that camera away!"

The linguist did as she told him and packed up the GoPro.

"Now, why don't you see for yourself? Reach in with your teacup. See what happens!"

Tariq hesitated. *Why can't the Waymaker just explain it? I don't like being tossed into things willy-nilly.*

"Here, let me show you."

She grabbed the teacup and took out an eyedropper filled with red dye. She cast a single red drop into the cup and then held it to the water. "Watch closely."

To Tariq's amazement, the cup filled nearly to the brim but it did not overflow. Below the cup, the bed of algae that would have caught the cup's water swelled to twice its previous size and new water gushed out of it. The flow of water from this bed down to the next was as seamless as if the cup had not obstructed it at all.

The Waymaker removed the cup and drank from it. "Here, take in a sip of Nature in its purest form." She handed the cup to Tariq. Amazed, he stood still a few moments before guzzling it down. *Unbelievable!*

"Look!" The Waymaker indicated a stream of red-tinted water that trickled from the algae as it shrunk back to its original size.

"But why was the red dye delayed?"

"Now *that's* the right question!" The Waymaker grabbed the cup back from Tariq and shook a few drops into the stream at their feet. "But your thinking is limited by the English word 'delay.' The algae don't delay anything; they simply move water through time. What I mean is that they can send water backwards and forwards through time in order to keep all events in balance, not too fast and not too slow. They are like a clock that can naturally compensate when the pace of the world speeds up or slows down."

Tariq smiled and listened to the gushing waters that poured forth before him. He thought of his conversation with the Windstepper and Gray Fin at the mall: *Muslims speed up time, Christians slow it down.* Now it made sense why they believed both religions were placing a strain on Nature.

"In Nature all things are connected," the Waymaker continued. "This is because all water is connected. It seeps through every cell in the human body, through dirt, through mist absorbed in the air, and through all life on earth. We breathe it, perspire it and even become it for a time! And in becoming water, we exchange with its past and its future; we become everything that it has been and everything that has yet to be. You, me, these algae—we are all streaming in and out of life through our intimate connection with water. Water is life; water is the lifeblood of Nature! And the exchange between any two lives is simply a matter of *when*."

Tariq stared into the waterfall, still not convinced that he was really awake. He touched the glass pen that sat in his pocket and softly gasped.

"So, what would happen if someone tried to hoard time by hoarding water?" he asked.

"Then Nature would chew him up and spit him out!"

The Waymaker set down her pouch and planted herself upon a mound of rocks. Her stout, old bones were tired from so much walking. She grabbed Tariq's attention and pointed.

"You should head up to the top of that hill, Mahatma. It overlooks our entire village. Go take a look."

Tariq made his way up the hill of thickets and into a clearing, which gave way to a steep cliff. Looking down, he could see the row of huts that lined the Quoquamish village. From the distance they appeared as humble dwellings, and yet each one of those homes, he imagined, contained its own stone tables and rocking chairs, animal hides and hand drums—authentic treasures of the tribe's way of life.

He then saw the Silent One come out of the leftmost hut. The Silent One looked up to where Tariq was standing and shaded his eyes with his blistered hand. Tariq raised his hand and delivered an unassuming wave hello. The old man grunted and waved back reluctantly, then turned to the side and spat emphatically in the dirt.

All water returns to the earth, Tariq observed, reflecting on the Silent One's spit. Absorbed in thought, Tariq lowered his hand and marveled again at the Waymaker's eloquent description of the water that connects all life. Although the Silent One no longer returned his gaze, Tariq felt a connection with him, an unspoken tie that tugged and invited his consciousness into the mystery of the Quoquamish way of life. *How much more I could learn from these people about nature and time and indeed, life!*

As he was absorbed in this reflection, a faint engine sound started to hum in the distance behind him. The hum grew louder and louder, bringing his pensive awareness back to the sight of the Silent One in front of his hut. The engine sounded so loudly that it silenced his thoughts just as powerfully as it silenced nature around him.

Silent One, do you hear that? Tariq pretended to ask. He kept still and focused on the noise.

Within seconds, a drone darted into view. Swift as an arrow, its metallic color likely would have rendered it undetectable if not for the noise.

Do you see that?

The drone sailed through the air above them, agitating the tops of the trees with its air propulsion, until finally, it dropped a round, black object from its metallic base. The object descended upon the village like an ominous ball of hail. Tariq panicked. It was a missile.

Silent One, get out of there!

But Tariq's tongue was tied in the stupor of his thoughts. The thought of a missile descending upon the village was too surreal and inconceivable for him to verbalize a reaction. Meanwhile the Silent One did not hear or see the missile coming. He stood silently looking up at Tariq. For a fraction of a second Tariq thought he saw the Silent One crack a faint smile. In any other circumstance Tariq would have smiled back. If not for the drone missile, his heart would have jumped at the Silent One's sudden show of camaraderie, subtle as it was. But in the heat of his panic, all the linguist could do was reach his hand out and wave again, this time more vigorously.

Don't you hear the missile? Run!

Tariq wanted to shout at the top of his lungs to warn the Silent One to run. He imagined himself standing next to the Silent One, grabbing him by the shoulders and prodding him on. He would have run to the nearby brook and jumped down into the divot it had carved in the earth, hoping the earth would shelter them both from the destruction to come. And the destruction was certain to come! But Tariq's mouth could not utter a sound. A moment of terror was erupting in front of them, and the linguist was helpless to stop it.

Can't you see you're in danger? Get away from there before the missile hits!

The missile struck the ground right in the middle of the village, sending a wave of heat to the top of the cliff where the linguist stood. The white shroud of the blast eclipsed each hut one by one like an ominous ghost. The sound from the blast echoed through and between the trees. Everything happened unimaginably quickly, and yet the moment seemed interminable.

Then, a stealth jet zoomed into view. Its powerful engine rocked the foundations of the wounded settlement. The jet launched a fierce missile at the drone, exploding it in midair like a firework meant to distract and conceal. The stealth jet vanished without a trace. Waves of shock pulsated from the nexus of the attack. The bombing felt as if it rippled through time as well as space, reaching back to generations of past elders and causing them to moan and cry.

Silence followed. The village was completely destroyed.

The Waymaker quickly arrived at the top of the hill. She stood next to Tariq, panting, placed her hands on her knees, and wept. Her sadness was like a song, crying out to all of history's unsuspecting victims.

Tariq stood paralyzed. *A terrorist attack on Canadian soil? How can this be happening?* These thoughts agitated the linguist's mind. *And I might have saved him. Oh, how I might have saved him! If only I had warned him!*

Tariq wrestled with what to say. Eventually he let out a sympathetic whisper, "I am so sorry, Waymaker. Do you think anyone survived?"

The elder snapped with a disdain in her voice. "You should really think before you speak!"

Tariq recoiled in fear of having done further damage through his words.

"Listen to me," she said, enraged. "This is the reality: war is always present, always sucking the lifeblood out of us. Sometimes it strikes us swiftly from behind! Sometimes it haunts us in the night and weighs down our hearts as we suffer. My people have seen war from all sides: skirmishes with the Makah, with the Haida; captives taken by the Russians; bloodshed with the English, the Canadians, and the Americans; terror from violent extremists—there is no end!"

The linguist nodded and kept quiet.

"Oooch! Kaanittwa!" she ejected furiously, pulling at the roots of her graying hair.

Some words don't need any translation.

Gradually the Waymaker regained her stillness, though rage still fueled her speech.

"These wars run deeper than tribal conflict and deeper than mere words, Mahatma. They happen when people turn their hearts from Nature, from the true way of life that moves us forward like water through a stream. We feel it in the present, and we feel it in the future and the past. It is no wonder people misunderstand each other!"

Briefly, Tariq felt the quest for this peace calling to his heart. He felt Nature coursing through his blood, and it felt like a rush for revenge. But the guilt of failing to warn the Silent One of the missile weighed painfully upon his conscience. From the blast site, mushrooming clouds of smoke and dust rose and dissipated. The Waymaker stood still, looking out at the remains of her village, completely unaware of Tariq's shameful secret.

"So, what do we do now?" Tariq asked.

"You should go home," the elder commanded.

"Just like that?"

"Don't meddle in our grief."

He could tell she was upset, but this time, he refused to hold back his words.

"But I can help you! Don't we need to fight? Don't we need to defend Nature?"

Without realizing it, he had taken out the glass pen from his pocket and gripped it like a weapon.

"Patience, Mahatma. We may hate what has happened, but there is no need to fight, at least not yet. The next step will be revealed to us each on our own."

Tariq loosened his grip on the pen, though his chest was still tight.

"What are you holding?" asked the Waymaker.

"It's a pen. But I believe it has some sort of power. When I held it, it guided me to write out a message."

"A message?"

"It said: *War in Seville. Find the Clepsydra.* Do you know what that means?"

"It means that you are beginning to find your way, Mahatma." The Waymaker reached up and folded the pen back into Tariq's hand.

"But how will I know the way?"

The Waymaker did not answer his question at first. She let him stand in silence again with her, looking down at the ruins of a village that was, now, truly lost. Everything inside those wooden huts—cedar baskets, rugs, teacups, rocking chairs, drums—all of it had been consumed in the fire of the blast.

Tariq wept for the Silent One. He wept for the Waymaker and hoped that no other Quoquamish had died in the bomb blast. He hoped that Gray Fin and the Windstepper were unharmed, far away, on the other side of Vancouver Island where he had seen them last. His throat was so tight he could barely breathe. And yet he continued to ruminate.

Attacks like these must be stopped. The two sides must be reconciled. If I am going to help bring them to reconciliation, then they will need a common language.

He winced again at his mistake.

And I have to be able to speak that language to them when the time is right. If I hesitate, people might die!

On the dirt below him, an army of ants marched in a loop around his shoes. The ants had no language, he observed, and yet somehow they knew where they were headed and directed each other.

I just wish I could see where I was going. If I knew which step to take, then I wouldn't hesitate.

Finally, at the perfect moment, the Waymaker spoke her answer:

"This journey, for you, may be pathless like a beach of sand; yet if you look closely, it is perfectly defined by the footprints you make."

Tariq looked down at his bootstraps and squeezed his fists.

You are a hero.

Chapter 7

The jeep's engine revved as Amara and the curly-haired zoologist zoomed through the Sahara. Seogo's beady, reptilian eyes gazed into the empty horizon while the caravan whisked him and the rest of crocodiles across the landscape like a bullet train, bound for a destiny that was written in the sands.

Gradually, the zoologist woke from the hypnotic spell and noticed that the sun was high again. "Where are we?" she asked in her raspy voice, tiredly rubbing the space between her eyebrows with the heel of her hand. "Did I sleep the entire day?"

"You slept two days."

"Two days! You're crazy."

"I'm not crazy. Look. We are exactly halfway to the North African coast."

The zoologist examined the surrounding ecosystem, realizing that Amara was right. They were in a region of the Sahara that was hundreds of miles from where they started.

"Two days! I haven't eaten, drunk, or showered—"

The robed one pulled the caravan to an abrupt stop.

"Naomi, We have a problem."

"What?"

"Do you see that ravine?"

"Yes, it's all sand and sandstone. No creatures in sight."

"We need to be on the other side of it."

"Okay, let's get to it," the zoologist said with enthusiasm. "Six cars, plus us. We need to cross."

They got out of the jeep and closed the doors. The zoologist darted toward the ravine, looking in all directions for a path.

"We should look for the shallowest incline," the zoologist proposed. "And put chains on all the tires. It must be at least a hundred meters deep."

"That won't be necessary. All we need is to build a water clock."

"A water clock? Is that your answer to everything?"

"I didn't ask you for opinion, only for your help."

"Where's the adventure in that?" Naomi stepped aside and lit a cigarette.

"You assumed we were going to cross it, but that is not the case. We will simply go around it."

"Around it? That could add days to our return."

"But a water clock will speed things up."

The zoologist shook her head. She didn't quite believe her, but then again, how could she doubt their whereabouts? Something about the nature of time was being changed with this mysterious Amara.

"With all this sand, why can't we just make an hourglass?"

Amara wasted no time responding. She pulled a jug of water and a tool kit from the back of the jeep, and then she laid out a cloth on the sand to start her project. The calm desert wind blew through the windows of the jeep.

"We'll need to dismantle the jeep."

"Good," the zoologist reacted facetiously, puffing out a cloud of smoke. "Tear it up. We're not going to make it out of here anyway."

"If you're going to whine, go talk to the crocodiles and not to me. I have work to do."

Amara knelt down and opened the toolbox. Her colorful robe pressed upon the soft sand as if giving it a kiss.

"Fine."

"But first, get up there and untie Seogo."

The zoologist did as she was told.

"Anything else, your highness?"

"No."

"I'm taking a break."

"Fine."

The zoologist disappeared into the shade of the caravan, leaving the robed one to build a water clock by herself.

In a hardworking flash, Amara disassembled the jeep and engineered a multi-chambered vat comprised of windows, tires, and scrap metal all held together with a dried concoction of makeshift putty. She poured water into it and reconfigured the camshaft to serve as a siphon. Then she placed it into the vat, holding it all together with a piece of chicken wire. Engine parts lay sprawled across the desert sand. Seogo watched gleefully as she poured herself a glass of water and wiped her forehead.

She took out a piece of paper and placed it on the sand. Then, she removed a small glass ornament from her robe's innermost pocket and dusted off the tip. *I hope you've still got some ink in you*, she thought, placing the tip upon the paper to write. *Time is running out. Who knows how long it will take for the Watcher to receive this message?*

When Amara finished writing, she turned around and observed Seogo trotting playfully around the desert, his tail swaying gracefully behind him. *The guide was right*, she admitted. *He moves like beautiful poetry.*

The zoologist returned from her rest, and her jaw dropped in bewilderment .

"I couldn't have been gone more than ten minutes! How on earth did you dismantle an entire jeep and build a water clock and in that short of time?"

"The only thing left is to activate it."

Amara walked back to the water clock and picked up the timing bath she had constructed using two of the hubcaps. Carefully, she placed the timing bath on the water's surface, letting it draw in water. Then she pulled out her pen and shook out a single drop of its seaweed-green ink into the vat. The water glowed a brilliant shade of green and swirled around like glitter in a massive snow globe.

"Is that a some kind of magical potion?" she asked, condescendingly.

"You don't need to understand, only to listen—"

At that very moment, a sharp buzzing sound arose. Both of them looked up and became still. It was a yellow-brown swarm of desert locusts heading directly toward them.

The zoologist made a mad dash for the caravan. "Take cover!"

But the robed one didn't move. She knelt down and prayed.

"What are you waiting for?"

Looking back at Amara, the zoologist hesitated. She realized what she had neglected to realize before: without the jeep, Seogo no longer had a seat in the caravan.

Amara stood up calmly and dusted off her clothes. She gestured for the caravan to come pick her up.

"Amara!" the zoologist shouted over the increasing noise of the locusts. "We have to get Seogo onboard!"

But Amara didn't respond. One of the drivers of the caravan pulled up next to her, and she threw in her tool set.

"Close the windows. You're giving us a ride."

The yellow-brown cloud of locusts drew nearer with every second. The zoologist frantically gathered the chicken wire and contemplated how she might tie Seogo to the top of one of the other cages. Amara and the driver pulled up next to her.

"Get in," the robed one ordered. "Now!"

"Help me get Seogo on top of the cage!"

"We must leave him behind. There is no time to waste."

"Do you think we can just leave him here in the middle of the desert? Let's quickly get him loaded."

The driver of the car eased off of the breaks as the locusts came into full view.

"GET IN! NOW!"

The zoologist's heart and breathing raced. She looked at the swarm and listened. The risk of death was invigorating.

"NO!

"GET IN NOW, OR I WILL LEAVE YOU BEHIND!"

"NOT WITHOUT SEOGO!"

But Amara couldn't allow it. Their lives were in danger, and she could not risk getting caught in the swarm of locusts to save the stray crocodile. Instead she closed the door and ordered the driver to take off.

"HEY! WHERE ARE YOU GOING!"

The car raced away toward the rest of the caravan, which was already fleeing the swarm.

"DAMN YOU TO HELL!" she cursed in Yiddish.

The zoologist's first thought was to chase after them. But she knew that it was impossible to outrun the locusts. She looked at Seogo, then gazed down into the ravine.

"Seogo!"

The crocodile closed its eyes and nodded, accepting his fate, as if he understood what needed to be done. The zoologist led Seogo to the edge of the ravine and tied herself to his scaly back with the chicken wire.

"Brace yourself!"

Right as the menacing plague of yellow-brown locusts reached the edge of the ravine, she hugged Seogo and leapt off. Never had nature beheld such an escape: woman and beast tumbling downward, clinging together and being beaten upon the sandstone, escaping an otherwise certain death.

Chapter 8

A long, rectangular rug spanned the main prayer hall of the Seville mosque, depicting a sequence of multicolored geometrical motifs. Starting from the hall's entrance, the rug's design began with gray lines and hooks intersecting at clever diagonals, and then as one walked across it these figures opened up into overlapping embroidered boxes of crimson, violet, and gold. Treading farther, the design's geometry grew more intricate as hundreds of beveled triangles tessellated their way down the rug, getting smaller and smaller with spurts of all colors threaded in. Beyond these forms, the design coalesced in a pattern of cascading waves dyed various shades of blue and green, weaving up and into every corner and fading gradually as the rug reached its end.

Yusef, the imam, paced slowly up and down the rug in solemn contemplation. He was dressed in a coarse, woolen garment that was expertly sewn. *Her message could arrive at any moment*, he thought. He pulled out his pocket watch to examine the time. *Almost sunset.* Yusef traced the elaborate rug with his steps once more until it ended at the base of a small fountain. Reverently, he dipped his hands in the water and used them to cleanse his face and forearms. Then he knelt down upon the rug facing the *mihrab*, an ornate alcove built into the recesses of the southeast wall, and prayed.

He began with the *Basmala*, Islam's beloved phrase that gave a name to the one true God: Allah, the Merciful and Compassionate. Then he recited a verse from the Quran with his eyes closed. Lines and letters and curves swirled behind his eyelids; for Yusef the imam, the experience of the holy recitation included not only spoken words but also indescribable whirls of polychromatic ink laying their indelible message upon the pages of his consciousness. These holy words were powerful beyond measure. They opened his mind to the truth that all Muslims knew, the truth of the Last Day—this was the written end to the struggle of humanity, the day when judgment would come and peace would prevail. These were the words of the true Islam, the way of victory through peace and through submission to the will of God. These words, Yusef believed, were his salvation.

As the imam lay folded in prayer, his attendant Ibrahim cleansed his face and forearms and knelt down beside him. His knees pressed into the rug with sweet reverence. When they finished, the two men rose and greeted each other as brothers in faith.

"*As-salaamu alaykum*," Yusef spoke from his heart. The greeting was familiar in Arabic: *May peace be upon you.*

"*Wa-alaykum salaam*," Ibrahim answered. *And upon you, peace.*

As they grasped forearms, a faint glow emerged from Yusef's pocket. He stood back and, with a sudden spark of excitement, reached into his pocket to pull out a luminous piece of paper. Glowing green letters appeared on the page in a familiar handwriting.

"What does it say, Yusef?"

The imam cloaked the document with his hands in order to read its illumined message:

My Dear Yusef,

Please inform the Watcher that the crocodiles are with me and that my caravan should arrive in Seville this week.

We hit an unexpected ravine, but the delay should not hinder us much. Never have we needed our Clepsydra more than now.

It is time to bring in the linguist and get him up to speed. We must make haste. The Last Day awaits us all.

Your Beloved Sister,
Amara

The imam folded up the paper and placed it back in his pocket.

"You must inform the Watcher at once," suggested Ibrahim, who snatched the paper in order to study it more closely. "He might be upset that she is taking so long!"

"I will do so in good time," declared Yusef. He stood at the fountain, thinking of his sister Amara.

With all his heart Yusef believed in Allah and in the Last Day. To him this Day was something not only to be feared but also to be embraced as the goal of all history, the end and triumph of all human endeavors. Like the edges of a brilliant tapestry, this Day would be the tassel at the end of time itself.

"But remember," Yusef added, "Allah's blessings are given to those who are patient and who persevere. Have patience!"

"Patience, you say, but how much patience can we spare? The Last Day is surely upon us."

"We are advancing time as quickly as we can, Ibrahim. Our war will be over soon, and the Watcher's army will be victorious. Amara, too, would do well to remember this, though already the desert air is getting to her. Have patience."

"I will try, Yusef."

Despite his show of calm, Yusef felt an inner whirlpool of anxieties about the Last Day swirling within him. In his community he was a rock of faith; he preached the wisdom and compassion of Islam as best he knew how. But what if that wasn't enough? What if his knowledge was incomplete? The only thing he knew with perfect confidence was that the Last Day was near. On this Day, all people would be judged by their earthly deeds and rewarded in Heaven according to their adherence to duty. Yusef's duty, so he believed, was to build an army for the Watcher, so that no one may stop this Day from coming—not even the Order of the Libraries, try as they might. Yusef's cause was pure and holy: to find the Clepsydra and use it to usher in eternal peace on the Last Day. This was the only cause that assuaged his burning anxiety day by day. It was the only cause that mattered.

"Begin preparing the baths," ordered Yusef. "We have a great journey ahead of us. It is only a matter of time before the Clepsydra reveals Allah's greatest power."

Ibrahim nodded and took the letter. He headed down a narrow stairwell, leaving Yusef to reflect upon the chain of circumstances that had led him to the present day. Yusef and Amara Tejedor were siblings descended from a long line of Andalusian weavers—known by the surname *Al-Hayek*—dating back centuries before the Spanish inquisition. In the 1400's, the invading Christians drove their family into secrecy; but rather than flee Spain or be persecuted, the family learned to blend in. They changed their surname from *Al-Hayek* to *Tejedor,* which in Spanish meant 'weaver,' and they dug out caves below ground to use as hidden chambers of worship.

Over the centuries, the persecution of Muslims continued. Bloodshed was rampant, and the Christian invaders showed very little tolerance. Village by village, home by home, Islam was virtually wiped off of the face of Spain like dust from a map. It was not until the 21st century that Yusef Tejedor acquired the mosque in Seville and furnished it with precious antiquities, including the thousand-year-old, 30-foot embroidered rug that now lined the floor of the prayer hall.

Most people attending the mosque, when they learned the history of the rug, became preoccupied with not damaging it. They would ask Yusef why he let common visitors walk upon such an important family heirloom. To this he always gave the same response: "This rug is a reminder. It reminds me that wherever I may walk, I carry my history, and how I tread upon this earth becomes my destiny. So I walk lightly and with every step demonstrate my constant submission to the will of God." To the rug's own credit, there was something about its masterful construction that lent itself to a timeless existence. Indeed, the thousand-year-old prayer rug was the finest symbol of the Al-Hayek lineage, and it was a constant reminder to Yusef of where he came from and where his path was leading.

As Yusef cleaned up the prayer hall, he admired his family's majestic rug. For a brief moment he thought he could detect his own footprint as it lingered ephemerally upon its surface. He knew that in such a rug no imprint was ever lost—all was recorded in the fabric of time and interwoven into his family's legacy. And yet neither Yusef nor his sister could know with certainty what the future of that legacy would be.

After Yusef had sat a while, thoroughly musing on all these matters, the stairwell door opened and in ran Ibrahim, out of breath, with urgent news.

"An attack has been attempted in Canada! It was a drone missile!"

Yusef stood speechless, trying to shield his fear from perception.

"A drone missile? How many have been killed?"

"As far as we know, no one was killed."

"Are you sure?"

"It landed in the middle of the woods on Vancouver Island, several kilometers out from the nearest town."

"But are you sure it was an attack? Who would fire a missile into the middle of the woods?"

"According to my sources, the drone was spotted approaching the city of Vancouver. Quickly a military stealth jet intervened in order to intercept the drone and destroy it, but not before it could fire a single, desperate missile."

"Hmm," pondered Yusef. Traces of the Quran's visual reverie sustained his trance-like state of spiritual confidence. "Even if there were no fatalities, Ibrahim, I think something is not quite right."

Ibrahim bit his lip. "There is more, Yusef."

"Have they discovered who was behind this attack?"

"You will not like the answer to that question."

"Answers are answers; it is only for Allah to like or dislike them."

"The Islamic State has claimed it."

Yusef's trance grew fierce. He had expected this was the case.

"They are desperate," his attendant continued, "to send a message of resistance to the west. Yusef! With the Last Day so very near, what are we to do?"

"We stick to our cause, Ibrahim, and deliver our message. We will not let terrorists get in our way."

"And what if they do get in our way? I fear for us all! How shall we defend ourselves against the Islamic State? Against those pretenders who wish to destroy our religion by devising such ungodly stratagems in Allah's name! They are true evil-doers, for they bring defamation to the name of Islam!"

Yusef paused briefly to collect his feelings. He adjusted the insides of his pockets, stirring up the thought of Amara and her letter. *She must get the crocodiles safely into Spain.* Then without any significant hesitation he reached out and clasped his attendant's hand.

"Ibrahim, my brother, remember the true meaning of the word *Islam:* it is our *submission*—above all else—*to the will of Allah.* We may not know why Allah lets the Islamic State take land and waste lives. Those are His secrets; and He has many more secrets to be revealed in time."

"Then I will listen and act according to His will. May His will alone guide our actions."

"As you should, my brother. But do so in secret, just as the Watcher has done."

"Why so many secrets, Yusef? Why keep the Watcher's identity a secret? Shouldn't the world be warned of the great dangers ahead? Shouldn't we share our plans and create new allies?"

"Absolutely not. They will judge us and soil the name of Islam just as the terrorists have done. Secrecy is the only way we can operate. The Watcher's army must be set in place and our message prepared. Only then will we open our faith to the rest of the world."

"Understood."

"You are a loyal friend," the imam sighed. "Let us honor this loyalty until the Last Day arrives. Come, let us pray again."

Derek Olsen

Chapter 9

In the middle of a rainy Seattle night, Tariq had difficulty sleeping again. Though he was home, the terror of the drone attack continued to haunt him. He felt the Waymaker's anger and her call to action. *There is no use dwelling on it*, he thought. *I must do something. I must investigate. But how do I start?*

Bursts of inspiration often came to him at night, impelling him to write or to do research. From these sensations his brightest dreams were hatched—dreams that might unlock the fundamental power of language to transform human beliefs. Now that thoughts of war and guilt were tearing his world apart at the seams, this dream dazzled before his eyes like never before. He got up and walked over to his desk. The GoPro camera was begging him to transcribe his fruitful dialogue with the Waymaker. He turned on his computer, loaded the GoPro recordings, and began writing a meticulous transcription.

As he watched the video footage preceding the attack, every image and sound was exactly how he remembered it: colorful, captivating, and utterly magical. He sank into a bittersweet nostalgia for those precious moments with the Waymaker before the drone missile destroyed her village. He imagined the Waymaker rocking in her chair, playing her drum while singing. He imagined the Silent one tapping along with his eyes closed and his long, gray hair dancing about on his shoulders. He longed hopelessly for time to be reversed and for the Silent One to be warned and saved.

After an hour of intense concentration, Tariq's attention strayed from the screen and landed upon the glass pen, which hung by its chain from his nightstand drawer. Illumined by the light from the computer monitor, the pen glowed a ravishing green.

I wonder what will happen if I write with it again?

He picked up the pen by its chain and held it tenderly in his hand. The seaweed-green ink streamed through its intricate pipework like blood through veins. Slowly, with eyes wide open, Tariq grabbed his diary, placed the tip of the pen to the page and wrote: "How do I start?"

Not long and he noticed the pen's remarkable effect. A message in green ink appeared, glowing on the opposite page. It was a letter addressing him by name. He quivered in astonishment and read its content:

Dear Tariq,

You don't know me, but I am in need of a linguist's expertise at once. Come to Seville as soon as possible. All arrangements have been made. I trust that your Spanish is not too rusty. Our peaceful future depends on you.

A stranger not for long,
Yusef Tejedor

Tariq closed the diary forcefully in momentary disbelief. He took a deep breath, and then opened it again. He studied its words carefully, repeating them in his mind like a restless refrain.

For several minutes he sat in a trance. He wasn't prepared. And yet he knew that this invitation was related to his call to participate in something greater than himself. By going to Seville he would find his way, just as the Quoquamish elders had told him. He didn't know where the journey was headed, but he knew without a doubt that it was meant for him to do something important, perhaps something greater than he could possibly fathom. Whether or not it was heroism, it was at least a way to use his profession to serve the greater good. Reading Yusef's message again, he realized that his path was about to steepen. He squeezed his diary and slowly inched it away from his face. As he looked up from the page, anxiety, fear, and hesitation overtook him. He worried about the cost, the time, how he would get to Spain, how he would find Yusef—all these concerns stormed through his mind echoing like the rain and thunder outside.

Then, he looked back at the page. New words appeared:

Don't lag behind.

Wasting no time, Tariq got dressed and threw together a suitcase. He raced out of his apartment and hailed a cab.

"Where to?"

"The airport."

The freeway was empty, which Tariq found peculiarly symbolic, as if the road before him was his own unique destiny. The cab driver kept silent for several minutes. She could see the anxious excitement in Tariq's eyes. Finally, she asked, "So, where are you flying to?"

"To Spain. I've just been called to go meet with a complete stranger, and I am not exactly sure where to find him or what to expect."

The driver nodded incredulously. "And you're just picking up and going, just like that? That's crazy!"

"I know. But it appears to be my path to follow."

"Just be careful. Terrorism makes the world a dangerous place, even for people like you."

People like me. Of course.

The cab exited the freeway and pulled up to the departures curb. Tariq pulled out a twenty to pay the driver. Just then, three shadows appeared outside the cab and stood in front of his door. Tariq could not make out their faces in the darkness, but he got out of the cab anyway.

As soon as he stood up, he recognized them. It was the

Waymaker. And standing beside her were the same Quoqua-mish elders he had met at the mall in Nanaimo: the Wind-stepper and Gray Fin. He was greatly relieved to discover that these two had not been killed in the attack against their village.

"It is good to see you again, Mahatma," greeted the Way-maker.

"You as well."

Tariq introduced himself to the others, though he realized they already knew his name. As he shook hands with Gray Fin, he noticed the same tattoo of the fish skeleton he had seen while they were in the print shop.

"We heard that you witnessed the destruction of one of our villages," Gray Fin acknowledged. His voice quivered with concealed anger.

Tariq nodded.

"I saw the bomb with my own eyes. The Silent One was—"

"His death is a outrage," interrupted the Waymaker. "The whole attack is an abomination!" Her firm lip tensed up, though her breathy voice remained calm and soothing. "But we cannot be too quick to respond. Or too slow."

Tariq tendered a long pause out of respect for the elder's words. But ultimately, his curiosity got the better of him.

"What are you all doing in Seattle?"

"We have come to track down the Order of the Libraries," answered the Windstepper.

"The nuns who slow time down?"

"Who else can we hold responsible?"

"I don't understand. It was a drone missile. What do the nuns have to do with it?"

"The Order of the Libraries has brought this imbalance upon us all. Surely, you can feel it. Why do you think you are called to Seville of all places? That is where the Order of the Libraries has its headquarters!"

"But Seville is so far away! What brought them to Seattle?"

"That is what we intend to find out. All we know is that

they are throwing off the balance of Nature. They are causing us to sink into the present moment, lost in thought and analysis, like a song repeating itself in an endless loop. They are making us lag behind!"

"Lag behind? You mean, like I was, before you sped me back up to time's natural pace?"

"Right, Tariq," answered the Windstepper, poking him in the chest authoritatively with her index finger. "Only for them, it is much more severe. They're not in tune with Nature like you are."

"Why can't you make them be in tune?"

"Because we are like the wind," she explained, waving her arms up in an outward spiral, "breezing loudly through the leaves and yet—" She held her finger to her lips and changed to a whisper. "Powerless to make a sound without the leaves."

Tariq furrowed his brow.

"What the Windstepper means," clarified Gray Fin, "is that in order to be in tune with Nature, one must be willing to bend and rustle with the changing of the times. No one who is rigidly set in a particular belief can be swayed by our influence. However, a rigid person can be snapped apart by the wrong influence."

"But if each person is left to their own beliefs, what can I possibly do?"

"You can use your words!"

"You are the hero, Mahatma!" the Waymaker reassured him. "Remember?"

A chill of guilt struck his rib cage as he secretly thought of the Silent One's death.

"I don't see how. I can't even speak to save a life."

"Developing language takes time. But once your message is complete, you will have the power to sway the world."

He grabbed the pen out of his pocket and showed it to his company.

"Will this pen make me a hero?"

"No!" the Windstepper shouted. She snatched it from the

linguist's hand and prodded him on the forehead with it. "The pen is a hollow piece of glass. It's what comes out of it that makes a hero. *You* are the hero!"

"But even so," added Gray Fin, "the pen is useful. It is an instrument of great influence. When you get to Seville, you will use it to open the channels of communication and make them understand what the religions are doing to Nature. If you keep mindful of the pen, then perhaps you will attract exactly the people you need."

Tariq nodded confidently. "The right people, at the right time."

"Exactly," the three elders agreed.

The linguist grabbed his suitcase and went in to catch his flight.

Chapter 10

The caravan pulled up to the border linking Morocco to Melilla, a Spanish city on the North African coast. This was fortunate timing, since there was barely a trace of gas left in any of the vehicles. Amara took out her Taser and planted it in a hidden compartment under the seat. She got out of the car and adjusted her colorful robe. Nearly exhausted, she approached the entry point where the guards were situated. She held all the necessary documents firmly in her hands.

"Your name?"

"Amara Tejedor. We are returning to Seville."

"How many vehicles?"

"Six cars."

"How many people?"

"Six drivers plus myself."

He squinted when he saw the cages.

"Are those...*crocodiles*?"

Amara handed over the documents with a gracefully authoritative gesture. "Everything you need to know is written here."

The officer perused the documents. "Domesticated crocodiles?"

"*Sí, señor.*"

"And what exactly do you plan to do with them in Seville? Are you breeding a zoo?"

"You could say that."

The guard squinted his eyes at her. "Are you, by any chance, carrying any weapons?"

Amara hesitated. She had been prepared to lie. But in the

magnitude of the moment she sensed disequilibrium in her mind. *Why am I hesitating? Am I questioning my duty to the Watcher to hasten the flow of time? How will I serve my leader if I give up my instrument of strength?*

In the end, she resisted the temptation to hide the truth. She retrieved her Taser from the car and handed it to the guard.

"Yes, I am."

He looked into her honest eyes and decided to give her a chance. "I will need some time to verify your documents. Your caravan will be searched." He took the documents and left his post.

A security team swarmed in to search the cars for additional weapons. They raided every car, opened every compartment, and inspected every cage. The crocodiles looked on with amusement, utterly confounding the inspectors with their calm intelligence. Then the officers ran metal detectors along the creatures' scaly backs. *Nothing inside their bellies,* they concluded.

While watching the search, Amara squeezed the embroidered edges of her sleeves and sank into a state of shame. *I was supposed to enter without being searched! How could I have been so fearful as to surrender my weapon before our mission has even begun?* She took a deep breath and relaxed her brow. *The Last Day,* she reminded herself, *measures us according to our faith in the word of the Prophet. Each time I doubt, I must accept the consequences.* She patted her robed knees and straightened out the wrinkles.

An hour later the officer returned. "You are all cleared to enter with your caravan. However, I must keep your weapon. Weapons are not allowed."

Just like that? She thanked Allah for this stroke of good fortune.

"I admit, I was skeptical," explained the guard. "But you made the right choice to come forth with it, *señorita*. May God watch over you."

"And also you, *señor.*"

With nothing further, she led her caravan into Melilla to fuel up. The crocodiles shifted around in their cages, and the drivers nodded their weary heads. The caravan stopped at the first gas station after the border. As each car turned off its engine, the crocodiles let out a restful sigh. Amara got out of the car and stretched her legs. *Almost home.*

Unexpectedly, a voice chimed from behind her.

"Amara," Yusef called.

She turned around and embraced her brother. "I wasn't expecting you."

"I wanted to take you to Seville myself. Ibrahim is here too. He will take the crocodiles across the channel for us."

"You are thoughtful." She crossed her arms. "But I didn't need you to come."

"I know," the imam sighed. His younger sister was never one to accept help. "How are the crocodiles? Are they as docile as we were promised?"

"Yes. We have all of them except one, named Seogo, who would not fit in the cages."

"And what about the zoologist? Where is she?"

"She is lost to the desert. A plague of locusts came out of nowhere. I could not save her. The rest of us barely escaped."

"I see." The imam lowered his head. "I will tell the Watcher to prepare a funeral. Naomi has served our cause well, and for that we shall honor her death."

Then he sensed some agitation in her demeanor. "What else is wrong? Did something happen at the border crossing?"

Amara rolled her eyes. She knew her older brother would interrogate her like this. "I handed over the Taser to the border patrol. I know it was my duty to keep it with me, but I panicked. I was worried that if they searched the car and found it, then our entire mission would be jeopardized."

Yusef nodded and smiled. "What you did was right. Not all weapons are necessary. To tell the truth, I was never very comfortable with you hiding it in the first place."

"But I could have been captured once we crossed the border! How would I have defended myself?"

"Have faith in the decency of people, Amara. If the true Islam is to win your heart, you must choose the path of peace."

"Thank Allah nothing went wrong! Didn't the Watcher tell you that only a perfect execution of our plan, God willing, would suffice? We can take no chances, Yusef!"

"The Watcher meant that we must embrace the path of holiness and reject the path of resistance. When you felt compelled to relinquish your weapon, Amara, that command came from your intuition. It spoke to you just as we are speaking now. You must learn to trust it."

"Trust it? You mean, like how you ask me to trust the Watcher? How can you ask me to place my faith blindly in someone I have never met?" She moved her hands to her hips. "And what makes you so sure the Watcher's goal is really the same as ours?"

"Because I trust Allah."

"How do you know all of our efforts will really lead us to the Clepsydra?"

"The time is upon us, Amara, for such secrets to be uncovered. Surely your intuition is telling you that as well."

"And what about this linguist, Tariq Kamal? What is to say he can be trusted?"

"You worry about what is beyond your control. The tides of time are already bringing him to us, and you must use your eyes of faith in order to see it."

"But our family has fought for so many centuries to keep time advancing toward the Last Day. If we err in our trust, how can we protect the world from these same doubts and hesitations? How can we prevent them from stopping time and delaying the Last Day?"

"The hesitations are already gripping us, Amara. Just like your faith, doubts also weave their way into your every movement." He took Amara's hand, which gently inched out of its long, patterned sleeve, and he met her eyes with his. "The person you must really learn to trust is yourself."

Amara heaved out a cathartic breath. "I know, Yusef. But why can't I meet the Watcher so I know for sure he is on our side?"

"Because the Watcher has asked me not to allow it."

"Humph."

"There are secrets, dear sister, that only an imam can know. And such secrets are absolute. Not even you can be brought in."

Amara stood up straighter and cleared her mind. "I suppose I will just have to become the next imam."

Yusef grinned wholeheartedly. "We just might have to arrange that someday."

Smiling at each other, they got in Yusef's car and headed home.

Chapter 11

The zoologist and her crocodile landed abruptly upon dry brush at the bottom of the ravine. Both were unconscious for several minutes. When the woman came to, a nagging impulse squeezed her heart and wouldn't let go. She needed to smoke. She looked right and left, frantically assessing her whereabouts. Then she spied Seogo chewing something. His chewing was a bitter reminder of how famished she was. In fact, her hunger masked the pain of the countless scrapes and bruises she had accumulated during their fall.

"Seogo, what are you eating?"

She made her way over to the crocodile and placed her hand below the docile animal's jaw. Inside, there were chewed up scraps of thin, white cardboard.

My cigarettes!

She attempted to reach into Seogo's mouth to retrieve them, but his swift, muscular tail whacked her and sent her sliding several feet across the sand.

"Seogo!" she scolded, enraged by this sudden show of force.

Seogo opened his mouth and clamped onto the zoologist's pack, removing its only bottle of water and swallowing it whole. Then, as if to torment his companion, the beast let out a loud, conniving burp.

"Curse you!"

Seogo turned around and scampered away.

"Curse you back to your filthy pond!"

The zoologist looked down at her knuckles and wiped off the blood.

"Hey! Where do you think you're going?"

Though barely able, the zoologist ran after the crocodile and pounced clumsily on his back. The beast grunted, then went motionless.

"The caravan is gone, and I have nothing. Nothing! This is all because of you. You've killed me, you bastard!"

She attempted to wrestle with Seogo while straddling his back, but the crocodile did not fight back. Instead he hardened in place like a sitting stone.

"What do you have to say for yourself, huh? You nasty little—"

Then the zoologist grabbed a knife from her pocket. Without thinking, she directed the blade at Seogo's neck.

"If I'm going to live," she declared desperately, "then I have to eat something. And it's going to be you!" She raised the knife slowly and braced herself to take a sacrifice.

But just as the zoologist prepared her grip, Seogo spun his head backwards and gave her an austere, penetrating look. His was a look of awe, an image of the rawest wrath of God. His teeth were an omen, his beady eyes a warning. But then he softened. His wrinkles sagged like the skin of an old wise man, directing her to a higher path. Indeed, the look he gave her was intended to save her, not to bring her harm.

The woman chucked the knife behind her without looking and collapsed. Her hands trembled, and her scraped-up knuckles bled. She then hugged Seogo and lay shaking upon his back. She wept forcefully, wishing her eyes were moist enough for tears.

"Forgive me, Lord!"

She gazed into Seogo's beady, sympathetic eyes and felt a surge of overwhelming calm. Almost instantly, trickles of sweat ran down her cheeks. The water within her was released. She sighed.

"Forgive me, Seogo." She slid off Seogo and planted herself beside her companion placing her hand lovingly on his neck.

Seogo responded with a deep, reverberating purr.

"I've always tested the limits and cheated death by a hair.

Maybe it's my nature; maybe it's because I have nothing to lose."

Seogo lifted his snout into a cobra pose and became still. The zoologist admired the crocodile's scaly physiognomy and rough jaw. She had never before come in such close contact with a large reptile for such an extended length of time without needing nooses, chains, or tranquilizers. But something about Seogo calmed her soul, bringing her into a deep state of trust.

"And yet I've never lost faith. I know the Lord has put me here to suffer, not to die. And this time, He has put you here with me." The zoologist tickled Seogo's chin and smiled. "He has given us both a heart. That's one thing we share. Let's not fight again."

Mentally revitalized, she stood up, gathered her knife, and began walking. Seogo followed. He grunted and held his head up, motioning for his friend to look around.

"There's a hell of a lot of desert out there. We'll have a greater chance to survive if we cooperate. We are partners, Seogo."

The crocodile snapped his teeth together.

"And that means no eating my cigarettes!"

She took the butt end of her knife and tapped Seogo on the nose in jest. He flared his nostrils and flinched.

If only I had any cigarettes left.

As they moved, Seogo's tail left a long, sinewy imprint in the sand. To pass the time, Naomi shuffled her shoes in the sand to mirror his trail.

We are partners, she reminded herself. *Seogo and me.*

Chapter 12

Tariq stepped outside of the Madrid airport and into a strangely unsettling place. He knew Spain quite well, having spent a year as an undergraduate at the University of Granada. But the air of Madrid felt thicker since his last visit, the people less familiar. Though he could not understand why, it was immediately clear that change was about to take place—revolutionary change—and that he had just descended into the midst of it.

On his way to the train station, Tariq stopped at his favorite park, *El Retiro*, to gather his thoughts. Often while visiting Madrid he had spend hours sitting beside *El Retiro's* vast, rectangular water reservoir, taking refuge from the busy demands of his academic life. There, he could watch busy locals rowing in rented boats and listen to the sweet hymns of saxophones played by street musicians. Perhaps it was no coincidence that the park's name, in English, meant 'the refuge.' Amidst the park's strolling distant crowds, the falling of leaves, and the quacking of ducks, one could hide away to contemplate the changing of the seasons.

The seasons were now changing faster than Tariq had ever experienced. As he walked Madrid's historic streets, smells of old stone buildings and artisanal hams wafted into his awareness, feeling somehow ancient and new at the same time. He had no idea what would happen, only that he needed to get to Seville and find Yusef Tejedor.

When Tariq arrived at the train station, he stood in line at the ticket counter behind two nuns dressed in their traditional black habits. They were speaking Spanish with what he gathered to be an Andalusian accent. *I wonder if they are from Granada*, he surmised, reminiscing about his college days.

"Two tickets to Seville, *por favor*," he heard one of the nuns request. Tariq's eyes widened. She paid the woman behind the counter, adjusted her habit and then polished her wooden necklace with her sleeve. *The nun I saw by the water clock in Nanaimo was wearing the exact same necklace*, he noted. *Maybe they are the Order of the Libraries!* As the two nuns left the line, they whispered to each other, though Tariq was unable to hear their words.

"Next!" shouted the ticket vendor.

Tariq approached the counter and asked to purchase a one-way ticket for the same bus as the two nuns. The man behind the counter met his request without question. Within minutes the bus pulled up and the passengers poured into their seats. By a stroke of luck, Tariq was seated directly across the aisle from the nuns. Soon the train departed for Seville. He tightened his fists, anxious about his next move. *It's a three-hour ride; I'll wait a while and then introduce myself.*

The Spanish countryside was a stunning juxtaposition of lush green foliage and bold, brown dirt. Tariq rested his cheek on the complimentary pillow and gazed out the window. Strings of long-unused Spanish phrases resurfaced and raced through his head. *The Spanish word for pillow, 'almohada,'* he recalled, *comes from the Arabic 'al-muhadda,' for which the root word means 'cheek.'* His eyes fell slowly shut, and within a few minutes, he was sound asleep.

He got his first wink of sleep in over 24 hours, ever since reading Yusef's letter. He thought about how the letter's green ink had led him to follow his intuition without lagging behind. Then he slipped into a vivid dream.

He was back at the University of Washington, sitting in the Suzzallo reading room. In front of him was a stack of enormous, old hardbound books. The library was desolate. Eerie streaks of light poured through the stained glass windows and danced upon the polished oak furniture. Wax candles lit up in flame atop the room's octagonal chandeliers. The vaulted ceiling and smoky gray walls loomed over him like those of an enormous, empty cathedral.

Two painted globes hung at opposite ends of the long, narrow reading room. Both globes were large and dazzling, like proud monuments to celebrate the world's progress in coming to understand itself. But they were placed so far from each other across the room that one could scarcely appreciate either one closely without losing sight of the other. *Like two opposing worlds,* he thought, *destined to remain at a distance from each other. Like two opposing worldviews.*

Then the linguist turned his attention to the stack of books, which gave off a soft aura of green light. They were made of the kind of vellum parchment used during medieval times, fashioned from animal hide, soaked, cured, stretched, and dyed the perfect tone to receive careful, calligraphic brush strokes. The books were like precious gems. As their aura grew stronger, Tariq felt an inexplicable notion that these books contained the answers to everything he sought to know in life: the deep structures of human language, the inner psychology of creed and reconciliation, the mysteries of what to say and when and how to say it—all this wisdom was densely, immaculately concentrated between those crisp, hardbound covers.

He stood up to reach for the books, and at that moment the sight of everything in the room felt heavy in his mind like a sailboat being filled with water, sinking. He tried to move, but his shoulders wouldn't twist and his arms wouldn't lift. He could think, but his body was completely numb. He couldn't even muster a twitch of his cheek. And yet the weight of the books somehow was drawing him in like an object floating powerlessly into a black hole.

Then the books began sinking into the table. The table's

oak surface sagged and bulged beneath them, and the entire room appeared to bend around their aura like the bending of space and time around a massive celestial object. Tariq felt himself being pulled slowly into the aura. Faster and faster he was drawn in. But this time, the thought of getting close to those books was horrifying—it was unbearable! Reading those books would mean learning the final truth. It would mean bringing an end to his research, an end to his quest, and an end to his mortal existence!

Yet the gravity of the books was inescapable. He couldn't look away; in a way, he wanted to suffer this death. He longed for it more than anything else. *I must know what is written inside!*

Then, just when he was about to touch the front cover of one of the books, streams of green, glowing strings of letters poured out of the book and spiraled around his field of vision. Words fluttered through the air as they filled the room. This happened for what felt like several minutes, and then instantly the words sped away from him, leaving a trail of fading stardust behind.

Now the books were empty. They had poured out their essence. All that remained in the tomes were those lifeless, decaying pages, forever bound to those rigid, decrepit spines.

Then, like the closing of a book, the entire room started to close in around him. The walls warped, the tables curved, and the books folded in on themselves. The two opposite ends of the room wrapped around the nexus of the lifeless tomes like a moving image in a convex mirror, until the two opposite ends of the room connected. The east became the west and the west became the east. The two globes that hung at opposite ends of the room met and converged into one. *One world.*

Finally, darkness consumed him, and all went black.

With a jerk, the train pulled up to its stop and startled Tariq awake. He was in Seville. *I slept through the entire ride? I may have missed my chance to meet the nuns, all because of that damn* almohada*!*

He grabbed his suitcase from the overhead bin and followed the nuns out of the bus. *Here I go again, following strangers to God-knows-where. But this time, I will catch up from the start and not lag behind.*

"Excuse me," Tariq addressed the nuns in his half-rusty Spanish. "I have just come from Seattle, and I am looking for a man called Yusef Tejedor. Do you know how I might find him?"

The two looked at each other, wide-eyed, and answered: "Come with us."

The nuns proceeded to lead Tariq on foot through Seville's historic downtown. Orange trees lined the sidewalks where locals made their way from place to place. Echoes of antiquity rang through the streets, as buildings of brick and plasterwork bore beauteous traces of the *Mudéjar* architecture of the medieval Moors.

Finally, they reached the plaza in front of Seville's famous palace, the *Alcazar*. They stood in plain sight and yet were completely concealed amidst the busy-mindedness of the crowds. The older, taller nun spoke first:

"I am Sister Clarinda, and this is Sister Belén."

"Pleased to meet you. I am Tariq Kamal from Seattle."

They kissed cheeks as a formal greeting.

"Let's get right to the point. What do you know about Yusef Tejedor?" Sister Clarinda asked him.

"Next to nothing," Tariq confessed. "I only received a message from him asking me to come to Seville. I have never even met him."

"You mean, you didn't follow him here from Seattle?"

"Yusef was in Seattle?"

"Yusef is a thief!" exclaimed Sister Belén. "He steals from you the most precious thing your soul has here on earth."

Tariq could only imagine what she was referring to.

"He steals your time," explained Sister Clarinda. "Imagine it. In one moment, you are at home listening to the faint sound of water trickling away, and in the next you are waking up hours, sometimes days later as if no time at all has passed at all!"

"This is happening in Seattle?"

"It is happening all over the world. Time is being sped up! We have already sent many of our Sisters abroad to slow it down and set things right."

"The Order of the Libraries," explained Sister Belén, "has seen every episode of turmoil going back a thousand years, since before the Crusades and before the Muslims sacked our city. We have kept the peace in Spain for centuries and have documented it for our records."

The Order of the Libraries. Tariq paused to reflect: *Christians slow time down, Muslims speed it up. But why?*

"I don't know why you are here, Mr. Kamal," added Sister Clarinda, "but you have come to the right place at the right time, and for that reason, you are a part of our struggle. Now you must slow down and weigh the truth of each matter carefully. Only in the eternal sanctity of the present moment will you find the answers."

Sister Clarinda paused and grabbed her wooden necklace. Now that Tariq was closer, he could see that it was engraved with a crucifix and the letters *INRI*, which he knew to be a Latin acronym for "Jesus of Nazareth, King of the Jews." For a few seconds, Tariq smiled in awe of how such a short string of letters could carry such a profound religious significance—a symbol of the divinity that was crucified when society rushed to judgment in their persecution of the Christ.

Suddenly, a voice thundered through the air as a woman in a striking, colorful robe darted across the plaza of the *Alcazar*.

"Do not waste another second here!" the robed one shouted as she approached them.

It's Amara Tejedor, the nuns nervously realized.

"Who is it?" Tariq asked them.

But before either Sister could answer, a string of gunshots deafened the plaza.

Tariq jerked his head to observe what had happened: three masked gunmen armed with semi-automatic rifles were charging the *Alcazar*, leaving wounded civilians floundering outside its gates. Bystanders screamed; children cried. And a mysterious robed woman stood before him somehow removed from it all. He felt the same implosion of his wits as he did during the bombing of the Quoquamish village. *This is an act of terror!*

"Come with me!" the robed one instructed Tariq.

"Are you talking to me?"

"Are you armed?"

Of course not, exclaimed Tariq's surprised eyes.

"Then you have to get away from the gunfire. Come with me!"

The robed one grabbed the linguist's arm and whisked him away from the scene. They headed straight for the Seville Cathedral, past frightened clusters of fortune-telling women carrying rosemary branches.

"Quickly, do not fall behind! The fate of Islam is at stake!"

She led Tariq around the back side of the cathedral and then diagonally through a tall, shady alleyway. There, they passed behind a rustic eatery and an abandoned church. When they were out of sight of all onlookers, she grabbed his arm and stopped. Her ornate sleeve waved in the air and she held him still.

"I think you are Tariq," she said softly.

"You're right," Tariq nodded, not wanting to question how she knew him.

"I am Amara." She pulled up her other sleeve and extended her hand. "My brother Yusef is looking for you."

"Yusef?"

"Yes, he is our imam."

"But what's going on? Seville is being attacked, and we're

hiding out behind an old church!"

"*Silencio!*" she commanded, covering his mouth with her hand. Then she grabbed his hand and marched onward. "We must get to the mosque quickly. These terrorists think they are fighting for our homeland, for Al-Andalus, but they are misguided—unbelievers! They know nothing of Islam or our past!"

"You know them?"

"Of course not." She shuddered at the question. "But I know their politics."

"I think we all do. Attacks like these have been going on all over the world."

"Precisely. But in Spain, there is something more. Do you remember the attack on Madrid's train station in 2004?"

"I remember it well."

"That attack was carried out by pretenders—radicals, who wish to avenge the *reconquista*."

"The *reconquista*? You mean the 15th-century expulsion of Muslims from Spain?"

"Indeed. And now, after all this time, the real threat is coming out of the woodwork: with support from the *Islamic State*, they will stop at nothing to re-conquer Spain in the name of the old caliphate, Al-Andalus."

"The return of Islam to Spain? Is such a thing possible?"

"Not by force, no. Each person's spiritual journey is for that person alone. Yusef and I are not after converts, only peace. This is why you must help us! We need to warn them, warn all of humanity that time itself will come to a standstill if we do not make peace."

Now, he thought, *things are starting to make sense.* The war of the religions was not just ideological; it was really happening! Each terrorist attack—from San Bernardino to Lahore—was simply an extreme example of humanity disrupting the flow of the river of time, speeding it up and slowing it down, diverting its natural course. Everything the Waymaker had described was now shown plainly in front of him.

"Amara!" Tariq exclaimed as he contemplated the signs of war. He pulled out his glass pen and showed it to her. "Maybe this pen can help. It was the instrument that told me about the war to happen in Seville."

"Let me see that!" Amara took the pen swiftly from his fingers and stopped in her tracks. She gripped it like a dagger and squeezed it energetically. While she examined it, she felt for her own pen secretly within her robe's innermost pocket as to make sure it was still there.

"I have seen these before. This kind of pen has a quantum power to it, capable of sending words over great distances in no time at all. Where did you get it?"

At the mall, he nearly said, realizing how silly that would have sounded.

"From a First Nations tribe in western Canada. I believe it contains powerful algae."

"Algae?" She had never stopped to wonder what made the ink green. "Well, never mind what's in it; bring it with you. It looks like we may have a full-on war in our midst. Are you ready?"

As she looked at him with her penetrating eyes, Tariq felt all the walls of his consciousness breaking down. He studied the bold, polychromatic designs woven into her robe. To him these designs signified strength and courage; the robe itself was a kind of fortress protecting the inner sanctity of her secret faith. Inexplicably he knew he was in the right place and that this woman could be trusted. Nothing else mattered.

"I think I'll have to be."

"Good. The role of the linguist is essential to our plan."

Though several blocks away, they could still hear the sound of shells being fired in the distance followed by the screams of unsuspecting civilians.

"Amara," Tariq began, trying to slow his breath.

"Yes?" She looked back as if waiting for him to say something profound.

"Do you think the nuns made it out of the plaza alive?"

"The nuns?"

"Yes. I feel bad for just leaving them there."

"They are fine, Tariq, don't worry about them," she responded. Part of her was impatient with the question, yet another part was strangely fascinated by this man's concern. "Just be careful not to get left behind. Spending too much time with Christians can leave you lingering, *para más INRI!*"

Tariq blinked his eyes trying to decipher what that expression meant in Spanish. Though he could not make sense of it, he admired the bold and passionate timber of her voice.

"Come. The mosque is not far."

Seville fell quiet. The shock of terrorism brought merchants and drivers, laborers and beggars alike to a standstill. Life was precious, and never was this truth better appreciated than in the circumstance of near-death. The people of Seville would dwell in the grief and perplexity of terrorism until the sun's last light. But not wanting to lag behind, Tariq and Amara continued down the desolate alleyway, hearing nothing but their own foreboding footsteps and the restless beating of their wondering hearts.

Chapter 13

"This place is a labyrinth!" exclaimed Gray Fin as he and the Windstepper wandered through Seattle's Central Library. "Why would the Order of the Libraries want to meet here?"

"How should I know?" she retorted, throwing her arms up as she led her companion up through floors of endless book stacks.

"Maybe," he thought out loud, "there is something about the architecture of this particular library. Or, maybe this library contains a book with all the answers. Or, maybe—"

"Shush!" she whispered. She closed her eyes and took two dramatic steps forward, looking left and right. "I think they are on the fourth floor."

"The fourth floor? Then why are we up here on floor six? Or, is this seven?"

"Since when does a fish question the wind?"

"Maybe," he mumbled, "when the wind starts to go against the current, hmm?"

"O, please! You know very well that it's sometimes necessary to meander around in the shallow waters before reaching the *heart* of the matter."

Though she was unaware of it, this was an impeccably apt analogy: the fourth floor was in both literal and metaphorical ways the heart of the building: all of its walls, doors, floors, and ceilings were painted blood red; furthermore, the entire floor was suspended within the vaulted third-floor atrium and had no outside windows. Everything within the fourth floor was concealed in the library like a red, painted heart locked away in secrecy.

"Very well," acceded Gray Fin with a hint of sarcasm. "I shall yield to your direction."

When they reached the fourth floor, the two elders circulated its blood red hallways until they came to an unassuming door marked *Meeting Room*.

"Hold onto your reel," the Windstepper warned, gripping the air with her fist. "You'll need all your energy to keep from lagging behind."

The door opened to reveal a candlelit meditation session. Two Sisters, Sabina and Martirio, sat facing each other with eyes closed, their faces illuminated by the flame. In the shadows the blood-red color of the walls seeped into the quiet darkness.

The energy between the Sisters was mesmerizing. The Windstepper and Gray Fin watched them sit perfectly still for what seemed like several hours suspended in the restful act of meditation. Their meditation was the kind that naturally dissuaded their onlookers from interrupting its silence.

Then, breaking out of the trance, the Sisters simultaneously let out the end of their prayer: "In the name of the Father, the Son, and the Holy Spirit. Amen." They opened their eyes and turned to face their visitors.

"Welcome to our meeting place. Come, join us."

The visitors shook off the hypnotic spell and sat down. They introduced themselves cordially as to not press the delicate intentions of their mission.

"You are the tribe's elders, no?" pronounced Sister Sabina in her gentle Spanish accent. "What did you say your tribe was called?"

"The Quoquamish."

"Who?" exclaimed Sister Martirio in a slightly thicker accent. "I have never heard of such a tribe."

"We have managed to stay off the maps for a hundred years," explained Gray Fin. "But now one of our villages has been destroyed! Who will answer for this?" He tightened his fists and held his lips firmly closed.

"I don't understand. How was your village destroyed?"

"By a drone missile!" shouted the Windstepper angrily and nearly leapt off of the ground as she made a gesture for the falling missile.

"I thought the drone fired into the wilderness!" sister Martirio exclaimed. "All of our sources reported that no one was harmed!"

"That is why we can no longer stay in hiding," the Windstepper continued. "Nature is in crisis. The world is destroying itself! You see that it has already begun to do so."

"Allow us the time," offered Sister Sabina, "and we will pray for you."

"A lot of good that will do!" exclaimed Gray Fin. "It is your prayers that are causing the problem!"

Sister Sabina furrowed her brow and calmly inquired, "What do you mean?"

"Have you ever watched the seasons change? Winter thaws, giving way to gushing streams; flowers bloom in the springtime while salmon hatch and rabbits bear their young. Nature is a fine balance. It takes only a slight deviation from the normal parameters of life to cause Nature to spiral out of control. Don't you realize that when you pray, time deviates from its natural course?"

Sister Martirio contemplated their response. After a moment of silence she spoke: "We mean no disrespect to Nature, Gray Fin. In fact, we too recognize how humankind is prone to violence and the destruction of the earth, and this is precisely why we slow down time in prayer. We do it so there is time to reflect, to surrender the need to proceed until we are sure of the correct path for our words and actions."

"We are scholars of the natural world," added Sister Sabina. "We take nothing for granted that we know or don't know. But when dealing with matters of grave importance, surely you can understand our duty to retreat into our libraries and consider all of the possibilities."

"But there is only one possibility," declared the Windstepper. "Gravity doesn't make things meander around, it pulls them straight down." She illustrated with her index finger. "Water, too, has only one possibility. It does not need to stop and consider which way to flow; it simply follows Nature's law. The more you study, you will observe this: the human heart already knows the way."

The Sisters hesitated, taking in the elders' explanations. *Do they have a point? Perhaps not, but let us pause and reflect. We have all of eternity in this moment to seek out the right path, and you can never be too quick to assume you are on the correct side of justice, the side of the Heavenly Father.*

"This is why you must stop," added Gray Fin. "You are making the world lag behind! All the while it is we who end up restoring the flow of time."

"We will have to consider this some more. After all, it was humankind's failure to consider that led to the eating of the forbidden fruit, the original sin."

In our eyes, Gray Fin wanted to exclaim, *religion is the original sin!*

"One other thing comes to mind," added Sister Martirio. "There is a man in Seville called the Watcher. He is connected with an imam called Yusef Tejedor. These two have us very worried. Word has it they are building some kind of army."

"An army?" the Windstepper repeated, pressing all ten fingers nervously against her chin.

"They are obsessed with the coming of the Last Day."

The elders turned and looked at each other. The Windstepper scratched her chin, agitated. *I wonder if this Watcher is connected to the attack we have suffered?*

"I have met Yusef," the Windstepper confessed.

"When?" cried a startled Gray Fin.

"He came to me two days ago."

Gray Fin was furious.

"I hope you did not invite him into our home!"

"Do you think my head is full of air?" The Windstepper crossed her arms. "It was here in Seattle." She stepped back and pointed at the sisters with both her index fingers. "Yusef warned me about you! He told me that the Order of the Libraries was responsible for exposing our whereabouts!"

"That's a lie!" exclaimed Sister Martirio. "We had never even heard of your tribe until this very meeting!"

"That is not exactly true," admitted Sister Sabina.

Sister Martirio was shocked.

"Sister, you knew about them?"

"I have been praying for the Quoquamish for a few weeks now, letting my prayers guide them in finding us here."

"Let's not get caught up in arguments about the past," insisted Gray Fin. "The past is all upstream. But your prayers must stop now."

"Do you even care that a village was destroyed?" shouted the Windstepper.

"Of course we do, Windstepper." Sister Sabina placed her hand to her heart.

"The problem seems to be Yusef," reasoned Sister Martirio. "The Muslims have no regard for your precious Nature. To them the created world is a distraction that delays the coming of the Last Day."

"To put it in your terms," explained Sister Sabina, "they want to speed time up so quickly that Nature might have no chance to nurse life at all! I don't know about you, but I would rather repeat this moment one thousand times over than miss out on it entirely."

Gray Fin put his arm around the Windstepper, who was growing more and more distressed.

"I think it is time we go to Seville and counteract the Watcher's army," Sister Sabina proposed. She could see that the Windstepper was on the verge of tears. "Will you join us?"

The Windstepper turned her hands into fists and pushed them into her chin to contemplate their offer.

"We will go with you to find Yusef," she answered, qualifying her statement with a raised finger. "But we will not *join* you."

The Sisters doused the candles' flames and locked up the meeting room. Spain, their homeland, was calling them back.

Chapter 14

In no time, Amara and Tariq arrived at the entrance of her humble mosque, which was built into the face of an unassuming townhouse with faint, white geometrical engravings etched into the building's original *Mudéjar* decor. In the presence of Amara's dazzling robe, however, the engravings stood out in full splendor, announcing to visitors that inside one might find words of truth and power. The door opened and the imam greeted them. He prompted them to remove their shoes.

"Yusef!" exclaimed the imam's sister. "The attacks are going on as we speak!"

"Attacks? Here in Seville?"

"They are shooting in the streets! I had no way to defend myself. But we got away as fast as we could and ran straight here."

Yusef's dark eyes grew large and severe as he glanced outside once more. "These attacks are not merely acts of terrorism, they are signs that all of human history is caught in an endless loop, unable to advance toward the Last Day. They are lost without the hope of enlightenment or salvation. But now you are here. It is time for us to embark on our long-awaited journey." He paused to observe the linguist. "I see you have brought our guest to join us for the ride."

"This is Tariq."

"Welcome, Tariq." He clasped the linguist's hand and placed his other hand on his shoulder. "They tell me you are a talented linguist. You don't realize how much you are needed here in this very moment."

Tariq smiled. "I still can't believe this is happening. And I don't see what I can possibly do to help."

"I understand. Follow me, and I will explain everything."

"Just tell me what I should do."

"First, pray with us."

Tariq followed the imam and his sister as they treaded reverently upon their family's thousand-year-old rug. Each foot pressed down upon its multicolored threading like the squeeze of an adoring handshake. Tariq felt as if he were trekking across time itself, following it to the very end. Water flowed placidly from the fountain at the end of the rug. The three of them dipped their hands to cleanse themselves, and then descended into kneeling position facing the *mihrab*.

"This may surprise you, Tariq," Amara said as she wiped her face and adjusted her robe to a kneeling position, "but we are a progressive mosque. This means that women and men pray together in the same line."

"Not surprising at all," he commented. "It's about time!"

Amara squinted her eyes and gave Tariq a faint smile of approval. "By the way, your Spanish is very good."

He returned the smile modestly, and they began to pray.

Tariq was familiar with the procedure of the prayer. He knew when to repeat the words, when to bow, and when to rise; his grandfather had taught him this as a young child. However, this time something about the prayer struck a new, vibrant chord. The way the imam's kind voice resonated through the prayer hall, how Amara's stillness protected him on his other side—all the elements of the religious experience coalesced within him, leading him to a truth that had to be experienced in order to be understood.

When they came out of prayer it was already dusk; but because there were no windows, not one of them was aware of the time of day.

"Tariq," Yusef began, "has Amara told you about our army?"

"Army?"

"Not yet, brother. I was getting to that."

"Fine. I will explain. There is time."

Yusef placed his hand on Tariq's shoulder again and gazed into his inquisitive eyes.

"You have seen the attacks; you have witnessed the violence that keeps religions at odds with each other. True?"

The linguist nodded. *Yusef has no idea.*

"The only way to reconcile these extremist ideologies is to unite them with an army—one that can send a message to all the world, warning them of the Last Day, warning them to let time proceed without trying to hold onto it."

"But why an army? Isn't that counterproductive?"

"Our army will use not the force of brute strength but the force of words. Words are powerful, as you well know! The army will weave its warning into the consciousness of all of humanity, preparing us for that Day when all believers are delivered from suffering."

"Have you heard of the Watcher?" asked Amara. "He is the one who will lead this army and stir the world into peace by delivering our message."

"What message?" asked the linguist. "What can an army possibly say to command the entire world?"

"That is exactly the right question," Yusef replied. "That is your job. You are the linguist. You will compose the message."

The linguist touched the pen in his pocket. Now that he understood the magnitude of the war he was fighting, it felt even more like a weapon.

"But there is one more problem," Yusef continued. "Even if we have the perfect message, we still need a means of transmitting it. That is why we need a timekeeping technology so vast and intricate that it can broadcast your message across space and time and restore all seven billion human hearts to their eternal state of peace."

"What kind of technology can do that?"

"The Clepsydra. It's a water clock. But it's one that has been lost to us for many centuries."

Tariq immediately thought of the waterfall the Waymaker had shown him. "Can this water clock be made from a waterfall?"

"Tariq," Amara interjected, "we don't have to make anything; the Clepsydra already exists! Somewhere in Spain, it is hiding, waiting for us to find it."

"It was built long ago by a wise man and hidden for protection," Yusef explained. "He knew that in this very moment we would need it."

He knew? But how could they know?

"Come. You will help us find it."

Yusef and Amara took Tariq down to a lower floor and into a long, narrow chamber. The chamber led into a labyrinth of caves, winding beneath the streets of Seville, lit by torches like a scene from the Dark Ages. The ceiling at times was nearly low enough for Tariq to bump his head, but with a little attention he avoided that error. Eventually, the narrow cave opened up into a large room whose ceilings were lined with ornate three clover-shaped arches. In the middle was a row of three oddly shaped baths large enough for a human being to lie down in comfortably. What made these baths even more peculiar, however, was their depth.

Tariq walked up to the first bath and peered into its still, clear waters. He could see a cavernous bottom with pores and crevices, irregular like the inside of Andalusia's Nerja Caves. In the very middle, a deep crack opened up into a lightless, elliptical pit. Without warning, a fist-sized air bubble erupted from the crack and rippled upon the water's surface. Tariq looked up at the other two baths. The same thing had occurred in those baths too, perfectly synchronized with the first.

"These baths are filled from an underground spring. Over time, water seeps in in gradual bursts. Then, at precise intervals it drains back down letting a series of sixty bubbles emerge before it begins to fill again. The water level of the bath, effectively, can be read as a kind of clock, so long as you know how many cycles of filling and draining have taken place throughout the day."

Tariq watched the baths with anticipation as he waited eagerly for the next bubble to appear. *These baths are water clocks!*

"What do you think, Tariq?"

The linguist paused a moment. His head was filled with questions rather than evaluative thoughts.

"Do you know the Order of the Libraries, Yusef?"

"Now is not the time to discuss them, Tariq. Such a discussion will only slow us down!"

"I ask only because when I met the nuns from the Libraries, they said you had been to Seattle."

"That is true."

"What were you doing there?"

"Looking for a linguist, of course."

"To write your message?"

"I found him, didn't I?"

"But how did you choose me?"

"How does Allah choose anyone?" Yusef adjusted his copper belt buckle and smiled. "Tariq, there are no coincidences. Even your name suggests you were meant to help us."

"My name?"

"It means a star that visits in the night."

"I know that. There is a chapter in the Quran with my name."

"Then you know that a star is fixed in the sky, Tariq. A star has a path that must be followed, and it does not dare deviate from its path."

"I think about this quite often."

"As you should," Yusef affirmed. Another bubble erupted from the baths in front of them. "And this means keep away from the Order of the Libraries. They are not in your path. They cannot be trusted."

"But why?"

Yusef sighed with his eyes closed. He put his hand on Tariq's back and motioned for him to sit down.

"It is time you knew about our family's history."

They all sat down on a woven carpet placed on the floor in the middle of the three baths. Then, Yusef began:

"A thousand years ago, our family was entrusted with the ability to accelerate time. All this began with our first water clock. Now I shall explain to you how it was created.

"Our ancestor, Umar Al-Hayek, was a weaver of textiles and tapestries. He used a loom to produce remarkable works of woven art, which made him quite well known during his time.

"One day, he was selling his goods around the outskirts of Seville. He encountered a government official who was using a water clock to keep his appointments. And though this water clock was simple—made of nothing more than a porous bowl placed inside a basin of water—Umar Al-Hayek was struck by an ingenious idea: *Maybe,* he thought, *if I can use the water clock to power the back-and-forth movement of the loom, then I can create even more beautiful pieces with superior precision.*

"When he got home, Al-Hayek immediately began building a water clock. He experimented with different materials, weights, water sources—everything! He fashioned an array of interconnected tubes and spouts so the water could be siphoned at the correct times to fill the correct chambers. Until finally, his invention was complete: a hydraulic machine that could move the ends of the loom at precisely the intervals needed to weave his great works.

"Al-Hayek attached the water clock to his loom and began weaving. Visions of colors and patterns enraptured his mind. Following these visions he was able to weave what he saw much more quickly and clearly. He could spin more colors and arrange more intricate designs than ever before. Thanks to his new invention, in the month that followed he sold forty times his usual amount. The water clock brought a surplus of food to his family's table and joy to their hearts.

"But over time, a strange thing started happening. Al-Hayek discovered that the patterns he wove were not merely decorations; they were symbols—deep symbols of the human experience. The more he wove, the more he learned to see and understand them: they were symbols of great wealth and extreme poverty, of abundant feasts and mass starvation, of the rising and falling of dynasties—he recognized the same experiences repeating throughout all time like patterns woven over and over again. He learned to see and feel them all.

"It was true, with the water clock, Al-Hayek could weave like never before. And yet he barely needed any effort to create new, ingenious designs. The patterns just came to him as easily as slipping on a glove. Because of this he knew that these were more than mere artistic productions; they were divine expressions from Allah.

"Through his weaving, Allah was teaching Al-Hayek to recognize the timeless unity of all the elements of life. He learned how sorrow threads its way into merriment and merriment into sorrow; how colors of friendship and colors of enmity intertwine and feed each other; how strands of love and longing bind people together; how children, men, women, animals, plants—all of Allah's beloved creations—are woven together in this world like threads in a magnificent tapestry. Indeed, with the water clock, everything that came out of his loom was an effortless, inspired masterpiece.

"Over the years, Al-Hayek discovered that he could not only read the symbols woven into his designs, but also read into people's hearts—he could read and understand the patterns streaming into their consciousnesses at every moment. But he could only do this with his water clock to meter the flow of divine inspiration. He could gaze into a person's eyes and weave a part of himself into them, influencing them to think, feel, and act, likewise according to Allah's design. He could even accelerate time for them, advancing them toward their destiny.

"Tariq, my good friend, I could spend a lifetime telling you of the wonders that our family has known throughout the centuries. But the Clepsydra we are seeking is the greatest invention of the Al-Hayek legacy. It is a water clock capable of reaching humanity as a whole and advancing all hearts to a final state of tolerance and reconciliation—provided we have a proper message to broadcast. But now we are at the end of the line. The Last Day is closing in, and the war has begun."

Yusef's attention turned toward the baths. Synchronized bubbles shot up again.

"There is only one person who can show us the way, Tariq. He is the one we must find."

"Who is it?"

"Umar al-Hayek."

Tariq's face grew pale. "Is he…still alive?"

"No, of course not. He died in the eleventh century."

"Then how—?"

"Put these on," Yusef instructed as he handed Tariq and Amara each a thin, white smock and a green mask resembling a snorkel. "You are going to see one of our incredible devices in action."

Tariq sized up the smock and nervously tested the snorkel's elastic band.

"It is written that Allah has the power to restore life to the dead. But it is not stated *whose* life will enter the dead when it is restored."

Tariq did not fully comprehend, but he nodded anyway.

"You see," Yusef continued, "just as water is the essential substance of physical life, consciousness is the substance of the soul's existence. Consciousness takes form in us and flows into our bodies like water into a vessel. Likewise, it can be siphoned out from that vessel and poured into a different one. Our mission, Tariq, is to travel back to the eleventh century and get Umar al-Hayek to show us where he has hidden the Clepsydra."

"Time travel? That's impossible!"

"On the physical level, yes, it is impossible. Your body was born in this era and it will die here. However, on the level of consciousness, it is quite possible! Using a water clock you can release your soul back up through the siphon of the Creator, and then let Him pour you back into life in some other time period."

"So," Tariq processed, "we will leave our bodies and be born as other people in the eleventh century? All to find Umar al-Hayek?"

"Not exactly," Yusef answered. "You will not be *born* into your new body; you will enter it at its moment of *death* and then be revived. It will be more like a resurrection."

Time travel, consciousness, resurrection—all this seemed far too mystical to persuade Tariq's scientific mind. And yet, at the same time, it was consistent with the Waymaker's explanation of how the algae could transport water through time. Everything was connected.

"When you arrive," Yusef continued, "you will be able to see as that person saw, feel as they felt, speak and understand as they spoke and understood. At times you will be able to control what you think and do, but at times your body and brain chemistry will take the reins, and there will be no way to overpower it. In effect, it will be like riding a horse that also rides you. But that is okay. After all, you cannot change history. You must respect what is there and learn to cooperate with it, to tame the horse, so to speak, and let it also tame you, without resisting."

"Let me make sure I understand. We are going to enter the bodies of those who have just died and bring them back to life?"

"Watch your language, Tariq! It is Allah who restores them to life, not us. We are simply along for the ride. When your eleventh-century body dies, your soul will return peacefully to the twenty-first century."

"Peacefully?" Tariq's heart was still ravaged by the attack on Seville that had taken place right before his eyes.

"And when your soul returns, you will wake up here again in the bath perfectly restored, as if you had never left." The imam shut his eyes and smiled proudly. "Allah is magnificent."

"But how long will we have before we die there?

"Not long. A few hours, I should think."

"What?" Tariq exclaimed.

"I know, it is a very small window of time to find Umar Al-Hayek, but it will have to do. Death cannot be staved off for long."

"Will it be painful?" asked the linguist. "Death, I mean."

"Most certainly."

Tariq grimaced and clutched his stomach.

"I have not done this before, either," Amara confessed, revealing an apprehension that Tariq had not yet seen in her. "We will be first-timers together."

"But how will I find you if I don't know what you look like? We will have different faces, different names—who knows where we will end up!"

Amara grabbed Tariq's hand and held it. "Look into my eyes. You will find me. You will know me, and I will know you. Now, calm your mind and change your clothes."

The linguist mustered up his courage. "Okay. Let's go."

The three of them showered, changed into smocks, and put their masks on. Amara's colorful robe hung vibrantly on a hook that jutted out of the stone wall. One by one, they stepped into each of the three baths.

The imam explained: "The way to release your soul is to become perfectly still and in tune with the universe. The water clock is the vehicle, but it is your mind that is the ignition."

Could it really be that easy?

"First, take a deep breath and float on your back. Let every organ in your body be completely relaxed."

Their eyes closed naturally. Lying in the stillness of the water they felt as if a black hole were sucking in all sounds, feelings, and thoughts. All that remained was the soothing, inaudibly low vibration of the earth's core.

"Good. Now let go of the edges of the bath. And as soon as you are ready, slowly exhale."

Tariq let go of the bath's stony rim. He floated so smoothly and timelessly that he scarcely made a ripple. He felt his chest, groin, and face take in the water, becoming heavier and heavier and making him sink slowly to the bottom of the bath. *It feels like drowning,* he thought, *except there is no pain.* Then he realized how imminently he was bound to feel his world collide with another world, and how soon he would suffer its inescapable death. The world as he knew it was ending, in a sense; it was sinking with him into the aquatic abyss. Mind, body, words, thoughts—all the elements that made up his worldly nature were being drained from him and returned, like water, to the cosmic source.

Then, his body awareness vanished. Thoughts of this world and the next were pointless, even laughable. His worries and fears instantly dissipated. He was pure consciousness floating in darkness, floating without any restrictions upon the waves of pure potentiality. It was a state of being without form, of Nature at its truest essence, unimpaired by the crude physicality of human life. It was a thrill beyond thrills, bliss beyond bliss. If there was any doubt about the existence of the soul apart from the flesh, that doubt was overtaken by a joyful, out-of-body ecstasy.

"At last," the imam declared, "it is time."

Slowly, they exhaled until there was no more air. The cave lit up with a phantasmagorical glow.

The universe was absolute nothingness.

Chapter 15

Living in someone else's body is a peculiar experience, Yusef reflected as his consciousness took root in a new form. *O Merciful One, let Amara and Tariq be at peace. No first-timer is truly prepared for how it feels.*

It's like getting a heart transplant, Amara thought to herself as eleventh-century blood raced through her veins. *Except, that it's me that is being transplanted into this new heart, poured between the backbone and the breastbone just as it is written in the Quran.*

Tariq's senses froze for an unimaginably long time as his mind acclimated to having a new nervous system. Memories of the soul's transcendence faded from his rational mind; bliss became pain, and emptiness grew full. Light stormed his blurry eyes but he could not begin to see. Sounds hammered his eardrums and yet he could not distinguish any one noise from the background of cacophony that droned on all around. *It is painful and overwhelming, like being grown in the womb and pressed through the birth canal all over again.*

Then the tastes hit him—some were putrid and unbearable; others were strange and intimate. He moved his tongue against his cheeks and noted each acrid impression. Then he realized that he could just barely feel his body. Sensory impressions were pouring into his conscious awareness one body part at a time.

Tariq could feel the weight of his head; he could sense which way was up and which way was forward. He realized he was breathing easily. He felt his jaw hang open on his face like a warm oven door. The air tasted smoky, like pitch and tar, but with a hint of a scented perfume. He couldn't quite move but he began to feel the presence of his legs and arms stretching out from his torso. He felt his hard, callused feet and soft, nimble fingers. And then he felt something unexpected, which shocked him indeed: his avatar was female.

With this sudden realization his eyes burst open. He was lying facedown on the dirt floor with a headscarf draped over his head. And right in front of his eyes was a snake.

Tariq recoiled violently, and the deathly omen slithered away. Then he realized that his right forearm was swollen and tingling with pain. *Snakebite. This must be how I died—or, nearly died.* He squeezed his forearm with his small, sinewy hand to test the pain. *I wonder how long I have left to live.*

Tariq stood up like a toddler finding his balance for the first time. *I am definitely built with different proportions.* He recognized immediately that he stood an entire foot shorter than his twenty-first--century self and was much lighter.

The room was light and airy. The scent of sweet orange enshrouded him. From what he could tell, he was dressed for a fancy occasion. Then the sounds of two female voices drew near.

"Yamina!" they called.

He felt a warm hand on his shoulder.

"Yamina," one of them said, "we were looking for you."

"I was just—" he stopped mid-sentence, startled by his new mezzosoprano voice. It felt hoarse and meek like the voice of one who rarely spoke.

"Did you fall asleep?"

Tariq knew on a conscious level that the women were speaking in an old Moorish form of Spanish called *Mozarabic*, and yet it sounded so natural to his ears that he hardly noticed the words.

"Egad!" the other woman exclaimed. "Yamina, what happened to your arm?"

"Uh…I don't know," he lied with his soft, scratchy voice, suppressing the pain of the poison and hiding his arm in his robe. "But I'm fine."

"You had better be! Sayyid is outside. He is ready for you!" The women headed back into the other room.

"Go! Sayyid is waiting!"

Unable to reply, he turned away and looked down at the floor. He was unsure whether his reticence at that moment was Yamina's or his own. *I'm Yamina, and yet I am still Tariq.*

It was late afternoon, and the vibrant green countryside shown through the open window. Outside, Tariq could see two men, one young and one middle-aged. The young man was dressed in silk with oils pasted into his hair. He was holding a basket filled with fig leaves and fruit.

Who is this Sayyid? My friend? My brother? My...suitor? With this thought, the finely dressed Yamina realized that if she met the man, he would never let her out of his sight. She would be stuck with him for the rest of her short life.

Tariq contemplated his situation. If he was to reunite with Amara and Yusef and find Umar al-Hayek, he would have to evade Sayyid.

Yamina looked down at her tiny, delicate hands. She held her swollen forearm and took a deep breath. In spite of her anxieties, part of her was intrigued by the prospect of meeting Sayyid, this handsome, well-groomed man betrothed to her waiting outside the window. How she had dreamed of the perfect man—one who could take her, protect her, teach her, and lock her up safely within his heart. Now that she could see his comely face in the distance, this fate didn't seem half bad.

Suddenly, memories from Yamina's past began pouring into Tariq's powerless awareness: picking oranges in the grove with her mother; playing games of sticks and ropes with her sisters; sitting by her father's side listening to him read from the Quran—each memory had a little flavor of emotion attached. But every thought and action in her life so far led to only one thing: the promise of marriage, the fulfillment of her sacred duty to Allah, the deed that would lead to eternal paradise on the Last Day.

Just briefly, as she stared with gawking eyes at the lusty Sayyid, the suitor's eyes caught hers through the window. *Does he see me? Does he want me?* Hormones coursed through her veins, making her weak in the knees. She pulled the headscarf over her mouth and crinkled it with her lips. Yamina had never been so much in love in all her young, sequestered life.

In the back of her mind, the eavesdropping presence of a twenty-first-century linguist sorted through these feelings. *This is all completely bizarre!* He observed Yamina's dainty fingers clenching the headscarf and felt her overwhelming feelings vying for his complete and undivided attention. *What would be so wrong if I just gave in? After all, what is better for the heart than love? What can assuage the wars of the world better than the surrender of all desire to the name of love?*

But then he remembered. *Yamina is going to die. Soon. And I need to get out of here so I can find Amara and Yusef.* He flexed what muscles he could control. His avatar broke into a hot sweat. *Come on, Yamina*, he begged her with his thoughts. *Snap out of it!* But it was no use. Even inside the girl's head his words had effect.

After a few more endless seconds in love, Yamina's knees locked, and she stood up a little straighter. *Yes, that's it, Yamina. You can do it!* She held her hand to her heart and pressed it in, digging her fingers desperately into her over garment.

And then, as she stared from the window, the second man made eye contact with her. It was her father. He was coming toward the window, and he looked angry. This would not be the first time Yamina's sluggishness had frustrated her father. Instantly, feelings of love eroded into a tumult of shame and fear and anger.

You see, Yamina? You can't stay here! We need to go!

"Daughter! Get out here!" he shouted impatiently. She hated it when her father yelled. It made her feel wrong and unimportant.

"No!" Tariq managed to shout through Yamina's tight

throat, though it came out rather as a grunt. The linguist tried his best to remain cool and composed. But the toll of Yamina's distress, combined with his own fear of experiencing this girl's excruciating death, overloaded his mind. *What if Yamina dies and I die along with her? What if I don't return?* He hoped his trust in Yusef was not in vain.

Certainly, Allah has the power to restore life to the dead, Tariq reminded himself. *Isn't the fact I am here already proof of this? Yamina should have died by snakebite, and yet here she is—and here I am—alive and breathing. Come on, Yamina, quickly! Your precious life waits for no one!*

Starting to run, Yamina's slippers slid across the finely swept earthen floors and wound around the circular well in the middle of the family manor. With a flick of her ankles she cast off her slippers and stepped into her favorite red sandals. Then she paused to catch her breath, wrapping her wounded forearm tighter in her robe. She squeezed the latch on the inside of the door and stopped to cry. This home had always been kind to her, like a warm embrace on a cold night. Wherever she went, the roads had always led her here, to her one and only home. But now, panicked for reasons she did not understand, she had to flee.

Yamina quietly slipped out the door and ran as fast as her legs could manage. She rounded the marketplace, past butchers and produce peddlers, and hid behind the walls of a narrow alleyway. She took her sleeve and squeezed it around her forearm hoping to stop the spread of the venom. Then she let out another stream of tears. *Where am I going? What have I done?* In the deep ocean of her psyche, the linguist Tariq lingered patiently, trying to still her racing heart.

Suddenly, a little girl ran out into the street in front of her carrying a basket of figs. It was Yamina's sister.

"Yamina! Where are you going?"

Without thinking, Yamina grabbed her little sister's hand and pulled her through the street. "Mayra! We've got to get out of here!"

Mayra held onto her basket and followed her sister. Yamina led her down a narrow diagonal staircase and into a courtyard where men and boys were smoking water pipes. The little one watched them, curious and intrigued.

"Where are we going?"

Yamina didn't know how to answer. She felt her thoughts gravitate to water. Unbeknownst to her, it was Tariq stirring up images of a water clock, trying to keep his mind on his goal of finding the Clepsydra.

"Come on!"

The air was unbearably hot. Yamina pulled Mayra into a little pocket of shade she found beside a tall fortress wall. Alongside the wall, the midday sun spared only a thin sliver of shade, and it stretched from where they were standing all the way to the city's gated entrance. Yamina followed the wall, agitatedly clutching Mayra's wrist. She let her tawny, melancholy fingers stumble upon the wall's rough, rocky edges.

"Let go of me!" Mayra screamed, squeezing the basket of figs against her ribs with her inner arm.

"We need to leave this town!"

"But we have never left Seville!" Mayra protested. "What will Father say? How many lashings will he give us when he learns we have run away?"

But Yamina did not concern herself with these questions. Tariq managed to point her mind in the direction of the water, and his avatar followed these images without looking back.

"When Father finds out, it's going to be your fault!" Mayra exclaimed. "And Mother will scream when she doesn't get these figs!"

After passing through the gates, Yamina and Mayra made their way down the slopes of the town's outskirts to where a river ran through. Alongside the river, a flock of sheep were strutting past them. There were hundreds of sheep and not a herdsman in sight. Yamina stopped and collapsed on the grass under the shade of a cypress tree. She wept into her hand and discretely cupped her snakebite. Mayra set down her basket and sat next to her sister.

"Yamina, what's going on?"

Tariq could feel Yamina's fear and angst saturate his nerves. He was caught in the drama of Yamina's life.

"I can't do it! I can't marry Sayyid!"

Mayra hugged her sister. She knew that one day she, too, would leave home and be wed to a complete stranger.

"But maybe Sayyid will be kind! Maybe he will give you gifts of sweet roses and honey!"

"No, Mayra!" Yamina sulked. "Do you think Fatima was so lucky? She used to be our sister, but then Abdul came and stole her from us. That snake! Now Fatima knows no happiness. I can hear her crying in my dreams."

"But it's the law, Yamina! A woman must give herself to her husband. It is the will of Allah!"

"Then why does the will of Allah cause so much unhappiness?"

Mayra didn't know what to say. She looked down at her figs and poked them one by one as she listened to Yamina weep. Mayra, too, shed a tear for her inevitable future. In front of them the river sang its song in trickling waves, and the sheep meandered by in a seemingly unending line. The breeze cooled their tears.

After a few moments of consoling each other, Yamina and Mayra spied a dark, round object at the river's surface. As it moved toward them they realized that it was the head of a boy wading out of the deep water and toward the shore. The boy's hands gripped his elbows as water streamed off of him. His bare feet stumbled on the river's rocky shore. He looked not more than five years old.

"Hey!" Yamina called to the boy. She stood up and ran toward him, all the while wincing at the pain in her arm. The moving line of white sheep curved around her courteously.

The boy looked down at first, blinking his eyes and letting the water drip off of his hair. Then he shook his head fiercely and patted down his soaked trousers.

"Tariq? Is that you?"

Yamina squinted and rubbed her eyes.

"Yamina!" Mayra called, still sitting beneath the cypress tree with her figs. "Who is that boy?"

The boy looked up at him and rubbed his head with his palm.

"Amara?" Tariq managed to question through Yamina's lips. His own excitement and desperation were beginning to win over the anxieties of the runaway Yamina.

"No, Tariq." the boy resounded with a confidence well beyond his years. "I am Yusef."

Tariq looked into the small boy's steadfast eyes and saw that it was true. This boy was Yusef. All that was good and reverent about the faithful imam was borne clearly in this boy's saintly disposition. His aura was peaceful and calm.

"Yusef?"

Without thinking, Yamina slid her arms around the boy's back and embraced him as hard as she could. She didn't know why, but something inside her was longing to hold him near.

Somehow, she felt, it was part of a higher plan.

Chapter 16

Naomi the zoologist staggered about in the sand, exhausted and stricken by cravings. She was determined to survive.

We are partners, she kept reminding herself as she led her crocodile companion through the desert. *Seogo and me.*

Knowing she was not alone gave her a strength she didn't know she had. It had been days since she had eaten, and in all that time she still had not come across any clear sign that they were on the right path. She fought a constant impulse to thrash about in the sand and beg for a miracle.

"Seogo," she panted. "Stay close. We'll find an oasis soon, I can feel it." She looked back at the scaly beast, who was in that moment her only friend in the world. "At least, I hope so."

Together they walked through endless mounds of blistering sand, which squeezed between her bare toes like hot honey pressed through the comb. The zoologist shook her head. "I still can't believe Amara would just leave us behind! I hate her for that! It's like all she cares about is getting a job done, and if you don't cooperate the way she wants, then there is no room for discussion! Or maybe, she's been brainwashed by that Watcher, whoever he is."

Seogo let out a flagrant hiss. By now, Naomi could read the crocodile's expressions remarkably well. She could tell his yawns from his laughs and his smiles from when he was merely squinting at the sun. She knew by his grunts and hisses when he was agreeing with her and when he was making a rebuttal.

"How can you say that?" she retorted.

Seogo sped up and kicked up sand with his tail as he passed

in front of her.

"Hey, don't walk away from me during an argument!"

The zoologist ran ahead and grabbed Seogo by the tail. The fierce crocodile coiled his nimble body and snapped his teeth at her face. His lethal jaw came so close to her nose that she caught the raw stench of his wild potency.

"You don't scare me, Seogo!"

The crocodile snapped at her again, this time striking her on the chest with his nose. Naomi recoiled and caught her balance.

"Well, don't I have the right to be angry?"

Seogo reached his snout to her chest again, this time as gently as he could, like the hand of a newborn babe reaching up to its mother's heart. Naomi sighed.

"Amara was my partner too. I realize that."

The beast huffed another pungent breath, and the zoologist coughed.

"If I had respected her as a colleague rather than just someone with crazy ideas who gave me a job, then maybe she would have treated me the same—so, now I'm a hypocrite? Is that what you're saying? You think *I* was the one not cooperating?"

Seogo grunted words of comfort.

"I know, you're right. Dwelling on the past will not move us along. If we're going to find a pond or a stream or some way out of here, then we have to keep our eyes forward. Amara or no Amara, we have each other, and we're going to show her we can make it home in spite of her."

The zoologist kept walking. Her legs trembled. Her stomach ached and cried out in hunger. Her tongue and cheeks burned with thirst. But she kept walking, even though she felt she was walking to her death.

Night fell, and day rose again. Though she had barely slept, the zoologist picked herself up and continued. *How long since my last cigarette?* The cravings only added to her misery. And all the while, the sky's brilliant, round menace began playing tricks on her mind.

In one instant, she imagined there were demons following her—shrouds of dark green monsters skating upon the sand coming to harvest her soul. After a moment of panic, she squinted her eyes to give them a hard look. It was only Seogo.

Another trick that tortured her mind was the image of water in her hands. Every so often she would cup her hands together expecting to drink from them the pure fluid of life, but only sand and dry air materialized.

Then there was the cruelest hallucination of all. It began with the sight of a beige canopy in the distance. *Could it really be? A shelter! Maybe there are people who will take me in.* As she drew closer to the canopy, it grew into a more elaborate camp. The zoologist imagined rows of tents filled with travellers, who were coming outside to bathe themselves in troughs of heavenly delight. She greeted the folks, but they ignored her. Then she spied an open trough filled with water and scooted toward it for a drink. But before she could reach the trough, a gust of wind pushed her to the ground—it howled and hissed, and soon its noise turned into gunfire resounding from all directions. Explosions hit left and right, which she barely evaded, and her fantasy was left in utter ruin.

At the end of this cruel daydream the zoologist collapsed in the sand. Her body slumped forward, hardly making a dent in the infinite desert.

Startled, Seogo jerked his head around. He had been oblivious to Naomi's hallucinations. He raced up to his companion's barely breathing body and nudged it a few times with his snout. He looked left and right, seeing nothing but sandy horizons in all directions. A gentle tear escaped his crocodilian eye. Then he scooped the zoologist onto his back and carried her onward through the Sahara. If she had been conscious, she would have understood in an instant the words implied by his grunt:

Let me carry you to safety, my child.

Derek Olsen

Chapter 17

Amara blinked her eyes and squinted. It was broad daylight. Her head was throbbing, and she was lying in the center of a large arena. A crowd of spectators cheered and hissed. As more of her senses returned, she began to piece together the mystery of her surroundings. She looked down at her dirty, white woven uniform held together with a sash. A nearly unraveled turban sagged upon her head suggesting she had been involved in vigorous physical activity. As it appeared, she had been pushed to the ground and hit her head.

Still dizzy, she massaged her temples. In the distance, she could hear a boisterous thumping sound. Amara turned around and noticed a massive animal charging toward her. She looked down and realized she had a large, red cloak draped around her. The thumping resounded, drawing shouts and whistles from the crowd as the animal sped nearer, its face appearing angrier the more visible it became. *Perfect*, she thought. *Of all the people I could have been in eleventh-century Seville, I had to be a matador.*

For a split second she remembered what Yusef had said: she would be revived during a moment of death and would die again within the next few hours. There was no stopping it. Like the bull barreling toward her, death too was swiftly approaching.

"Aha!" she shouted as she wove the red cloak masterfully around the bull and evaded its fearsome path. "Have at it again, you brute!"

The matador danced theatrically as the bull plowed into the empty air, scaring the horse back to the sidelines. The crowd thundered their applause. Trumpets blared close by, carrying the exuberance of the moment to far-distant places. *I admit, I've never been much of a bullfighting fan; but it's quite exciting when you're actually in it!* Amara delighted in the muscular agility of her new matador body, leaping about and egging on the bull a second time.

"One more chance for Seville! One more chance for Andalusia! Try as you might, you will never catch Husain the Swift!" The matador spat out the refrain so effortlessly that Amara knew with certainty this was her new identity; she was Husain the Swift.

Husain the Swift turned his back on the bull and squatted down close to the dirt. Rage flared in the beast's nostrils as it darted toward him again, kicking up thick clouds of dust. Without a horse, Husain was just a few seconds from being pummeled to death. But the matador remained with his back turned and calmly looked up. He raised his arms up in prayer declaring, "God is the greatest!"

Never before had Amara said these words with such raw enthusiasm. They had scarcely left her lips when, at the last mortal instant, she spun around and flashed the cloak in the bull's eyes and darted out of harm's way. Husain the Swift was a sensation! The crowd roared and blasted their trumpets even louder than before. "Allahu Akbar!" she repeated in Arabic and raised her hands at the spectators. "God is the greatest!"

In the heat of the moment, Amara lost awareness of who she was. The vigor and adrenalin of the bullfight had won her mind. The chemistry of Husain the Swift's brain had taken over. The bull thrashed about fanatically in the arena. The animal was utterly bewildered and even more peeved.

Soon, Husain spied another matador entering the arena. His head was uncovered, and he wore a black robe displaying the Christian cross. He also carried a pair of javelins.

"Now, let the conquest begin!" shouted the approaching matador. "Make way for Alfonso the Cruel!" He ran gallantly toward Husain and passed one of the javelins to him.

Husain the Swift stood up tall and puffed his chest out, catching the javelin with ease. Alfonso the Cruel drew the bull's attention the opposite way. He waved his cloak and lured the charging beast to within a horse tail's length away. In that moment he thrust the javelin into the bull's meaty left side. The bull squealed in pain but kept running, more furious and frightened than ever. "In the name of God Most High!" shouted Alfonso in Mozarabic.

Husain the Swift sprinted toward the bull with his javelin. "Now, let's finish him off!"

Amara watched the scene closely from behind the eyes of Husain the Swift. She felt the stiff, wooden handle of the weapon in her avatar's hand. And she felt the terrific rush of Husain's adrenalin, which locked her willpower to one thing only: the long-awaited killing of the infuriated and unfortunate animal.

In a flash, Husain the Swift speared the bull in the rump, causing it to screech to a halt. Dirt clouds erupted as the animal landed with a giant thud. Then, he and Alfonso the Cruel gathered near. The javelins were stuck in the bull's thick skin. The matadors began to count. "One! Two! Now!" Both men yanked their blades from the bull's hide simultaneously, unleashing thick streams of blood. The audience roared with excitement. Alfonso the Cruel immediately stabbed the bull again, sending shocks of agony through its flesh. Husain the Swift joined in without hesitation. And somewhere back in the shadows of his mind, an imam's sister watched it all.

Amara was not unfamiliar with the sight of blood and gore; but the killing of this bull was unlike anything she had seen before. These two men mutilated the poor creature beyond recognition, puncturing the eyes, stabbing at the stomach, and maiming it without any shred of decency. What had begun as a mere sport—indeed, a proud pastime of Spain's Moorish heritage—showed itself to be nothing more than a malicious, ungodly slaughter. Worst of all, she had no choice but to enjoy it! Bound to the matador's brain and nerves, she could feel every rush of sickening pleasure as he laughed at the kill.

Desperately, Amara tried to hold back the urge to stab. *Stop it, Husain! Control yourself!* She exerted her will with every ounce of strength she had, and yet it was still not enough to override his brain's command. She was a prisoner, caught in the inner trappings of the matador's act; and worst of all, those actions made her feel guilty.

But Amara Tejedor was not one to give up. When she could not control her external environment, she knew to look within and refocus: her mission was to find Al-Hayek and to ascertain the location of the Clepsydra—the one chance her family had to broadcast their message of peace as the Last Day drew near. *Don't you see, Husain? There is a greater plan to be enacted!*

Overcome with guilt and frustration, Amara knew there was no way to persuade the matador to quit. The choice of violence was already made. The question was, how to deal with that choice and bare its effects with grace. *If you will not spare your violence, maybe you can redirect it.*

"Let him have it, Husain!" sneered Alfonso the Cruel as he kicked the beast theatrically. "Long live Seville! Long live Andalusia!"

Husain gripped the javelin, shook it and let it teeter above the dying creature. He stood tall and looked up at Alfonso the Cruel. Alfonso's dark, hazel eyes swelled with bloodlust, and inexplicably, this angered Husain like nothing else. *That man is a brute! He's no better than the bull!*

Without thinking, Husain launched the javelin directly at Alfonso, who was quick enough to jump out of the way. But when Alfonso found his bearing, he erupted in a vengeful rage.

"What's the meaning of that, you Muslim fool?"

In that instant, Husain became confused. *Why did I do that? Am I trying to get killed?*

Alfonso lashed out at Husain, grabbing at his neck. But

the swift one escaped. He darted anxiously toward the sidelines. *What have I done?*

Amara's plan was working, though not exactly as she had anticipated. Remorse was setting in—a painful, agonizing remorse in a matador's conscience. *Generations of peace with the Christians, and now I have tried an attack! Allah, forgive me!*

Alfonso tried to chase after him but gave up quickly. "May God Almighty smite you to your grave!" he called, shaking his fist.

Husain the Swift hurdled a tall fence and was down the other side. The crowd became unruly; Christians and Muslims bickered over who caused what. This matador, by attacking Alfonso, had started a skirmish and led the entire arena into chaos. But Husain did not look back. His conscience told him to bear the guilt with grace. The terror of the bullfight only validated Amara's cause to bring peace to Spain and to the world through the Watcher's army. *I have only a few hours to find Umar al-Hayek.*

The matador removed his turban and ran through the empty street. Seething pain from his near-fatal head trauma struck him again. He slowed down, seeing that no one was chasing him. When he found a sturdy stone on the side of the street, he sat down and rested a moment. A refrain of self-belittlement beat down upon his brain. *I am a coward. I am no champion, for I have run from the fight!* Saddened with defeat, Husain squeezed his temples with the heels of his hands and winced at his lack of remedy.

Nearby, a beggar rolled over from slumber and lifted his drunken eyes toward Husain. The beggar was scrawny and barely clothed. Even the rags he wore were tawdry linens, suspended over his bare, bony shoulders by a pair of frail ropes. Moreover, they were drenched with sweat from the inescapable burden of the Seville heat. Everything about this man stunk of poverty and earthly despair.

"Can you help me, brother?" the beggar muttered. He staggered toward Husain and clumsily capped his shoulders, falling into him from behind with the weight of his whole sickly body. In his drunkenness the beggar didn't realize the potential danger of accosting a matador from behind. Then again, Husain himself did not recognize it either. Amara's consciousness was beginning to take the reins, and she was in a mind to be prudent.

"Can you spare a coin, brother?"

"Brother?" Amara turned around and examined the sinewy beggar. She had never been called that before.

"Maybe a scrap of food?"

"I don't know. Let me see what I have." When she looked closer she noticed that his bare torso was lined with lash marks. This beggar had been beaten, and recently.

"Please, I haven't eaten in days."

Amara smiled compassionately upon the poor man. Her faith compelled her to act. She stood up as tall as her avatar could stand and put an arm around him in good faith.

"Come with me, my brother. I will get you cleaned up and fed. What is your name?"

The beggar opened his mouth and stuttered. He was probably not quite as drunk as he behaved, mostly just hungry.

"My name is Christian."

By Allah, your sign could not be clearer! I have failed in bringing peace upon the Christian in the bull ring, but let me not fail to live by the pillars of Islam: I shall give to the poor, I shall help this man whose name is Christian. Between Christians and Muslims, the convivencia *will stand true. Peace will prevail!*

"I am Husain," she proclaimed.

Amara noticed she had a string of prayer beads around her neck. She took it off and placed it in the hands of the beggar.

"What is this?"

"It is a gift of God. Use it to pray."

"But I am not Muslim!"

"There is only one God; Christian or Muslim, He is there."

Christian ran the beads through his hands like a rosary.

"Would you believe it?" the beggar began. "I once lived in

a nice home. Well, I suppose it was not too nice, but we had enough. Then the plague came and took my wife. I lost my home to a fire. And just when I thought only hell awaited me, do you know what I found?"

Amara shook her head.

"The Virgin Mary. I saw her, Husain, like a ghost in a mirror! She was right there smiling at me from behind, whispering that everything would be alright, if only I would believe. And now, oh, heavenly blessings, she has sent you to me!"

"That sounds like the ghost of your intuition speaking to you."

"What? No! It was the Virgin! Don't you believe it?"

Amara searched her thoughts for words that would reach his faith while staying true to her own:

"The Virgin gave us Jesus the man, the prophet—yes!— but it was God who gave you your Christ. And if Christ is your God, then have faith in Him. It is Him who you must look for in the mirror!"

Christian scratched his cheek and coughed.

"But maybe," Amara continued, "we should find food and leave spiritual matters for another time." She reached into Husain's thoughts and discovered an idea. "I know of a butcher who owes me a favor," she explained, not fully sure what she meant as the words left her avatar's lips.

"You are most kind, Husain."

Amara led Christian to the butcher, where they shared a hearty meal. The butcher didn't say much but simply left them to eat the meal he had begrudgingly prepared. The beggar devoured his plate of partridge and mutton, and Amara listened and observed. Then she scanned the matador's brain once more for a place to get him cleaned up. The only thing that came to mind was the mosque.

"I want to give you one more thing," she told him. "I stand by my word, and I told you I would get you cleaned up. That is why I want to take you to the mosque."

Christian's eyes bugged out.

"The mosque?"

The beggar picked his teeth with his soiled fingernail.

"You don't have to pray with us, but we do have water to wash with."

"Take me there and I will pray! Muslim or Christian, He is the same God, as you say!"

Amara smiled and put her arm around the sickly man. She thanked the butcher and escorted Christian outside. In the distance, she could hear the passionate wailing of the *muadhin* calling them to prayer. *Perfect timing. It is time for the evening* salat. *Surely this act of kindness will lead me to Umar Al-Hayek. It is part of God's plan.*

When they reached the mosque, Husain was greeted by several familiar faces. One was Farhan, his childhood friend; he and Husain had caused many a boyish nuisance in their day. Another was Malik, Seville's most notorious prankster; Husain and Farhan looked to this puerile man for constant confirmation that they had matured from their mischievous past. Surrounding these two were Muhammad the bricklayer, Rashid the glassblower, and Kassim, who in his affable way had become branded the village idiot.

"*As-salaamu alaykum.*" Husain's heart raced with excitement to see his friends here once again.

"*Wa-alaykum salaam.*"

They greeted each other in turn and removed their shoes.

"Who's the white-faced wanderer?" joked Malik.

"I bet he stole his clothes off the skin of a goat!" cracked Muhammad. Kassim bobbed his head and chuckled.

"Be nice," suggested Farhan. "Visitors are welcome here. What is your name?"

"Christian."

"Christian, eh?" Rashid repeated with a sinister tone. "So you're an idolizer!"

"No, no, fellows!" laughed Malik, snapping the beggar's humble threads against his chest. "He's the actual idol! And to think, your face wishes it could be seen in Allah's house!"

"Brothers, stop this!" shouted Husain.

"Do you call this a face?" gestured a menacing Muhammad. "Filthier than the pigs who raised him!" The men roared with malicious laughter.

Husain couldn't believe his ears. *How can my brothers stoop so low as to cast such insults?*

"Just let him in. He hasn't washed, and he wants to pray with us."

"Are you sure that's wise?" questioned Farhan.

"Of course it's wise," Malik harassed, inching the poor beggar backwards against the wall. "This heathen will burn up as he enters and save us the trouble of sticking him with a torch!"

"Please, please, no!" Christian screamed.

"Brothers, listen to yourselves!" implored Husain. He stood up and puffed out his chest. Husain was the tallest and mightiest of the group, and yet even he was struck with a touch of fear for what might happen to this defenseless man. "We are about to pray! Can't we be in peace?"

"Have you gone soft, Husain?" mocked Malik.

"Why did you bring this hellion, anyway?" scoffed Muhammad. "What does he want?"

"He's a man in need," explained the frustrated matador. "And I'm ashamed of all of you! Have you forgotten what our faith has taught us about giving to the poor? And about honoring Allah with your words?"

"Who the hell do you think you are?" exploded Malik. "You think you're such a good Muslim? Bah! You invite a filthy wretch here and think you've done a good deed! That's one deed you could have done for a brother. But no! You waste your precious favors on this scoundrel!"

"He's not like us, Husain!" Rashid interjected.

"I think I know why you've adopted this heathen," proffered Malik, pulling up his sleeves and feigning a brief interval of merciful contemplation.

"Don't do it, Malik!" cried Farhan. "Can't we sort this out

later?"

Malik pushed Farhan out of the way and tackled Christian to the ground. Husain quickly grabbed his hot-tempered friend by the waist and attempted to drag him away.

"Whose side are you on?" shouted an outraged Muhammad, who then then laid a punch to Husain's muscular stomach. The matador turned and slapped Muhammad in the face, prompting Kassim to lunge at Husain with a choke hold.

Behind them all, Christian scampered away.

"Wait! Come back!" shouted Husain. "This is not who we really are, I promise!"

But it was too late. Christian was gone, and Husain's head trauma reignited, making the rest of the brawl a blur in his memory. He had beaten his friends and suffered several bruises himself. And when he finally awoke he was lying in the street, battered and abandoned by his brothers. His eyes poured out Amara's tears along with his own.

Amara wept for Christian. She wept for the violent reality of the human condition and for man's rage and prejudice. *The Quran teaches us to glorify Allah morning and evening*, she reflected, still in pain. *I sincerely hope I was just in defending that Christian. I hope that, in this unsaintly way, I have brought perhaps an atom's weight of glory to the Merciful One who will judge me on the Last Day. Allah, forgive me for my sins.*

After a few minutes, the matador's strength returned. Amara stood up and sighed, snuffing out the pain from her bruises as if she were pinching out candle flames, one-by-one, until all was dark.

Indeed, the sun had nearly set. Faint stars dotted the fading sky.

This is not at all how I imagined the convivencia, she thought, enraged. *Muslims and Christians coming together in sport, only to mutilate innocent animals? Grown men taunting each other for no reason other than blatant prejudice? It's madness!* With that thought, the tale of a peaceful and tolerant yesteryear—the history that Amara had owned without question—began to break down before her. The unabridged history of the *convivencia* was revealing its paling truth.

The bold and daring Amara was sickened to learn that the story of the *convivencia* was incomplete, perhaps even misleading! Not only was Spain's eleventh-century Muslim society imperfect, but also it contained the very elements of violence and destruction she and her brother were determined to stamp out of the human condition once and for all. *My mission to bring peace among the religions is not a matter of returning to the past,* she realized, *but of using the past to create a more tolerant future. The future is imminent! I have to find Umar Al-Hayek. I just know he will help me make sense of what I see here. And perhaps this unfriendly detour with Christian will lead to him.*

In the distance, Amara noticed a tall, torch-lit building and decided to move toward it.

Husain the Swift is strong, she affirmed. *Surely, I will succeed in getting to Umar Al-Hayek and asking him where he has hidden the Clepsydra.*

Amara nodded to herself confidently and started taking larger strides.

Besides, it could have been much worse. I could have been the bull.

Derek Olsen

Chapter 18

"Yusef! It's really you, isn't it? I barely knew you in our own time, and now here you are as a child. And here I am as this young woman, called Yamina, and...it's so strange being here!"

"It is strange, Tariq, I agree. But we must stay focused and find Umar Al-Hayek quickly before we die." The boy noticed Yamina's swollen arm. "What happened to you?"

"I...I...was nearly betrothed to a man called Sayyid. My father yelled at me! But I got away. I was so frightened!"

"What I mean is, how did your arm get swollen?"

"Oh, yes." He massaged his throbbing arm. "A snake bit me."

"Is that all?"

"What do you mean, is that all?"

Yusef scratched his head and placed his other hand on his stomach.

"It appears that I drowned in this river. Either that, or I fell into the river after collapsing from hunger. I sense that I have been fasting for weeks."

"Weeks?"

"That is not unusual for an orphan."

"An orphan?"

"You seem distressed, Tariq."

"Distressed doesn't even begin to describe it! How can we be here? How can we die and be restored?"

"The works of Allah are difficult to imagine. They are like secrets. They are uncovered only by removing the veil that is our attachment to worldly forms."

"Worldly forms? Is this a reference to the physical reality we live in?"

"Yes, it is. All sciences developed by our Muslim predecessors—astronomy, chemistry, algebra and so forth, even linguistics!—are sciences of the senses and the worldly forms that make up our reality. But beyond this world is the world of the soul. That is a world you have now glimpsed by being here!"

"But where is the soul? All I see here are different variations on the same worldly forms."

"You assume the existence of the soul is a matter of *where*."

"I know," the linguist sighed. "I can't seem to break that assumption."

"Allah reveals His secrets in due time. But the true secret is the soul itself! And this secret will not come fully to your awareness until you fall into the arms of death for good."

"That's another thing, Yusef. You speak of death as if it were something comforting, but I just can't see it that way. I feel so unprepared! How can I take comfort in this world knowing that my soul will disconnect itself from everything I see and hear and feel?"

"The only way to do it is to believe."

"In what?"

"What kind of question is that? You are a Muslim, are you not?"

"Well, my family is Muslim. I practice the religion sometimes. And I have high esteem for all that our people have accomplished."

"Esteem is not faith, Tariq. Not even close! Faith is your unwavering belief in Allah and in the cause He has written in the Quran for you."

"But how do I know my cause?"

"You know it by your faith," explained the imam. "By your submission to the will of Allah above all your other desires."

"*Submission to the will of Allah*—you are referring to the definition of Islam."

"Islam is a constant practice of discerning the soul from its worldly forms, the will of God from the desires of the flesh. Each soul has a path, and that path must be tended to with the utmost devotion."

"I know that! At least, I know it intellectually. My grandfather taught me about the faith."

"What did he teach you about Islam?"

"He was an activist. A successful one, too! He taught me that in the end each of us will be judged by our actions, and that everything we do that is righteous will decide our fate."

"Yes, that is the judgment we call the Last Day."

"But if we are judged by our actions," Tariq argued, "then what does it matter what we believe? What kind of God would judge us by our thoughts?"

"What kind of God? Now, you are speaking like an agnostic."

"If the term fits, then call me an agnostic if you wish. I call myself an academic. But these labels are beside the point. I really do want to learn from you."

"Then open your eyes to this new evidence. The evidence is your experience! How else can you explain being in 11th-century Seville? How else can you explain how Allah restored you to life after your snakebite?"

"I want to believe it, Yusef. But it feels like a dream."

"Compared to the glory that awaits us after the Last Day, all of life is like a dream!"

"Then what's the point? Why fight terrorism? Why try so hard to make peace?"

"Ay, Tariq." The imam shook his head. "You are asking the wrong questions."

Tariq turned and looked back at Mayra, who was licking her fingers after munching on a fig. The shade of the tree billowed back and forth around her as the wind blew. Then, Yusef spoke:

"You argued that a good God would not judge us by our thoughts. To some extent that is true; He does not judge us by the *content* of our thoughts necessarily. But He does judge us by our *intentions*."

"How do you tell the difference between thoughts and intentions?"

"A thought is unformed. It occurs just as a reflex, and it has little value except that it may lead to an intention."

"What makes intentions more important than thoughts?"

"Intentions lead to actions."

"But not every intention leads to action."

"Yes it does, Tariq! From the first moment of each intention either we act upon it or we act in order to *avoid* it. One path leads to the full expression of our thoughts and of our soul, while the other path leads to hesitation, denial, and repression."

"But if we allowed all our intentions to be uninhibited," Tariq argued, "how would we stop ourselves from acting incorrectly? How would we keep on the right path? How would we avoid making errors that cause harm to ourselves and others?"

"By remembering that Allah is merciful and compassionate. He *wants* to keep you on the right path. He wants to give you the right intentions so they will turn into the right actions. Your faith will tell you that. Your grandfather would tell you that."

Tariq looked back at Mayra again. She was standing up this time, petting a sheep that had strayed from the flock to greet her. As he looked at her, the wind picked up and tickled Tariq's soft, dark eyelashes.

"My grandfather took me on the *hajj* when I was five years old. He showed me for the first time—maybe the only time—how people who come together in prayer can create a kind of consciousness that is greater than anything we can own individually. He showed me how Pakistani and Saudi and American boys can come together and make a pilgrimage to Mecca. He showed me how sheiks and paupers, the healthy and the sick, the strong and the frail can stand side-by-side and speak to the heavens as one. I suppose this is why I still call myself a Muslim in spite of being secular. I believe in being part of something greater than the individual. And I believe that the true Islam is a path that brings us together to share in the wonder of being alive."

Yusef pressed his head to squeeze the water out of his hair.

"Then that is where you will start to find your faith, Tariq. That is your proof that Allah will restore us to life."

Suddenly they heard Mayra scream. Tariq whirled around and looked. Yamina's father was standing at the city gates. His fine woolen trousers flapped violently in the growing wind. He scolded his daughters with his terrorizing eyes, and from those eyes Yamina's greatest fear was manifesting right before her. Fear was taking the reins of Tariq's 11th-century avatar and leaving no time to think.

"Mayra, run!"

Mayra threw up her basket of figs and obeyed her sister. Yamina led Mayra and Yusef up a hill of rocks. Tariq was surprised to discover Mayra was such an adept climber. All the while, the barefoot, five-year-old Yusef straggled behind.

Mayra was first to reach the top of the hill. "Is he still behind us?" she cried. She looked down upon river valley lined with sheep and saw her father inching toward them. She was careful not to snag her trousers on the rocks.

"Yusef!" called the still-cognizant Tariq, who was nearly at the top of the hill. "Can you make it?"

"Go ahead, don't worry about me!"

"Yamina, watch out!"

Just as Yamina reached the top, Mayra grabbed her hand and pulled her in the opposite direction. It was worse than she feared: a herd of wild goats was guarding the top of the hill.

"Slow down, Mayra! You'll only make them chase us!"

And as those very words were uttered, the herd of goats assembled as one and charged toward the sisters.

"Over there!" Mayra pointed to a small cave down below.

"I see it. Yusef, get to that cave!"

In a matter of a few moments, the three of them scurried into the cave, and Tariq pulled a large, round stone to close its entrance. Only a sliver of light remained through which to look out. The herd of oblivious goats stampeded past them, and when they were gone. Mayra poked her head out and looked for her father.

"He's gone for now. But he hasn't given up looking for us, I'm sure."

Tariq heaved a sigh of relief.

"Where do we go now, Yusef?"

"I think we should ask Mayra."

"Why me?" Mayra sized up the young orphan boy. "Who are you anyway?"

"This is Yusef," Yamina explained, strangely confused as to why the boy was with them.

"Ah, yes, my dear, fortunate sister," Mayra joked. "You have found your suitor after all. Well done!"

"How mean of you to mock me like that!" recoiled Yamina. "I'm a grown woman, and you'll have plenty of proof of that when I marry Sayyid!"

"Ouch!" exclaimed Mayra. She stubbed her toe on a rock, and then fell down laughing. "See what you made me do, little Yusef? It's all your fault. Haha!"

"Look!" pointed Yusef.

Tariq came to his senses and looked at the rock. It was wet. And not only that, but water was coming up from the ground beneath it. He picked up the rock using both hands, and a stream of water sprayed out. It filled the cave with a violent mist.

"It's a hidden geyser! But how?"

"Haha!" laughed Mayra. "What are you waiting for? Let's get out of this hole!" She pushed the large round stone away from the cave opening and frolicked outside. Tariq and Yusef followed.

"Have you seen the obvious signs, Tariq?—I mean, Yamina?"

"What do you mean?"

"Mayra is the key to finding the Clepsydra"

"How do you know?"

"She is a sign from Allah that could not be clearer. Think, Tariq!"

Tariq searched his mind for associations. Then, it dawned on him:

"Of course! Mayra's name, in Arabic, means *water channel*. Mayra is quite literally our divining rod! All we have to do is follow her, and she will lead us to Umar Al-Hayek."

Quickly, water flooded the cave, and out poured a roaring stream.

"Unless," Tariq ruminated, with some excitement, "the Clepsydra is right here under this cave! Mayra has activated it by kicking it open!"

"No, no, Tariq. There may be an irrigation channel beneath us, but it is hardly the Clepsydra. The Clepsydra is the size of a lake! How else could we use it to transmit our message of peace to the entire world? It will not be as easy to open as merely kicking a rock. Whoever designed the water channel beneath this cave was an amateur. And certainly not the work of an Al-Hayek."

"Yamina, listen!" Mayra pranced around and dipped her toes in the emerging stream. "This water is singing my name! Such a pretty song, like this pretty stream. It's a song to me! Oh, Yamina! I love everything about this stream!"

Mayra began to sing and skip around in the stream. Tariq gazed down at the bottom of the hill where the nascent stream poured into the river. Bewildered sheep forded the shallow stream, not wanting to get left behind by the rest of the flock.

"My figs!" Mayra exclaimed, stopping her singing. She ran over to snatch one that was carried by the stream. "And there's the whole pile!" She ran over to the basket on the ground, and gathered the figs as quickly as she could. "They're dirty. But we can wash them in my new stream!"

Tariq and Yusef smiled and went over to help her. The

wind still wailed from the east, making the tree branches' shadows dance above them like a ghostly cloud.

When they finished, a new shadow appeared. It was the shadow of a burly, middle-aged man standing over them. The two girls looked up at him naively through the veils of their headscarves. A frightened Yusef grabbed a fig from the basket and stuffed it in his mouth, whole.

Yamina stood up. She couldn't speak, yet she was certain of her need to defend Mayra and Yusef. But as she made eye contact with this man, she recognized the look he was giving her. It was desire. It was that force of attraction summoning feelings of being wanted, even needed. The longer she kept eye contact with this man, the closer he came toward her.

"Yamina, he's going to grab you!"

The man took a look of caution to the side, and then he snatched Yamina callously by the arm.

"Leave my sister alone!" Mayra kicked at the man's shins a few times without much effect. Yusef was helplessly in shock; warm water streamed down his still-damp pants. Yamina flailed and tugged, but the man had twenty times her strength. He grabbed her jaw with his large, ill-mannered hands and yanked off her headscarf.

Tariq could not believe his senses. Frantically, he racked his brain for a solution. *I don't have the strength to overpower this man, but maybe I can call for help.* So, he attempted to scream at the top of his lungs. But all that came out of poor Yamina's mouth was a splash of vomit.

Surprised by the vomit, the attacker recoiled and softened his grip; and in that moment of hesitation Yamina slipped her slender arm out from his fist and leapt back toward the stream.

"Be careful, Yamina!"

All of a sudden, the man turned to Mayra and snatched her instead.

Mayra! No!

"Sister!" Mayra shouted as the man carried her away. "Find

me, quickly!"

Yamina stood, frozen, as the man carried struggling, helpless Mayra away. *Give her back! I hate you!* But these unuttered screams were useless. In a matter of seconds, Mayra was gone. The man had taken her. Yamina sat down in the stream and wept for her sister. Yusef gulped down the last remnants of the fig in his mouth. He, too, was speechless. And in their silence, all they could hear was the echoing sound of the stream calling Mayra's beautiful name.

"I can't do this, Yusef," declared Tariq, once he had a mind to speak.

"Yes, you can, Tariq. And you must."

"But we've lost Mayra. We've lost our divining rod. How will we find Umar Al-Hayek?"

"Have patience, Tariq. Allah will give us other signs."

"And even if we find the Clepsydra, what makes you think I can write the message? It's no coincidence my soul took on the form of this meek and ineffective Yamina. I can't even speak to save a life!"

"Stop thinking that way!" The boy swatted her on the head. "Do you think Mayra would have survived even if you had saved her?"

"Well—"

"There is no survival! As the Last Day approaches, only the soul survives. Don't you see, Tariq? As long as I am the orphan boy and you are Yamina, we will not survive. We will be buried beneath the sands of time."

"But I told you, I can't take any comfort in that!"

"Then take comfort in this: before we entered that cave, there was no stream. And now, water pours forth in abundance."

"What does that have to do with the soul?"

"I am no linguist, and my way with words is limited. But I am certain whatever message you will end up writing for us will explain how the water knew to find us at that exact moment. Mayra is not the only divining rod, you see!"

"I just hope we can divine our way back to the 21st century."

Yusef sighed at the linguist's lack of faith. "Allah will certainly restore us back once we complete our time here."

Chapter 19

Husain the Swift approached the building and looked up at its front gate. A minaret ascended from its walls lit by a torch from the inside. He could just barely catch a glimpse of the inner courtyard through the cracks.

As darkness descended, Amara took command of the champion's arms and knocked upon the gate. After a few seconds the gate creaked open, and the light from inside crept onto the outer wall.

"Who is there?"

"It is I, Husain the Swift. May I come in?"

The gate opened wider, and a bearded man with a wrinkled face answered. "Of course, my child, why shouldn't you come in?"

He invited the champion in and closed the gate. They stepped into a well-illumined corridor lined with alcoves. As Amara followed, she realized precisely where she was. It was one of Seville's medieval synagogues, built by Moorish workmen and commissioned by the town's well-to-do Jewish sector during the late tenth century.

"You are a lucky fellow tonight," the bearded man began. "The rabbi is out, and I am here in his place. This means we will have no other guests."

"Who are you?"

The bearded one looked into the champion's eyes and grinned.

"You don't know who I am?"

"Should I?"

"We have met before, but that was in a different age. You

may call me the Mystic."

"The Mystic?" She was disappointed. "But I have never heard of you."

"Haven't you?" He stroked his beard and adjusted the *kippah* on his head.

"I don't see how I could."

"My child," explained the Mystic, "I have walked your path—it is the path of spiritual pilgrimage, the path of a seeker of God."

"That may be true, but please hear me. I have come here on a mission. Do you know where I can find Umar al-Hayek?"

The Mystic gazed farther into her eyes. Amara sensed he knew something more, though it seemed impossible.

"Yusef told me you would show up. But I never imagined you would come like this—sweaty with the smell of blood on your clothes!"

"You know Yusef? How?"

"My child, I am like you, a visitor from a different era. Though my stay is much longer."

The wrinkled-faced man was beginning to annoy her. *Why can't he just tell me what is going on?*

"Where is Yusef? Did he bring you?"

"You have it all backwards, Amara. It is I who brought Yusef."

What is he talking about? It was clearly the Watcher who brought in Yusef. Unless...

"Are you the Watcher?"

"Certainly not! That is ludicrous! Now, come here and take a seat."

The Mystic pulled out two small rugs and placed them on the floor for them to sit. The white walls of the alcove stretched up and met in an archway lined with frescoes. It was a stunning interior; however, there was no time to appreciate it. Amara's headache was getting worse, and it took all the energy she had to ignore it and concentrate on the man's words.

"You have learned faith from your lineage," the Mystic

began. "For a thousand years, the Al-Hayeks and Tejedors have devoted their lives to Islam. But in all this time you have come to see your religion misused and distorted, hollowed out by litigious words and archaic laws. You have come to see it abused by extremists and neglected by disbelievers. Like many other seekers, you have come to look within and discover a path beyond your own tradition. You are seeking the way of the Mystic."

"No, no, that's not true; I am a seeker, yes, but I am firm in my faith. I am here because terrorism has struck Seville—in fact, it has been striking all over the world! We have built an army, and all we need is Al-Hayek to show us where he has hidden the Clepsydra. The Clepsydra is the only thing powerful enough to weave our warning into the hearts of all the world and bring peace to all."

The Mystic looked up to catch a thought. "In a sense, I suppose, you are right. The two goals are one and the same."

"Hardly! These thousand years have only reinforced our religion—not the misguided version, as you describe, but the true Islam. It is precisely for the glory of Allah that the Watcher is leading us to victory."

"And what is victory to you, eh? Winning the Lord's favor on the Last Day? The triumph of one religion over the rest?"

Amara's hands grew restless. "Please, Mystic, just tell me where I can find Al-Hayek. Do you know where he has hidden the Clepsydra?"

"Amara, listen to me. What you are seeking is the origin of your lineage, not merely for your ancestor's inventions but for your capacity to know the truth of all things. How else will you convey your message to the world? Al-Hayek would tell you the same, only he might phrase it differently."

"Please!" She ran her callused fingers through her hair and pulled it taut away from her scalp.

"Every religion has its own line of spiritual teachings, some of which can be traced back millennia. Each religion has its language, its sacred texts, and its brand of followers at any given time. But the more deeply you trace each spiritual tradition—beyond the words themselves, beyond the histories, beyond ritual and beyond fellowship—there is a mystic center, a core of spiritual truths that transcend religion."

"I understand that, but—"

"The way of the Mystic," he persisted, "is to reach God through direct experience rather than by doctrine or even by faith."

"Direct experience? How can experiences possibly improve upon a doctrine when one's faith is already complete?"

"Do you think you could have learned the truth about the *convivencia* without coming here to witness its cruel reality?"

"I...I don't know."

"Without first-hand experience all knowledge is useless. All words are useless. And without first-hand experience, all the names of God are mere words; they are shallow, meaningless breaths of air."

"The names of God are meaningless? How can you say that?"

The Mystic snickered. "Yusef didn't like this idea either."

"Because it's false! It's blasphemy!"

"In your tradition the names of God are invoked to express the unknowable; the Quran is recited in order to lead you on a path back to Him. But here is where your understanding has failed you: the experience of God is the *source* of faith, not the result."

"With respect, you are wrong," Amara asserted without hesitation. "Without words for God and language for understanding His nature, what hope do we have of knowing anything? It is the holy Word that instructs us. It fills us with knowledge of His divine will. We rely on the accuracy and fidelity of language in order to know the truth."

"But what is language, Amara? Words are based on our experiences with reality. As any linguist could tell you, a word does not create its meaning; the meaning has always existed. It is our *need* to express that meaning—to express a truth about a direct experience—that led to the creation of any word."

Amara's 11th-century brain couldn't process the Mystic's explanation as quickly as she wished. Instead, it dwelt upon the fear of spiritual inadequacy. *Direct experience with Allah? When have I ever achieved this without the aid of words?*

"The way of the Mystic," he continued, "is to realize that all religions, at the deepest level, are essentially one and the same: Islam seeks submission to the will of Allah; Christianity seeks salvation through the Christ; Buddhism seeks freedom from the cycle of birth and rebirth—but whether you choose to call the thing you seek 'God' or some other name, there is a transcendent meaning that lies deeper than the goal. And that meaning has always preceded the word."

"If that were true," Amara rebutted, "then why would God create language in the first place? Why would God enshroud the truth with meaningless words that do not lead back to Him?"

"Because these words lead *from* Him. That is the distinction! Words themselves are meaningless, for they reflect our limited understanding; but what our words express is not. Language is necessary to organize the structure of our thoughts so that we can express the inexpressible."

"But you are contradicting yourself! First you said words were meaningless, and now you say they are necessary. How can they be both meaningless and necessary?"

"Let me explain. Do you know the story of the Tower of Babel?"

"Of course."

"Humans have always known deep down that with God's strength behind them there is nothing we cannot do. You also believe this, I think."

"As firmly as I believe you and I are here in this synagogue."

"The people of ancient Babylon did too," the Mystic explained. "According to the Torah they banded together to build a tower to the heavens. They wanted to reach God directly and create for themselves a name in His image. Due to the precision and fidelity of their shared language, they might have succeeded! However, God did not want to allow them to succeed in this way, so he picked the Babylonians up and scattered them around, creating many different tongues to confuse them. You see, it didn't matter what language they were using. Language does not raise one's direct experience with God. It was futile to try and use language to ascend to His level. But it was also necessary for them to try. In attempting to reach the heavens and then losing their common language, they were forced to communicate with their hearts instead. They were humbled before God. This is how they gained the direct experience they lacked, the experience that renders all mere words meaningless in the end. You see, we cannot know God through words alone."

"But how can you claim to know this, hmm? If direct experience is required to know the truth, then what is to say the Tower of Babel isn't only a myth?"

"Only a myth, you say?" He picked up his copy of the Torah and weighed it in his hand. "Are the words in this book simply ink on a rotting page?"

Amara continued to listen.

"There is nothing wrong with seeing the Tower of Babel as a myth, as long as you look *beyond* the myth, beyond the tower itself. What the story really teaches is how to build our experiences in life into the highest possible expression of God. *Life* is the tower!"

"Sure, it's a metaphor."

"More than a metaphor—it's a metaphysical truth!"

"What's the difference?"

"Our nature is to seek unity in a common language, to speak what we know and to preserve it in words. This is how magnificent works of poetry and art are created. Even religions are created in this way, inasmuch as they are founded on words: the Quran, the Torah, the Gospels—these are all, in a metaphysical sense, spiritual towers ascending to God!

But however high they may reach through their words alone, these towers will crumble before any of us can reach the heavens. This is because language does not last forever. Religion also does not last forever! Like a weary, flowing river it trickles down and decays, morphing and evolving with the times. It diverges and confuses itself the longer it stays in use. Religion may be the language of the soul, Amara, but it did not create the soul. On the contrary! It was the soul that brought forth religion, and it did this through direct experience with the original Creator, the One who existed before He was given any name or any religion."

Amara considered the parable closely and was unable to find fault. But it still did not bring her any closer to finding the Clepsydra. If anything, the Mystic's discussion of language only made her anxious to reunite with Tariq the linguist.

"But Mystic, that is precisely why we are seeking the Clepsydra. Like the Babylonians, we want to construct a message of peace that can tower its way into the high reaches of the human heart. For us, this is necessary."

"You listen well, my child," the Mystic applauded.

"And once we have our message, we will be victorious! Allahu Akbar!" Husain staggered to his feet and raised his fist in the air, before plopping back down like a sack of potatoes. "I think I need to lie down. This pain in my head is getting more intense."

"No! The pain is temporary. Snap out of it!" He slapped the champion's muscular shoulders as a show of encouragement. "I will take you to Al-Hayek. Follow me. You can still walk, no?"

"God willing," she muttered in Spanish.

"Follow me. You are ready for a direct experience with God."

"*Ojalá,*" she repeated.

Chapter 20

Yamina didn't know what to do. She could not look away from the shadows of the kidnapper who took Mayra. *Bring her back!* she wanted to exclaim. *Please, Allah, bring her back!* Yamina clutched her stomach and looked around. Everything around seemed foreign to her now—those familiar hills, those inviting fields—all was now rife with evil and fraught with pain. All she could see was a reality distant from the dreams of her youth.

"Why are you so quiet, Tariq?" asked the boy Yusef.

Yamina had no tears left to cry. She squeezed her stomach and knelt down in front of the stream.

"Listen!" She placed her ear close to the gushing water. "I can hear Mayra's name. We have to go get her back!"

"Very well, Yamina. Go. Find her. Call out to her."

Yamina looked up at the boy, who was crossing his arms. She froze. The bubbling sound of the stream poured through her awareness like a timeless melody, numbing the pain of her sister's capture."

"I...I...can't."

"Tariq, in the short time we have known each other, I have watched how you react to things."

As Yamina calmed down, Tariq regained control over her words and thoughts. "What do you mean, Yusef?"

"You analyze your circumstances so intensely that you often fail to act when you are called to do so. Even now! Your heart told you to chase after Mayra, and you also expressed that intention through words. But even in that you have failed! You have hesitated."

"But that wasn't my fault! It was Yamina!"

"It was you, Tariq, believe me. Why do you think your soul chose Yamina as its carrier? She is a reflection of the state of your soul."

"But what is wrong with stopping to analyze?" Tariq countered. "Maybe, because I waited, I have come to a more rational decision. See? Didn't you say it was pointless to act here in the 11th century? Didn't you say we would not survive?"

"Perhaps, if you analyzed it further you could justify your hesitation. Perhaps all people in the world can rationalize their reluctance to act upon their destiny!"

"Destiny? How do you know what destiny is?"

"That is not the right question, Tariq. Just look. Many people in the west like to sequester themselves in their rooms and question whether their circumstances are destiny or not. The Order of the Libraries is very good at that! But whenever you overthink something, it ceases to be your destiny. When you overanalyze, you hesitate! And it is through hesitation that fear, urgency, and the tendency toward violence are born. You can see it in violent extremists who have lost hope for society's advancement. They are caught in a rationalization that holds time back, and so they lash out and attack at all the wrong moments. Be mindful of your inaction, Tariq!"

Tariq examined Yusef's words. Barring a few notable exceptions, they were accurate descriptions of his psychological pattern.

"There was one time recently when I did act," Tariq confessed. "I was at the mall in Nanaimo. It was the first time I stood near a water clock. It spoke to me. The clock told me to follow Gray Fin and the Windstepper. It said, 'go with them.' And I listened, I obeyed. That is what brought me to Seville, to you!"

"Yes, Tariq. That was your intuition speaking to you."

"So it wasn't the water clock after all?"

"God speaks to us in many ways," explained the imam. "Sometimes it is enough to hear His voice as your own intuition. At other times it comes in the form of something more tangible that you may recognize. But the more you follow this intuition without question and without hesitation, the more you learn of Allah and the closer to Him you will become."

"And the closer we will come to the Clepsydra," Tariq inferred.

As he uttered these words, his avatar's wandering eyes caught hold of the last of the sheep passing over the stream. "My sheep are leaving!" Yamina shrieked. Quickly she got up, wiped the dirt from her clothes and ran after them. Yamina had always been fond of animals. The sight of these sheep made her smile despite her grief. "I love you!" she shouted as she ran playfully after the flock and touched one of the animals' soft, wooly coat. The sheep ignored her, but she kept walking alongside them. "Come on, little boy!"

Tariq marveled at how quickly Yamina was able to forget Mayra's capture. He, however, could not stop dwelling on it. To him, it was like watching the Silent One be killed all over again. *Could I have saved Mayra?* But Yamina's emotions, which he was getting well acquainted with, were more fleeting, like those of a child. So, he didn't try to force them. Instead, he tried to heed the imam's advice and listen to his intuition rather than dwell upon the hypotheticals.

As the river rushed placidly by, Tariq composed his thoughts. "Yusef, We need a plan. You said that Umar al-Hayek was a weaver. So, maybe if we follow these sheep to their herdsman and find out who buys the wool, it will lead us to Al-Hayek."

"I think we shall soon find out if you are correct!"

Directly behind them, a herdsman appeared. He stared at the young woman and the boy.

"Don't you know, it's dangerous for a young mother and her child to run around outside the city walls? Does your husband know you are out here?"

"I don't have a husband. And Yusef is not my child!"

"Are you feeling okay?" asked the herdsman. "You look

like you are in great shock."

"You're right!" exclaimed an anxious and impatient Tariq, trying to show the imam he could act. "And we don't have much time. Look!" He showed the herdsman his swollen forearm.

"What happened to you?"

"A snake came into my home. I nearly died."

"You poor girl," he sighed. "You look like you've run away."

"We need to find Al-Hayek, the weaver. It's urgent! He is the only one who can save me."

"Not a doctor?"

"Only Al-Hayek. Can you help us find him?"

"Of course. Come with me. I will take you to Al-Hayek."

"You know him?"

"He is the finest weaver in Seville!"

Relief poured through Tariq's weary soul.

"Thank you."

The herdsman lifted the petite Yamina and placed her upon his donkey. The barefooted orphan boy managed to scale the back of the donkey without much difficulty. The donkey already carried a hefty load: ropes, linens, water jugs, and baskets of garlic cloves and spices, all carefully hidden from the sun under colorful, albeit faded blankets. They continued walking slowly along the river as it wrapped around the town. The sheep lined up ahead of them as far as they could see; in the distance they looked like long, vibrating threads.

"Look, *Yamina*," assured Yusef, "we are on the correct path."

She nodded her head and placed her hands on the donkey's back. The little boy put his arms around her and held on. The donkey trotted docilely alongside the river.

Perhaps there is hope after all.

After about ten minutes the herdsman spoke again: "What is your name?"

"Yamina."

"Tell me, Yamina, what are you and your brother doing

out here?"

Tariq didn't want to lie again. "I told you. We need to find Al-Hayek the weaver."

"Do you know what time it is?"

"That's just it!" Tariq improvised. "Is there a water clock around here?"

"A water clock? What do you know about water clocks?"

"Well, my family used to have one. Do you have one?"

"Why, they're all around us! They fill the channels that water all those fields. Without the water clocks, all the wells and streams might dry up."

"Mr. Herdsman," Yusef shouted to the herdsman. "How far outside the city are we going?"

"My boy, we are just following my flock. We'll get there."

"Are we almost there?"

"It's just around that hill." He pointed ahead and to the right. "It won't take us much longer."

The sun began to set. Sleepy Yusef rested his head against Yamina's back. It was such a pleasant ride atop the donkey that Tariq was able to put Mayra's kidnapping out of his mind for the moment. He was able to escape from the attack he had witnessed in Seville that very morning. Lost in the orange glow of the sunset, Tariq nearly forgot about the Waymaker and that wondrous timekeeping waterfall; not to mention the fact that the venom in his arm was drawing death closer to him every second! Instead, he smiled and didn't dwell on these things. The herdsman had a certain grandfatherly nature that resonated with him deeply—the kind he had not experienced since his grandfather's passing. He relished every moment of his sunset ride atop the donkey.

When they rounded the hill, the herdsman stopped and grabbed the donkey's saddle. Tariq jumped off and stepped closer to the building in front of them. The door opened, and a stranger came out carrying a sack of coins.

"Is this one for me?" the stranger asked, scratching chest.

"Yes, sir," replied the herdsman, removing her from the

donkey and gripping Yamina by both shoulders. Yusef jumped off of the donkey and stood behind Yamina. He rubbed his eyes as he peaked out from behind her waist.

"Yusef!" whispered the linguist.

"Shut up." The friendly herdsman's voice turned coarse and shady. His hand inched eerily close to Yamina's neck.

"She has no husband," he told the man with the coins.

"Is that so?" The man with the coins sized up Yamina's fine clothes. "Who is the little boy?"

"It's her brother."

He smirked and fiddled around with the coins in his bag. Then he took a quick, decisive breath. "I'll give you two hundred for them both."

"Two hundred? You've got to be joking! Look at her! She's from good stock. Surely she's worth at least eight hundred without the boy!"

"Bah! Three hundred, no more."

"She's clever too! Claims she knows about water clocks. I won't part with her for less than six hundred."

The buyer leaned in. "Are you a clever one, girl? How about learning a thing or two from me!" He took Yamina by the torso and slammed her hard upon the ground. Yusef crouched in fear. The buyer turned to the herdsman and let out a callous, sadistic laugh. Yamina tried to scream, but like her eyes, dried of all tears, the words in her throat had also evaporated.

"You liked that, didn't you, girl?"

The herdsman picked her up by the waist and stood her up for the buyer to strike her again. "Answer the man!" he commanded.

But this time, Yamina was not fazed. Her words were whirling around inside her, ready to emerge. Her fingers curled into fists. Her leg muscles tightened. She stood up to face her aggressor.

Okay, Yamina, we can do this!

"I have a better idea," Yamina answered. "Run!" Swiftly, she kicked the donkey in the rear with her knee, sending it braying frantically down the street. The jugs of precious water it carried sloshed and spilled onto the cobblestones.

But the buyer was not distracted. He seized Yamina's forearm and squeezed it hard. "Your ideas are about to get you into trouble."

As he gripped her arm, he noticed the swelling.

"She's a cripple! You're scamming me!"

"No!" claimed the herdsman. "I wouldn't dare!"

"Take this!" shouted Yamina. She removed the scarf from her head and covered the buyer's face with it, causing him to drop his bag of coins. The herdsman then snatched it from his feet and chased after his donkey. Then she grabbed Yusef's hand and darted in the opposite direction.

"Thieves! Both of you!" The buyer stomped the ground, not knowing which of them to run after. "I'll have your hands for this!"

Tariq and Yusef charged through the uneven cobblestone streets as quickly as they could. When Yusef could not keep up, Tariq picked him up and carried him. Tariq's entire right arm was throbbing with pain up to his shoulder. There was not much light in the streets, but in the absence of vision, a different kind of sensation struck him—a feeling of being pulled forward by an invisible thread, ushered in that direction with purpose and knowing. Indeed, something was threading its way into his destiny. He obeyed without resisting.

Tariq followed this feeling until he saw the faint light of an oil lamp illuminating a window. He laid the boy down in front of the window and hugged him as tightly as he could. The oil lamp lit both of their faces with a glow of splendor.

"Yusef, can you hear me?"

By now it was pitch-black. The clouds cleared and starlight filled the space between the horizons. Yamina and the young boy huddled around the oil lamp, blanketed by the glow of the night sky. Yusef blinked his eyes and awoke.

"Yusef, you're still alive!"

"Tariq?" The boy groaned with hunger and fatigue.

"I thought we were finished, Yusef. But there was this impulse that arose within me. It was Yamina! She knew what to do, and I didn't even need to control what would happen."

"It was you, Tariq, believe me."

"Do you really think so?"

"I do. It is the will of your heart. Controlling the heart is like riding a horse. You have to listen, spur it on gently, and don't over-think it. Sometimes, as you are riding it, you let it also ride you."

"Right, I remember."

"Believe it or not, your grandfather learned this same lesson from Islam."

"You knew my grandfather?"

"It is no coincidence that the Watcher chose you and sent you to us. You, like your grandfather, are a thread at the seams of God's great tapestry. That is why you must surrender your hesitations, follow your intuition."

Tariq might have had a myriad of questions for Yusef about his grandfather. But it was late, so instead he yawned. "Right now, my intuition is telling me to watch the stars."

"Then let us watch."

As they looked up reverently, a bright Venus and a brazen Mars shown next to each other like two eyes in the heavens keeping constant vigilance. The silence of the eleventh century was stunning, even refreshing. Here, they were free from the modern interruptions of electricity and radio waves. They were free of the tangled web of ideas and concepts that defined human thought in the 21st century. For the first time since awakening as Yamina, Tariq was fully able to open his senses.

Yamina's hair waved in the nighttime air. After a while, she muttered the only thing that remained on her mind:

"I think I'm going to die."

"Well, of course you are. This is only natural and is the will of Allah."

"I mean, I'm going to die very quickly."

Tariq felt the poison permeate his chest; the pounding of

his heart rang through him like a swift knock upon the gates of Hades. Then, like a blanket of shadows, death fell upon Yamina. Her head dropped to the cobblestones. Her time was up.

Above the poor Yamina, who would never wed or see her sister again, Tariq's soul hovered and watched. *It is a fact of life that all must die. After all, there is a time for everything and a season for each activity under the sun. But Yamina has died so young! Like countless others throughout history, she has fallen victim to the pernicious specter of death. She has reached her judgment day, her Last Day. Mortality itself,* the linguist wept, *is a greater threat to life than any living terrorist.*

And yet Tariq, too, had died in some form. He still felt real, though his soul was a ghost. He looked around, but the streets remained dark and dismal. *Isn't Allah supposed to restore me to life? Nothing is happening! How do I get back?* The faster Tariq tried to move, the more still his ethereal body became. *Help! Yusef! Help me!* But no matter how loud he screamed, the boy Yusef could not hear him. The oil lamp grew fainter, and the vision of 11th century Seville grew dim. The linguist had no physical form; he was between substances—an essence without a container, like meaning without words.

In the darkness, visions overtook his visual field. First was a prayer chamber, dark and ornate. Shoulder-high partitions made of gold contained fine inscriptions of a hundred different names for God, spelled out in a devout, calligraphic Arabic. The floor was lined with pale, blue tiles, which appeared dark gray in the dim light. Behind one of the partition walls, Tariq caught a glimpse of an old man with a long beard. The bearded man's presence was overbearing, even terrifying. In that quick glimpse, Tariq spied the man's coarse, gray woolen robe, and unordinary, albeit immaculately clean, turban. He was sitting still in meditation, and yet the aura of his soul seemed to whirl and dance around his body like a sufi dervish. *Are you the Watcher?* Tariq called out with his mind. The bearded man peaked half of his face out from behind the partition and glared at Tariq with one visible eye. Tariq's heart skipped a beat.

But the image of the mysterious bearded man left him as quickly as it had arrived. The gold partitions of the prayer chamber blurred in front of his squinting eyes and turned into gold-leafed trees. Deep brown soil appeared beneath him, and the leaves became clearer and more discrete in his mind's eye. He found himself outside in the woods near a river. Then he noticed that the leaves were falling. The wind roared, and gold leaves blew at him until he too was cast down into the earth. He felt as if he were the rain. He felt like water pouring down from the sky and beating upon the soil.

Then, like a stream of fallen rain, he seeped across the earth and caught the leaves in his flow. The leaves turned red, then brown, then green, and then yellow again. The colors of four thousand turning seasons streamed through his consciousness as he moved upon the earth, pouring through and ever downward toward his future. Four thousand seasons of loss and hate, warmth and uplifting, death and rebirth became him, left him, warmed him, and died within him. Each one drew him closer to his own heart. *It all ends here*, he suddenly thought. Not knowing how he knew it, he sensed that he was about to slide off of a cliff like a massive waterfall.

Help me! Yusef!

The imam was nowhere in sight. Nothing but nature surrounded him—the dear Pacific Northwest of his childhood. And just as he braced himself for the fall, Tariq found himself plunging into a lower river. The waters slowed, and he looked around. He had drifted from the raging part of the river into a shallow riverbed.

What is that awful smell?

Lifeless salmon floated in the water like icebergs in a frigid ocean. Some were long deceased with white, moldy debris growing on their silvery skin. Others were still alive, starving and sedentary, and yet already they had begun to rot. Two younger, middle-sized salmon scurried by. Seeing the dead ones, they swam away scared. Then, the quick hands of an elder scooped one of them up and gripped it tightly.

"Waymaker, it's you!"

She gently squeezed the fish to keep it from shimmying out of her hands.

"What are you doing here, Mahatma?"

She tossed the fidgeting fish into a dirty, red cooler beside her.

"I...I don't know. I don't even know where I am, or even what I am." *And how can you see me?*

"What you are? Bah!" The Waymaker pulled out her teacup and raised it in Tariq's direction. "You are the same as every living thing. Remember?"

River mists wafted into the space in front of him. He longed to see it with his human eyes and feel it with his fleshy cheeks.

"I have met many, many wayward souls in this river," the elder continued. "Like salmon returning to spawn it seems they come to me to be reminded of Nature."

"Is the Silent One here with you?"

"No, Mahatma." The Waymaker cast down her eyes. "He was killed before it was his time to die. We have no way of knowing how long it will take for his soul to catch up with the river of time."

Tariq sensed that she was not as upset as she had been before. Still, he recognized that the loss of her husband was not something to meddle in. The Waymaker's grief was personal, shared among her tribe alone. And so the linguist redirected his thoughts to a more practical manner:

"Do you know how I can get back?"

"Back to where?" asked the Windstepper, who entered the scene from behind. Gray Fin, too, was there.

Tariq felt a cosmic rippling inside him. *Where are we? Of course, that is probably the wrong question.*

"Back to Seville!"

"You are already there, Mahatma," Gray Fin explained. "It is only your perspective that has changed."

"You were racing quite fast through time," the Waymaker said, shaking her head. "Four thousand seasons all at once! But worry not, we have caught you and returned you to time's natural pace."

Tariq recalled how Gray Fin and the Waymaker had done the same for him after the nun beside the water clock had made him slow down. *And all the while it is we who end up pulling the two worlds back into balance*, Gray Fin had said.

"Thank you for that. But I really do need to find Yusef. He has my body in a timekeeping bath in a cave under his mosque. That is how I got here. How can I get back?"

"Be careful of Yusef!" exclaimed the Windstepper. She swished her hands through Tariq's ghost-like form, though he felt nothing. "His god may seem appealing to you, but be mindful of Nature! Sending you back a thousand years in time is proof that his religion disrupts the natural flow of life."

"All life must flow downward, following gravity," added Gray Fin. He reached into the river and caught another salmon to throw into their red cooler. The fish skeleton tattoo on his forearm seemed to wiggle as if it were alive.

"But what about the salmon?" argued Tariq. "They are part of Nature, and yet they swim upstream!"

"And they must also die, Tariq. That is their unavoidable fate."

"Then why am I not dead?"

"Because you have a message in you," answered the Waymaker. "Words of peace are flowing within your heart, ready to be poured into all human consciousness. You are helping us, remember? That is why your life must be brought back to balance. Our lives are dependent on yours, just as your life is dependent on all of ours."

"I understand that. But Yusef says—"

"Listen!" she interrupted, irritated by his loyalty to the imam. "What you must do is focus your thoughts on the one thing connecting all souls to Nature. It is the very substance that flows within you and permeates the earth. It seeks the depths because gravity is the only law available to it; that is how it never gets lost. Do you remember what this substance is?"

Finally, the answer dawned on him.

"Water."

"Water is the lifeblood of Nature!" she exclaimed, as if Tariq had answered incorrectly. "The exchange between any two lives..."

The Waymaker sipped from her teacup and waited for Tariq to complete her sentence.

"...is simply a matter of *when*."

As Tariq bathed in this all-encompassing thought, he felt his consciousness being siphoned up into space. The river of time was flowing through him.

He was returning.

Chapter 21

"Are we close to Al-Hayek's shop, Mystic?"

"It's on the other side of that aqueduct," he answered. "But first, put out your torch. Al-Hayek's wife can smell a flame six houses away."

Amara snuffed out the torch with her muscular elbow. "How will we see?"

The Mystic did not answer. He led Amara around the aqueduct, which might have been a stunning architectural sight for her if the night had allowed her to see it.

"How is your head?"

"It's getting worse," she answered. "I don't think I have much time left."

"Then let us hurry, my child." He grabbed her shoulder and guided her into an alcove where a rounded door was just barely illuminated by the moon and stars.

"Go ahead," the Mystic went on. "Give it a knock."

Amara lifted her large matador hands, but before she could touch the door she heard a sound.

"They hear us!"

The door opened, and Al-Hayek appeared.

"Umar Al-Hayek!" shouted Amara. "We've found you!"

She leaned in to embrace him, forgetting that she was Husain the Swift.

"Get off me! Who are you?"

"It's me, Amara!"

"Go away. I am a weaver, not an oracle. I can't help you."

"But—"

"I don't care what they told you at the bazaar—I don't

do readings!"

The wrinkled-faced Mystic stood idly by with a sagacious grin.

"We don't want a reading. We need to ask you about the Clepsydra."

Al-Hayek's temper raged. "Who told you about that? Scoundrels, all of them! I take one person in, trying to do a good deed, and now the whole town wants to profit? Pshh! May Allah smite you to your grave!" He slammed the door in their faces.

"No!" Amara pleaded through the cracks in the door. "Please, Al-Hayek, let me speak with you!"

Behind the door they could hear the whispers of Al-Hayek and his wife. They sounded angry. Amara knocked once more. The pain in her head continued to throb.

"Now, get away from here at once!" The door thrust open revealing Umar al-Hayek with a dagger pointed straight at the matador's neck.

Al-Hayek, what are you doing? I'm your descendant! Don't you recognize me?

The wrinkled-faced Mystic took Husain in a gentle choke-hold and pulled him back. "I'll take care of him," he assured Al-Hayek. "Go and get some rest. I will send for protection so you won't be disturbed again."

Al-Hayek reluctantly withdrew his dagger and went inside. Amara sagged in the Mystic's arms, not fully recovered from the shock of Al-Hayek's threat. Her head felt as if it was being compressed by an anvil.

I've failed! Al-Hayek won't see me, and now we will never find the Clepsydra!

She looked down at her hands covered in dirt and blood and wept. Her perceptions had changed so fast, and yet now it was all over. The ingenious ancestor she had esteemed all her life was now nothing more than a surly wretch unwilling to open his door. Her entire worldview was unraveling faster and faster the longer she spent in this foreign time. Dazed and hopeless, she laid her tortured head to rest in the Mystic's cold hands.

The Mystic stroked her forehead to comfort her. "Be at peace, Amara. Now you have a real, direct experience with God—the god called *existential angst!*"

"But why didn't he listen to me? I told him who I was!"

"You did, and quite forcefully, I might add! But the message you gave him was incomplete."

"What do you mean, incomplete?"

"If every human interaction were simply a matter of announcing who you are and what you mean, then everybody would understand each other already! There would be no need for language at all! But remember the Tower of Babel? A good piece of communication is not fixed, Amara; it constantly needs to check its foundation so understanding can be built upon it. Each time two people meet, it is as if they begin building a new Tower of Babel together. That tower is the language through which their souls can communicate. And the tower they share will only stand if the message is made in partnership, not by force."

She looked out through the matador's eyes for the final time. The Mystic gazed back at her with a cool, almost reptilian smile. His eyes were wise, like twin stars burning brilliantly in the background of the night. Amara breathed heavily. Her hands and arms trembled in order to bear the pain in her head.

"You might not have succeeded in the way you thought," he reassured her, "but you will find what you seek. I promise."

"Aaghh," she tried to speak, but her brain could not make words.

"Don't forget, my child, to make your message in partnership, not by force. That is the true victory."

She could hear his words, but her mind was growing numb. Her soul was preparing for departure.

"You recognize me now, don't you, Amara?"

As her eyelids fell shut the image of the Mystic's beady eyes and wrinkled face remained in her mind. She had seen those eyes before; somewhere in the swamp of her memory they were still staring back at her, beckoning her to remember. And then, like a beam of sunlight, it dawned on her. She knew who the Mystic was and who he had been. And as her avatar slipped into the throngs of death, she let her insight resound:

"Seogo!"

Chapter 22

A gray heron landed upon a massive, floating rock. The rock was warm, and it grunted as the heron clamped its talons down on its fleshy surface. To the heron's delight, the rock was nothing less than the head of a hippopotamus nearly fully submerged. The portentous roar of the Nile silenced everything else around the two creatures like an ominous lullaby. And yet while their symbiotic encounter was barely started, a second head—twice as large as the first—fired up out of the water, sucking the heron into its jaws and devouring the bird whole. Sharp, unforgiving ripples emanated in all directions. The hippopotamus backed away in fear. This was the Great Nile Crocodile, king of the river.

The Mystic had been here before; in fact, his life as a crocodile had led him to the Nile many times. During some of these visits, the Mystic would bathe in its waters as a way of centering himself spiritually after weeks of tiresome desert wandering. During other visits, the Nile became a place where he faced his fears. Here he had come face to face with crocodiles twice and three times his size—creatures that would eat him without a second thought! But this time, now carrying the unconscious zoologist upon his back, the Mystic's mission was as selfless as an animal's could be: to deliver this withering woman to the next stage of her spiritual journey. Perhaps all the pain and agony would lead her to a direct experience with God. The Mystic could only hope.

Menacing waves from the Great Nile Crocodile's feast of heron still pummeled the riverbanks, though no sight of the beast was evident. Seogo found a shallow river inlet in which he could rest. He laid the curly-haired zoologist face-up in the water and then rolled her into a shade of thickets.

Naomi the zoologist coughed and shivered as she came to. Seogo plucked a nearby branch of tree nuts and tossed it upon her lap.

"Where are we, Seogo?" she asked; or, at least, that is what the Mystic presumed she was asking. Naturally, his ears were presently not attuned to recognizing human speech beyond slight variations of pitch and volume. The crocodile relied on gesture and context.

Eat up and rest, my child, he said to the human. *You will need strength to cross this river.*

"I don't think we'll be able to get around this river without crossing it," remarked the zoologist as she chewed on the nuts.

Seogo placed his claw upon her knee and made eye contact, tilting his large head to the side with a sigh. The zoologist understood his meaning as clear as day: *You can do this.*

"I guess you are right. Moses led the Jews through the desert and across much more difficult stretches of water than this."

Naomi smiled for a moment, appreciating the elegance of the Torah's teaching. Then she realized the difference: the Jews were returning to Israel, claiming their holy land, a mission commanded by God. But what was the grand purpose of this lonely zoologist in the wild? What was her importance? She shook her head in disbelief.

"How do we cross?" the zoologist pondered in frustration. "I'd swim, but suicide is already out of the question." She plucked the last nut from the branch with her teeth and discarded it at her feet. "And we don't have a boat."

The crocodile growled. *Isn't that what you humans are good for?*

The zoologist took heed and quickly got to work building. She gathered long sticks and sturdy blades of grass to tie together. "If Amara can build a water clock from nothing but a few odd car parts, then surely I can build a raft for one person and a crocodile." She looked up at the mighty river and gulped. "I just hope I can navigate the way."

The Mystic wrapped his tail around the zoologist's feet and pulled her in, pressing the tip of his snout onto her chest, comforting her with the unspoken words of friendship.

Stay strong, my child, for soon you will reach your promised land.

Chapter 23

Tariq opened his eyes and shut them again. He was floating in the bath. He instantly recognized that he was back in his 21st-century body. His brain and heart once again rested in familiar anxieties. And yet he also carried memories of Yamina's life. As he further awoke, his feelings were saturated with blissful echoes of that state of nothingness as his soul had left his body. He felt himself flowing like waves in the river of time. But the more conscious he became, the more that feeling trickled away into the realm of the forgotten. The bliss of formlessness receded, making way for the thoughts and sensations necessary for physical life.

The linguist was grateful to be alive. He was inspired! Feelings from Yamina's heart lingered in his own heart. Though she had puked and stammered at her sister's capture, she also found the courage to speak out and avoid being sold into slavery. *What a metaphor for finding one's voice!* Tariq remembered that moment as vividly as memories from his own life. He replayed it, felt it, and reveled in it from the inside out. He removed his snorkel and gazed upon the inside of the faintly illuminated cavern beneath the mosque. Amara, too, was waking up. He could hear her splash as she got out of the bath next to his.

"Tariq!" she shouted, grasping the rocky edges of the bath.

"Amara!" The linguist scrambled out of the bath and grabbed a towel.

"Where is Yusef?"

The two of them looked to the third bath and saw the imam laying still, suspended in perfect tranquility upon the waters of the cavernous bath.

"He isn't back yet," Amara said with a slight sigh of relief. "That means we still have a chance. I found Al-Hayek, but I wasn't able to find out the location of the Clepsydra. Did you have any luck?"

Tariq looked up to try to recall everything that had happened.

"No, I didn't make it. Yusef and I were talking, and then I—"

"You found Yusef? What did he say? Was he close to reaching Al-Hayek?"

Amara noticed that Tariq was taken aback by her abrupt questioning. Then she remembered the Mystic's final words of advice: *Make your message in partnership, not by force. That is the true victory.*

"I am sorry, Tariq. I didn't mean to speak so forcefully. We are working in partnership."

"I know that, Amara. But if you and I both failed to find Al-Hayek, then I don't think Yusef stood a chance. His avatar was a five-year-old boy!"

"Hmm. Maybe five-year-olds are wiser than they appear. Let's just hope that it was all part of Yusef's plan to come alive in such a form. It must have been the only way to gain Al-Hayek's trust." *Which is what I failed to do.*

A latch opened from the door behind them and the imam's messenger entered, followed by a pair of crocodiles.

"Ibrahim!" cried Amara. She reached out to hug him.

"What are you doing?"

Amara withdrew and composed herself. She had never greeted Ibrahim in this way before. "Thank you for bringing the crocodiles."

"I have done my part, Amara. It is all part of the Watcher's plan." He turned to size up the linguist. "You must be Tariq."

"Yes. We have just returned from our trip to—uh, Amara, does he know?"

"To the eleventh century? Yes, I know. I would have gone

myself, but then who would have looked out for the Watcher's army?"

Tariq jumped when he finally saw the crocodiles. But then he quickly fell into a state of calmness. He could not understand it; the two crouched, even-tempered beasts seemed to radiate peace and tranquility all around them. Indeed, there was something about the presence of these docile reptiles that made his soul smile. And he could swear the crocodiles were smiling back at him.

Suddenly Amara remembered the Mystic. "Seogo!" she exclaimed. "Where is Seogo?" Her eyes lit up as she knelt down to greet one of Ibrahim's crocodiles. She stroked its neck and chin as one might a household pet. This crocodile was much smaller than Seogo but no less stately. It purred and leaned its head to the right as she massaged its chin. She gazed into the animal's wise, swamp-green eyes and whispered to it. "Whose soul is hiding in there? Another Jewish mystic?" The crocodile gazed coyly back and gave a subtle nod.

"Amara? What kind of crocodiles are these?" asked a bewildered Tariq.

"Dwarf Nile crocs from the sacred ponds of the South Sahara," Ibrahim interjected. "The Mossi people have been domesticating them for hundreds of years."

"They are our army, Tariq."

The linguist never imagined that the army she and Yusef were referring to was a band of peace-loving crocodiles.

"These crocodiles, I believe, were sent to us from another age." She was excitedly piecing together their significance in relation to the Mystic. "But Seogo is missing—I left him with the zoologist. I left them both, Tariq! I left them to die in the desert! What kind of partnership is that? What kind of message? I may as well have just thrown them into a bull ring without any defenses!" She grabbed a towel and began drying herself off. Her hands and arms trembled with repressed angst.

"They are with Allah now," Ibrahim said consolingly.

Amara turned around with a jerk and ran over to Yusef's

bath. Her brother's eyes were hidden by the dark-lensed snorkel as he lay floating in the bath. "Brother, why won't you come back? Please! We need you!"

A thought then dawned upon the linguist. He approached the imam's sister and took out his pen.

"Do you think this pen can help?"

Amara looked up and snatched it from him.

"Of course!"

With haste she laid her wet towel on the floor and began sketching on it a large map of eleventh-century Seville. The markings glowed a brilliant hue of green, and instantly she knew her brother had received the message and could read the map. *This will lead you directly to Al-Hayek*, she explained with her thoughts. *May it be Allah's will that you find him.*

Seconds later Yusef's hands began to twitch. He was coming out of the coma.

Amara smiled at Tariq. "I knew there was something I liked about you." She leaned in to peck a kiss of gratitude on his cheek. Then she stood up and pointed, dumbstruck, at the green markings she had drawn. Ibrahim stroked his beard. *What has gotten into her?*

"This is made of algae, you say?" Amara asked.

"Something like that," Tariq answered playfully.

Yusef splashed around and removed the snorkel from his face. Amara and Tariq each offered him a hand and led him out of the bath. The imam dried himself off and composed himself. They waited eagerly for him to speak.

"You have made it back," he congratulated them. "What did I tell you about Allah? He is magnificent!"

Tariq nodded, secretly wondering if he would have made it back if not for the Waymaker catching his soul in the river of time and returning him to balance. Amara leapt up and hugged her brother. Surprised, he hugged her back.

"Yes, dear sister, I missed you too."

"What about Al-Hayek? Did he tell you the Clepsydra's location?"

"I found Al-Hayek, yes," answered the imam, "thanks to your map. But before I tell you anything more, let us go back up to the mosque."

The three of them grabbed their clothes and headed through the narrow, torch-lit passageway and toward the mosque's underground entrance. Yusef and Ibrahim embraced hands and exchanged comments in Arabic as they ascended. The crocodiles trailed behind.

Soon they emerged from the cave and into the mosque. Dozens of crocodiles were waiting in the main prayer hall. Tariq's heart jumped again when he first saw them.

"Stay calm," advised Yusef, though his instruction was unnecessary. Sweet vibrations of the crocodiles' gifted presence filled the room. Inwardly, Amara marveled to think that each crocodile contained the soul of some long-departed mystic saint.

The four of them proceeded down the Tejedors' ancient woven rug and toward the fountain. Beneath their feet the rug displayed its multifarious design: triangles and hooks, curves and tessellations, colors woven in and upon one another in exquisite dynamism. Walking down Al-Hayek's masterpiece was like entering the holiest of sanctuaries.

"To tell the truth," remarked Ibrahim, "I was beginning to worry. After last week's attack in Seville, I thought you would have made better haste."

"Last week?" exclaimed Tariq. "But we were only asleep for a few hours!"

"You slept for nearly four days."

Tariq was stymied. *Maybe the Order of the Libraries had a point when they accused Yusef of stealing time.*

"The army has awaited your return and we are ready for battle, Yusef," declared Ibrahim. "Now, tell us where to find the Clepsydra."

"Wait!" Amara interrupted. "What about the Watcher?"

Tariq's eyes widened and angled upward in recollection. He had only glimpsed the face of the mysterious bearded man for a moment, and yet he was certain this man, whether or not he was the Watcher, was wise and discerning, even more so than Yusef.

"He will join us later, Amara," responded Yusef.

If he even exists, she thought, still frustrated at her brother for not letting her meet this mysterious man.

"But it may not be as soon as I had hoped. When I met Al-Hayek, I asked him about his Clepsydra. But he lied and said he hadn't yet created it, nor had he any idea of how or why he would do so."

"How can this be? Did you miscalculate the year you sent us back?"

"No, there was no miscalculation. We know he had already created the Clepsydra; there is no doubt about that. He was lying to protect our family's secret. But this is understandable. After all, secrecy is the foundation of our community. It is not just anybody we invite into our closest circles."

"So you have no idea where to find it?"

"Al-Hayek may have hidden the truth on the surface, but he did offer two hints: first, that such a complex design for a water channel would need to be enclosed within strong walls; and second, that this channel would become a pivotal place of influence in human history."

"Are those the only clues you have?" asked a dejected Amara.

"I'm afraid so."

"But where was he referring to?" prompted Tariq.

"I can only speculate. But, I have an idea."

"What is it?"

"During the Golden Age in Spain, Seville was the center of trade and commerce with the Americas. It was the wealthiest city in the land! All of Spain's ships bound for the New World would pass through Seville, and all the incoming ships filled with gold and silver and sugar from the Americas would likewise find their harbor here."

"The Tower of Gold, of course!" Amara exclaimed. "It was

built beside the river canal in the early 1200's as a guard tower to fend off the invading Christians. But three hundred years later, when the conquest of the New World began, this was precisely the spot from which all trade and exploration emanated. Do you think this is what Al-Hayek meant by a pivotal place of influence?"

"I think we should explore the area and look for signs of an underground water channel."

At the imam's command, the four of them led the band of crocodiles out of the mosque and locked the door. The war was on, and the hunt for the Clepsydra exact location had begun.

Amara's face shimmered with excitement. She made eye contact with another one of the crocodiles. It moved its jaw and wiggled its cheeks, casting a tender, knowing glance in her direction. She smiled back, and before her attention could be diverted, the crocodile winked at her.

Don't forget, my child, she imagined the crocodile saying, just as the Mystic had said. *Make your message in partnership, not by force. That is the true victory.*

Chapter 24

The wind was still, and the stench of fallen oranges filled the streets. The imam led the march across Seville, followed by his sister, his attendant, his linguist, and their troupe of dwarf Nile crocodiles trained to work their mystical prowess. Victory, in the eyes of the true Islam, was upon them.

Inexplicably, very little public inquiry arose as to why the crocodiles were following the imam and his entourage through the streets. As they marched through the *Plaza de España*, curious children ran up to pet them, and their parents followed. Everyone who looked upon them agreed: the crocodiles were smiling. And the more people were drawn in, the more expressive their smiles grew. But the march proceeded, and the crocodiles did not stop to linger with the passersby.

Amara walked beside the linguist. Her colorful robe appeared even brighter than usual. "Have you thought about your message, Tariq?" she asked.

"Message?"

"Have you forgotten? Your job is to create the words that we will broadcast through the Clepsydra once we find it."

"Yes, of course," he hesitantly agreed remembering what he'd been told was his contribution.

"So? What will the message be?"

Tariq looked out at the canal that circled the plaza. The midday sun glistened on its waters like the twinkling of stars.

"I think you will have to wait and find out."

She winked at him and continued walking by his side. A warm breeze coursed through their strides.

"Can I ask you something?"

"Yes," she replied. "But I cannot promise I will answer."

"Now that we're getting acquainted a bit, I am curious. What is your job, exactly?"

"I teach Arabic at the University of Seville. But my real interest is comparative religion."

"That sounds right up your alley," he tried to say, but the idiom didn't translate into Spanish.

"What?" She laughed pleasantly. "It's serious work, Tariq!"

"To tell you the truth," Tariq responded, "I have only just begun to contemplate it seriously. Growing up, Islam was present in my life, but I've always been more of an agnostic."

"Do you believe in God?"

"I don't know. What is your definition of God?"

Of course, a linguist would ask this question.

"Well, in Islam, God is the Magnificent Creator of the universe, the one true power and knower of all things. In other religions, God may be a mythological figure, a force of nature, or even a code of ethics. But, I suppose, belief in God might boil down to something as simple as the belief in a presence and a power greater than oneself: an all-encompassing, supreme being."

"If that is your definition," reasoned Tariq, "then it would be impossible not to believe in God!"

"True, unless you believe yourself to be the center of the universe. As Yusef says, believing in God is part of our nature."

"Did you say Nature? I know some First Nations people who would disagree with that."

"Then examine your definition of nature," she sneered.

"Okay, Amara. I suppose, the easiest way to explain it is to use the metaphor of water. Nature, like water, is the source of life. It gives birth to life, carries us, and becomes us. We cannot exist apart from Nature any more than we could exist apart from God. It is our lifeblood, so to speak."

"If that is your definition of nature, then my definition of religion is the same."

"But they are completely different!"

"Listen to me with a fluid mind, my dear linguist." She maneuvered behind him and came up on his other side. "Religion weaves itself into the cultural body of every society; there is not a village on earth that is not bound by some kind of collective belief. Religion, or shared belief, you could say, is the lifeblood of collective consciousness."

"Hmm…I suppose I can understand that metaphor."

"It is just like sharing a cultural tradition or honoring family loyalty. Justice, too, works through collective belief. The particular ways these beliefs are acted out varies by society, of course, but without some kind of core beliefs, such as these, a community cannot function."

"You could also make an argument," Tariq conjectured, "that religion gets misused just as Nature does. Just look at what the terrorists have done! Look at *jihad!*"

"That is not the same!" she shouted, stopping in her tracks. She looked both ways as they stood at a traffic intersection.

"Of course it is! Terrorists take our religion and modify it to their own advantage, but it is still a religion, don't you think?"

"No, Tariq, it is not. The difference is this: true religion is a glue that binds people together and makes a society cooperate, not for a particular aim but for the betterment of life as a whole. Terrorism is an ideology that destroys cooperation. It is *not* a religion; it is the very antithesis of religion! And here's another bit of study for you: *jihad* does not mean *holy war*, as you translate it. You use the word in that way because you see it accompany the use of violence. But what it actually refers to is a kind of inner struggle against the weaknesses of one's own heart. It's a struggle for self-defense against aggressors who are working *contrary* to the practice of the religion."

"Self-defense? Then why do religious extremists go out of their way to attack, planning elaborate, aggressive schemes?"

"In that question, you are making another presumption based on words. Am I right, Tariq? What you are calling *reli-*

gious extremism is, in fact *anti-religious extremism.*"

The linguist furrowed his brow as they crossed the street. She was sailing him into uncharted waters of analysis.

"Take this example: a Muslim town in the Middle East is under attack. According to the precepts of Islam, the victims should respect the lives of their attackers and do no harm. They would try to use words to resolve the conflict peacefully. Let God cast light upon their sins on the Last Day! But when the threat of death is imminent, each person in the town is faced with a terrifying moral crisis, in which one option is to use violence for self-defense. This internal struggle is the true meaning of the word *jihad. Jihad* is the war within one's conscience, the question of whether your life is threatened seriously enough that you must use force to save yourself and your family."

"Okay, but now compare that to a case where a First Nations tribe in the Americas who lives by the religion of Nature has had their home destroyed in order to profit from natural resources. Wouldn't they fight back? Don't Islamist extremists also believe their world is threatened by the west?"

"Ideological threats are not threats to life, Tariq."

"Unless you define your life by them."

"The true Islam is tolerant of the beliefs of others because one's own righteousness in the eyes of God is not dependent on what others do, even on the scale of the whole society."

"Isn't it? Aren't we all connected?"

"Not when it comes to the Last Day," she answered with a passionate breath. "Each of us is judged individually. You could be the only 'good Muslim' in your town, and you may be persecuted for your beliefs, but so long as your physical security and that of your family isn't under attack, then you accept it. And you remain kind to those who are misguided. That is where the terrorists have gone astray! The ones who travel overseas to destroy and take vengeance are doing so because they incorrectly perceive themselves as under attack. They don't understand that the words and customs of the west are not a true threat to the religion that one practices internally. Words can be no threat in God's eyes."

"Now, that is something I believe in," remarked the linguist, *"con todo mi corazón."*

Ahead of them, the imam pointed the way to the Tower of Gold. "Keep moving, you two!"

Overhead, spirals of cumulus clouds streaked across the heavens. Tariq looked up and noticed the sky divided in half: to the east, the clouds resembled fiery arrows being blown around without a clear direction or target. To the west, they resembled rows of soil tilled and planted with seeds. As these white, foamy cloud bodies met in the middle, they blew their way into Tariq's consciousness, soothing the hot airs that still lingered within him and uniting the dual nature of his yearnings. Indeed, on this day in Seville, the streets were paths of serenity.

"Tariq, now I have a question for you."

"Ask me."

"Have you ever had an experience, maybe a supernatural experience, that you couldn't explain?"

Tariq thought for a moment about flowing through the river of time with the Quoquamish elders—how he had no physical form, and yet he could speak and interact with them as they guided his soul home from the 11th century. He considered how he would put to words such an indescribable experience. It seemed to defy everything he knew, as if it were only a dream! But something in the back of his mind—his intuition, perhaps—was inclining him to share a different experience, one even more powerful from long ago.

"When I was a child, I went with my grandfather on the *hajj*. We had been traveling on foot for what seemed like an eternity. When we arrived at the Grand Mosque, Grandfather and I joined thousands of other people in our procession around the *Kaaba*. And as we finished our fifth circle around the *Kaaba*, I had a vision. I didn't know if it was due to fatigue or something in the desert air, but I saw the black box open up from the top, and out came a bluish-white cloud of dust. The cloud took the shape of a giant hand with five fingers. It pointed at me. I started walking faster. I went ahead of Grandfather, worried that this hand was out to get me. Then, as I looked back, it was moving toward me, palm facing up, and it scooped me up and carried me away."

The robed one followed his story enthusiastically. "Where did it take you?"

"It took me soaring through the sky, higher and higher. I could see the top of the *Kaaba* and the heads of the masses as they filled the Grand Mosque. The hand then became invisible, and it was my own legs that made me fly. Once I realized this, I panicked. 'I shouldn't be able to do this,' I thought. But then I started speeding up, and I couldn't stop. It was the giant hand, pushing me through the air. Then I saw the most terrifying thing of all."

"Was it Satan?"

"It was a face, bluish-white like the hand, but incomprehensibly immense. I stopped and hovered in the air. The face was hard to see directly. I couldn't make out any eyes or a nose, but I knew it was a face. I knew the eyes and nose had to be there even though I couldn't see them. Just then, I heard an enormous boom thundering out of its mouth. I felt as if the face was scolding me, pronouncing all of my weaknesses. And its words wrapped around my body like sky-colored strings. They felt coarse at first, but they became gentle once I gave in and let them grip me tight. Then, the strings started coming out of my mouth. They were my own words."

"You were speaking with the face?"

"Not exactly. It felt more like my words were being squeezed out of me. I couldn't control it! I watched them shoot out of my mouth and spiral into the immensity of the mouth in the sky. Seeing these strings, I felt connected to the sky, connected to everything. For the first time, I felt like I belonged in the world, that I didn't need to argue or prove myself, because my words were with a higher power. Words no longer tied me down. I was left completely speechless."

Amara stopped in her tracks. She, too, was speechless.

"So, Amara, what do you think? Was it a supernatural phenomenon, or was it the desert air playing tricks on my mind?"

"I think maybe," she said humbly, shining her admiring eyes upon the linguist's face, "you had a direct experience with God."

Tariq squinted, trying to play back the vision in order to comprehend her interpretation.

"Quickly!" shouted Yusef ahead of them. The Tower of Gold was in sight. They crossed the riverfront boulevard known as the *Paseo de Cristóbal Colón* and made their way to the tower.

"Good. Now, let us look for signs of the Clepsydra. But be discreet!"

The crocodiles circled round the tower, searching it out, obeying the instructions. Tourists stood by gawking at them, pointing and taking photos. *Did they forget that an attack was made on Seville only days ago?*

"I hope the crocodiles are getting enough to eat," remarked Ibrahim. "What ever happened to the zoologist?"

Amara bit her lip and squeezed her sleeves with her fingers. She thought of Naomi lying in the desert being consumed by locusts.

"She is with Allah now."

Ibrahim panicked. "But I have not heard from her family. Four days have gone, and we have still not contacted them!"

"She gave us no contact for any family," Yusef clarified. "Perhaps she has none. Let us give a call to the university and explain her disappearance. I wish we had done this before taking our trip in haste."

"I have an idea!" Amara interrupted.

The two men stopped and looked at her. Ibrahim stepped aside to make the phone call.

"This pen might serve as a divining rod." She equipped her pen and held it out for all to see.

Tariq's eyes opened wide. *She has a pen like mine?*

"It's algae, right?" she whispered to the linguist.

"Yes, try it," her brother answered. "Maybe it can tell us if we are close to the Clepsydra. I will enter the tower to get a view from the top. Look after the crocodiles, Amara." Yusef used an antiquated metal key to unlock the tower's door and entered.

"Let me see that!" Tariq pulled out his own pen to compare the two.

"Yours is similar," Amara noted, turning his hand to show the backside of the glass pen. "But look at the difference."

Tariq examined her pen and noticed that the ball bearing inside Amara's was rough and imperfect, whereas his was more precisely spherical. In addition, the glass had a different curvature. Compared to his, Amara's pen looked like a cheap knockoff.

"Where did you get it?" he asked.

"I bought it on eBay."

"Seriously?"

"Well, technically, I did. But it was Yusef who tracked down the seller."

Tariq chuckled.

"Is that funny to you?"

"No, no. It's just that these pens have inexplicable powers. They should be hard to find! And yet, you got yours off the Internet, and I picked mine up at the mall."

Amara hit his shoulder with the back of her hand. "Get out!"

Just then, a crocodile butted in between them and snarled.

"Okay, be serious," she said, regaining her focus on the mission. "We don't know how much time we have until the next terrorist attack. We need to find the Clepsydra, and quickly."

Tariq nodded. Amara shook her pen gently and held it up in the air. The linguist did the same.

"Now what?" he wondered out loud. *We look awfully silly holding them up like this.*

Then, a voice arose in the distance.

"There!" shouted the voice. "There they are!"

Amara and Tariq turned around to see an old woman and a nun walking side-by-side.

It's the Waymaker, thought Tariq, excited to see her.

It's Sister Sabina, thought Amara, dreading a confrontation with the Order of the Libraries.

The Quoquamish elder approached them and snatched the pen from Amara's hand. "Let me see that!" she ordered, in English. The Waymaker examined the glass ornament and showed it to Sister Sabina. Its green ink swirled inside, giving an illustrious glow.

"What is it?" the nun asked.

"It is an abomination of Nature! A forgery!" The Waymaker heaved out a grunt and launched the pen into the river.

"Oye!" its owner exclaimed. She then switched to English. "What was that for?"

"It must be returned to the ocean."

"Who are you?" asked a peevish Amara.

"I am a guardian of Nature and of time. And I will not let you and Yusef manipulate and destroy the earth!"

"She is the Waymaker," Tariq explained to Amara. "The chief elder of the Quoquamish tribe."

"We have come to stop you from speeding up time," declared Sister Sabina.

Amara's voice climbed a notch. "And how will you do that, hmm? Will you slow it down and hold us as prisoners? I think, you wouldn't dare be such a thief as to take our future from us!"

"We are not the thieves!" cried the nun in Spanish. *"You* are the thieves, stealing the past right from under us in order to hasten the Armageddon! Why can't you appreciate what little time we have left on this earth?"

"We are already in the Armageddon! Don't you see? War and terror are enwrapping the globe! Yusef and I are only trying to advance us beyond it."

"Okay, okay," Tariq interjected in English. "You both have a point. I think we should all calm down and sort this out."

"Very good, Mahatma," the elder commended him. "We will not resolve our differences until our dialogue has found a balance."

Sister Sabina took a deep breath, rubbing her wooden necklace. "You are right, Waymaker. Forgive me."

"You'll be forgiven once you stop being a disgrace to Nature. Time is meant to flow naturally, like a river."

As swiftly as she could, Amara snatched Tariq's pen from his hand and smashed it on the ground in front of them. Tiny green drops spattered onto the foot of her robe.

"Ooooh!" exclaimed the Waymaker. "You murderer! You have just squashed a sacred giver of life!"

"You mean your algae? The Giver of Life *created* them! How can they be sacred? It is you who disgrace the Creator by praising Nature in place of Him who made it!"

"What creator? Do you know where you come from? Nature has born you, raised you; water has filled you and given you life; and yet you invent these concepts—these religions! The Earth is the only Giver of Life."

"Stop!" chimed Sister Sabina. "We must be still and contemplate all sides of the issue. Nothing can be learned in the haste of an argument."

Amara looked at Sister Sabina's face. Her words rang true. They reminded her to watch her own words.

The Waymaker was furious. "Argument? This is no argument. It is an attack! Did you not see this woman destroy our precious algae?"

Amara guarded her silence. The nun tried to calm the Waymaker down. "If you will just take a breath, you might see it from a larger perspective."

"No!" the elder asserted. "There is no larger perspective."

"Waymaker, please—"

"You can conquer and colonize our land, Sister, but you will not make slaves of our intelligence. Come, Mahatma. Let us escape from this torrent and find still waters." She raised her arms and stormed off.

Tariq hesitated. He looked at Sister Sabina, at the Tower of Gold, at Amara's glowing face, and then down at his shoes. *Where are the crocodiles?* he wondered.

"Are you coming?"

Then Tariq looked at the river. *There they are!* The crocodiles were bathing. Amara also turned to watch them. *Their every splash is like a song; their every movement, a poem.*

"Tariq! If you stay with them, you will lose your balance. You will lose your way!"

At the top of the Tower of Gold, the imam emerged.

"Yusef!" Without thinking, Amara grabbed Tariq's arm.

Tariq looked up at the imam, then back at the Waymaker. He could neither speak nor move. It was exactly as he had felt when seeing the Silent One for the last time: nothing he could have said or done would have kept her from leaving. All words were rendered useless.

"Fine. Make your own way. You are no hero, no Mahatma." The elder proceeded down the riverfront alone. Like a flame in the dust, she vanished all at once.

"Amara!" called Yusef from above.

"*As-salaamu alaykum*," she greeted him.

"*Wa-alaykum salaam.* I am coming down." He disappeared from the turret of the tower, and in a few moments, he emerged from the old, rusted door.

Ibrahim approached them as he put away his cell phone. "I put out a notice to the university and to the embassy about the zoologist. Have you found any signs of the Clepsydra?"

"No," Yusef answered. "The Tower of Gold is not the correct location."

"What clepsydra?" inquired Sister Sabina. She received no reply.

Amara stepped forward. "How can you be sure?"

"The Watcher has sent me a message."

The Watcher? Bah!

191

"He says that we are still far from finding it. We may need to look outside of Seville."

"And go where? Let me talk to the Watcher! If he is so knowledgeable, then he should answer my questions."

"Be patient, Amara."

"Tariq, what are they talking about?" asked Sister Sabina.

Tariq started to explain: "They are talking about the Clepsydra. The Clepsydra is a water clock that—"

"Hold it right there!" exclaimed Yusef.

Tariq had never heard the imam speak so sternly.

"You were about to divulge our family legend! To the Order of the Libraries, no less!"

"No! I didn't—"

"I thought you understood our mission. I thought you understood the need for secrecy and the sanctity of Islam!" The imam shook his head. "I was wrong."

"But Yusef!"

Yusef's brow ridge became stiff and horizontal, like a storm front charging in echelon across the sky.

"No, Tariq. You will not be participating in our mission any longer."

"But I've come with you all this way! I've suffered death in another age for you! You need me!"

"My decision is final. A linguist is no longer required. You are finished here."

Tariq looked to Amara, whose eyes were downcast.

"You should go, Tariq," she conceded. A cloud passed over her, softening the colors of her robe. "Perhaps our fates will intertwine again someday."

Is it all over? Just like that?

"I told you not to trust Yusef," reprimanded Sister Sabina.

"Amara?"

"Just go."

"Come with me," the nun invited. Her wooden necklace, engraved with the word *INRI*, hung around her neck like a lovingly placed ornament. Tariq shrugged and gave in. How he longed to pause time and figure things out! How he longed for a rest! He followed Sister Sabina back across the street and out of sight.

Meanwhile, the crocodiles moseyed out of the river and gathered around the imam.

"It is time to move forth with our army," declared the imam. "The Last Day is upon us, and the Watcher needs all of you to be loyal to me."

"Again, you speak of the Watcher as if he were here. But you refuse to tell me anything about him!" She turned to the attendant. "Ibrahim, have you met the Watcher?"

"Well, no, but——"

"Then how do you know he even exists?"

"You have just seen me demonstrate the importance of secrecy to our cause," Yusef explained stringently. "And yet it works just the same within our circle. Little sister, you must trust me on this! Trust me as you would trust Allah."

"Forgive me, dear brother, but *you* are not Allah."

"My relationship with Allah is clear to you, Amara. You are unwise to doubt your faith."

"No, Yusef." She gestured with her index finger. "For the first time, I am not doubting my faith. I am honoring my faith by standing by what I believe in. No person should treat others as if he were the exclusive channel to God. This is not right!"

"Of course, it is right! It is the Quran. It is Islam. Or, have you forgotten?"

"But how can anyone hold a monopoly on God? It's not natural!"

"Do you deny that Islam is the natural religion?"

"I do not deny that we are all connected to Allah and must follow His will alone."

The imam stared fiendishly at his sister. *She is betraying me! She is turning her back on Islam!*

"I hope you will reflect deeply on the path you are choosing."

"Believe me, brother. I will."

Yusef prodded his attendant and called the crocodiles to follow him along the riverside. Amara watched them gradually leave her sight. Not one looked back to console her. She was left completely alone.

The robed one sunk onto the pavement beneath the tower. *It is all crumbling to the ground! The great peace I've believed in all my life—the* convivencia, *as I knew it—was a sham. Umar al-Hayek was right in front of me, and still I failed to win his trust. I forced my words instead of building a partnership. How far have I fallen from the path of my ancestors? How severely have I strayed from the straight and narrow? What will the Last Day hold for me?*

Amara looked down at a bed of grass where a handful of gnats hovered around a fallen orange. The clouds above had dispersed, revealing a lofty, azure sky. Seville had been Amara's home for most of her life, and yet she never grew tired of these simple sights.

Then she remembered another one of the Mystic's lessons: the Quran—the entire religion of Islam—was a kind of tower, ascending to the knowledge of God. And like all towers, it was never meant to last forever. Like a language changes naturally over time, the religion too would shift and adapt. *This may be a good thing*, she decided. *After all, if Islam remained permanent, exactly as it is, then we could never climb any higher than we are now. We would simply stop building our knowledge of God.*

Amara picked up the orange and pulsed it with her fingertips. The gnats scattered, and she looked up to follow their path.

To reach the Magnificent One, the seeker must transcend the tower.

Chapter 25

Seville was a metropolis teeming with finely adorned abbeys and cloisters. But for the Order of the Libraries, none of these magnificent places suited the unpretentious depths of their devotion to God. Theirs was a tiny spiritual refuge, a chapel hidden in plain sight whose bells sounded only for those with ears to hear.

"Spain is rich with history," the nun explained to Tariq. She set a brisk pace as they headed east from the *Plaza de España*. "Saint Isidore of Seville once called our nation the *ornament of the world*. Have you visited any of our cathedrals?"

"I visited many of them while I went to school in Granada years ago. Which one is yours?"

"Ours is not on any of the tourist maps. It is not easy to find!"

The chapel was nestled in an obscure corner of the historic city center. An administrative building dwarfed the adjacent chapel, while walls of crisscrossed gardens acted as camouflage. Even the few people who knew about the hidden chapel found it difficult to locate. And for this reason it had become the Order's intimate, pristine meeting place to rendezvous with God, removed from the mainstream, and free of loyalty to any worldly organization.

Sister Sabina opened the doors and invited Tariq inside. "Bow your head!" she whispered. The linguist obeyed.

Each nun of the Order of the Libraries had her own story of how she found the chapel. Some, like Sister Martirio, spied it instantly in a moment of pure synchronicity. Others, like Sister Belén, sought it out like a paleontologist sifting through dirt for bones. And others still, like Sister Clarinda, found the hidden chapel while fleeing from another cloister. But no one knew Sister Sabina's story. She was thought to be the oldest living nun in all of Spain, although her appearance would not have suggested it. And whatever her past contained, she kept it immaculately concealed behind her still, gentle face.

"Why are there so many books in here?" asked the linguist.

"Knowledge is the nourishment of the soul, Tariq. What better way to honor the Creator of all knowledge than by immersing ourselves constantly in books that carry His wisdom?"

As Tariq made his way around piles of books stacked up to his knees, he remembered what Sister Clarinda had said when they first met: *Only in the eternal sanctity of the present moment will you find peace.* He imagined how she must have spent years, even decades of life in seclusion, studying the Word of God and its many interpretations. This was the way of the Order of the Libraries, the Christians who slowed time down.

"Is it only us in here?" he asked, only too soon. Beneath the altar, he saw that the three other Sisters knelt praying. *They're so still*, Tariq thought, *they look like an image drawn straight from one of* El Greco's *paintings.*

Sister Sabina lowered her head at the altar. Tariq relaxed his shoulders and slowed his breathing. Time seemed to stop again. Finally, the three Sisters stood up and greeted him. The room slowly sank into darkness as the dull, colored light faded through the unkempt chapel windows. Sister Sabina lit a candle.

"Now, Tariq, tell me. What is this Clepsydra you are looking for?"

Tariq looked at the nuns, who were eager and patient to hear his words, and he began to speak:

"Yusef and Amara, as you know, are concerned with the Last Day. They have built an army—the Watcher's army—to warn humanity of the perils of hesitating too much in life. Yusef taught me that hesitation breeds fear, and that fear causes us to lash out, sometimes violently, in order to make up for the time we have lost. He preaches that one should follow one's intuition, heeding the voice of God and holding nothing back."

The Sisters nodded and continued to listen.

"But I can understand your perspective too. Taking the time to reflect does not necessarily mean stopping time from advancing. Sometimes intuition tells you to stop your course of action. Pausing to reflect is a way of savoring the time you have."

"You understand well. Better than most people, in fact!"

"I have also learned from the Quoquamish people, who believe that both religions—maybe all religions—may be obstacles to peace because they cause us to forget the role of Nature. The Waymaker taught me that the flow of time, like the flow of water, penetrates us at all levels of being. She teaches that we are all connected, and that if we become aware of this connection—and if we have a mind to utilize it only while respecting Nature—then, we can navigate through time, backwards and forwards, as one would through a stream of water."

"I could not have explained the secret property of water clocks any better. Well done! But now, what about this Clepsydra that Yusef is seeking?"

Tariq looked down, reluctant to tell anything more. *But,* he considered, *Yusef already thinks I have betrayed him. If I can still find the Clepsydra—maybe with the Order's help—then I must tell.*

"The Tejedors have an ancestor, Umar al-Hayek, who was a kind of legend. He is said to have created a water clock as large as a lake that has the power to influence the hearts of all of humanity at once, should one ever find and use it."

"*And* if one has the right message to send through it," surmised Sister Belén.

"That's right. Creating this message was my job. I was their linguist. But to tell the truth, I am not completely convinced that the Clepsydra exists. If it does, why would Al-Hayek have hidden it from his own family? And why has it never been used?"

"Those are good questions," affirmed Sister Martirio. "I think you would do well to meditate on them. You should also ask yourself what the Lord is teaching you through this entire experience."

"That is the hardest question of all. I have seen so much and felt so much pain. And I have made horrifying mistakes! I have watched people die!"

Sister Sabina lifted her hand to draw his eyes toward her: "Do you feel responsible for the deaths of others?"

"Well, yes. It was my words that could have saved the Silent One from being killed in the bombing. It was my actions that could have saved Mayra from being abducted. But I said nothing! I hesitated! And in this, I believe Yusef is correct."

"Finding the right time for words and actions is not easy," Sister Sabina assured him. "Even the wisest among us makes mistakes. But consider this: how many times have you done good by succeeding to act on your words? Indeed, how much more good will you do by waiting until the time is right in order to speak, hmm? Sometimes the moment is sooner, sometimes it is later. *There is a time for everything and a season for each activity under the sun.*"

Restfulness overtook Tariq's heart as he remembered hearing this verse the first time he stood near a water clock in Nanaimo. Sister Sabina, he realized, had been the one leading her class of students through the recitation. He felt his thoughts and feelings slow down, and he let go of his haste.

"The Lord has a way of playing with us sometimes," added Sister Clarinda. "Some people get to experience the highest joys a human life can offer. Others are left to flounder in misery. But it is no surprise to Him that our circumstances hinder us from making good decisions, especially in the heat of the moment. We can never know His true plan."

Sister Sabina grabbed Tariq's shoulders and met his eyes. "Yusef will proclaim that it was the Christians who eradicated the Muslims from Spain five hundred years ago. In this, he would be correct. And yet, who lived here before the Muslims? The Visigoths—earlier Christians—whom the Muslims had pushed out of Spain in the eighth century. And who was here before the Visigoths? The Romans! And who, before them?" She dropped her arms to her side. "History is endless. You can lose yourself in trying to understand it all. But what I have learned from decades of meditation on the issue is that God's power is absolute. He could drain an entire civilization from the Iberian Peninsula just as easily as you pour wine from a bottle. And He can also pour us back in, as He has done with Christianity in Spain. It was a miracle how our faith was restored! I think your Quoquamish friends would agree with this one point at the very least: human migration has always occurred in waves."

"You just have to find the wave that is meant for you," added Sister Belén.

All of this makes perfect sense. The will of the Lord commands us to search out the truth in deep reflection and wait for the right time to act. And yet I can understand Yusef's philosophy as well. The Last Day compels us to act upon our intuitions, upon the will of God without delay. But how can both be correct? How can I reconcile these two opposing worlds?

"I can see the conflict inside you, how it divides your heart and taxes your spirit. But I think I can offer you a way of sorting through your thoughts," offered Sister Sabina. "It will involve you returning to the past."

"You mean, time travel?"

A unified grin dawned upon all four Sisters.

"The Tejedors are not the only ones with ingenious inventions."

They took Tariq up a turret of winding stairs that ended at a lookout point. Through the open window he could see Seville's urban landscape resting beneath the celestial lights. He saw the belt of Orion hovering over the horizon, pointing the way to the seven stars of the Pleiades. In the distance, the towering spires of the Seville Cathedral held their luster in the night.

"Good, Tariq. You have activated our water clock."

"You have a water clock? Where?"

"Look around," instructed Sister Martirio.

He tried to find it. He looked up at the octagonal vaulted ceiling that opened into a bell tower farther up. He looked down at the dusty stone floors that smelled of bygone centuries. Then, at last, he noticed water leaking from a window on the opposite side of the chamber. The window was not open at all, he realized. Instead, a thin, invisible film of water veiled the entire opening. And the film was moving, trickling downward like a paper-thin waterfall. Watching it closely, he could see it give off very subtle vibrations, precise like the ticking of a clock.

"It's running water!" the linguist exclaimed.

"It is not running. It is regressing," explained Sister Sabina. "These are the tears of your past. They are the waters of time leaking back from where you once were."

"But what good will come of returning to the past?" *I've already been there, and I much prefer the present, thank you very much.*

"It is human nature to err, to sin," explained Sister Belén. "But the disciples of Christ showed us that venial sins can be absolved. This is how you rid yourself of these past errors."

"You mean, I can change the past? I can correct my mistakes?"

"Not all of them," she clarified. "Maybe one. Some interpret this to be what Christ meant by being *born again*."

"You mean, a kind of baptism?"

"Not officially, but yes, it is similar."

Tariq's muscles tensed at the thought of baptism, much in the same way he hesitated to invite the word 'Christ' into his heart's vocabulary. *How can I do this, just start using 'Christ' as a name for God? Will what little faith I still have as a Muslim be wiped clean from me if I participate in a Christian ritual?* He continued to hesitate. The nuns circled around him, as patient as could be.

"Are you okay, Tariq?"

"Yes, it's just—"

"Do you understand what we are asking you to do?"

"I...I think..."

The linguist relaxed his mind. *What is baptism but a word? What are any of these things but words? Baptism is just a concept defined within a context of other Christian concepts. Plus, she said it isn't an official baptism. What really matters is the intent behind the words I put into action. How can mere words possibly destroy my native faith?*

"Is something wrong?" they persisted.

He continued to reason it out. *For example, I could choose to define 'being born again' as the same feeling in the heart as 'submission to the will of Allah.' The only difference between the two phrases is the religiosity of the concepts. The intention is the same, even though the concepts are different. And what are concepts but mere words leading back to a meaning that preceded the concepts? And if it is just a matter of words, then why couldn't I do it? Yes, I can do it! The true Islam would not judge my heart by mere thoughts, only by my intentions. Therefore, my thoughts may entertain Christian concepts, but my intention is universal. My intention is to discover my past and reveal my true nature.*

"Okay, I think I can do it."

"Are you sure? You shouldn't agree unless you are completely—."

"Will I be born into another person's body?" he interrupted.

"Of course not," answered Sister Clarinda. "You will be yourself. But you will be younger, reliving a past event that was significant to you, one in which you sinned. You will even have the ability to make different choices that may change the course of your life! When you return, you will be born anew as a version of yourself who is forgiven, rectified, perhaps even saved."

"Wow." Tariq didn't know what to say. His mind raced to think of all the pitiful moments of shyness he could erase from his past by simply baptizing himself in this water clock. *How can I choose just one?*

"You must be wondering about how to begin," Sister Martirio surmised. Tariq nodded. "You will need a prayer—a mantra—something you can repeat to yourself while you hold your head under the running water."

"How many times do I say it?"

"As many as it takes to slip you into a state of complete trust in Christ."

Trust in Christ. She means, 'submission to the will of God.' It is only the language that sounds different.

"I know exactly what prayer to choose."

"Are you sure? You don't want to rush into—"

"Yes. I have formed my intention. Now, let me pass through the veil."

The nuns grabbed his head and guided it slowly into the thin film. He closed his eyes and recited his prayer:

There is a time for everything and a season for each activity under the sun.

A time to be born and a time to die, a time to plant and a time to uproot,

A time to kill and a time to heal, a time to tear down and a time to build up,

A time to weep and a time to laugh, a time to mourn and a time to dance,

A time to scatter stones and a time to gather them, a time to embrace and a time to refrain,

A time to search and a time to give up, a time to keep and a time to throw away,

A time to tear and a time to mend, a time to be silent,

And a time to speak.

Chapter 26

"Where are we going?" Ibrahim asked the imam. The crocodiles trailed behind them. "Shouldn't we return to the mosque?"

"We must go to Cartuja."

People in Seville called the Cartuja neighborhood an island, though it was technically a peninsula. Still, to reach it from the city's historic center, one had to cross the river by way of a long suspension bridge.

"Why? What is in Cartuja?"

"Look!" The imam answered, pointing to the island's famous replica of the space rocket, *Ariane*.

"The *Ariane?* How will that lead us to the Clepsydra?"

"I don't know. But my intuition is telling me to pay attention." Yusef stopped halfway across the bridge and looked out at the *Ariane*. "Look, Ibrahim. This was the rocket that supposedly marked Europe's expansion into space. It is a metaphor, don't you think? The rocket soars toward its destiny, breaking all barriers with the earth and ascending into the heavens."

Ibrahim scratched his head. The crocodiles held still, feeling the vibrations of the bridge beneath their claws.

"Yusef, I am concerned."

"With what?"

"Amara's words were blasphemous and a disgrace to our cause. Do you think she will come back to us?"

"I do not concern myself with such questions."

"But she is your sister! Is it not your duty to protect her?"

"Amara makes her own decisions. Only her internal compass, God willing, can redirect her. Besides, she brought us the crocodiles and helped us find Umar Al-Hayek. Her work is already complete."

"And what about Tariq's work? The role of the linguist was to create with words what you and I could not manage. He never questioned our faith, and yet in an single instant you eliminated him altogether without any second thought. You didn't even consult the Watcher!"

"We are in the final hour of the Last Day. There is no room for a second thought. Especially from you."

Yusef glared at his attendant, who bit his lip.

"But if it helps you be at peace," the imam continued, softening his gaze, "then I will explain. The Watcher has had his eyes on Tariq Kamal for quite some time. His grandfather, Baruq, was our main contact in Seattle for many years."

"Ah yes, I remember Baruq Kamal. He was certainly a key participant in the Muslim integration movement."

"True, my friend. His devotion to the faith was unlike any other. He knew that there are two paths in life: a steep path—the difficult path that leads to God—and a low path of ease and temptation. Baruq never shied away from attempting the steep."

"Then why did you fall out of contact with him?"

"For the same reason any of us falls out of contact: each of us is judged by our own actions, not by our belonging to groups. Activism has its place in society; after all, it is written that the steep path is one of compassion and generosity toward the poor and needy. But after much time I realized that I could not wade into the waters of western politics and still hold my values. There is no compromise with those who oppose us, especially the Order of the Libraries. The Watcher affirmed this in me. He told me that I must keep to the path that leads outside the system, outside the realm of politics and activism. The Watcher commanded me to build an army that would transcend mere laws and creeds and speak directly to the heart. That is the only way we may reach peace between us all."

"But do you think Tariq is no longer capable of creating this message?"

"Tariq made a choice, just like Baruq did, and it has led his judgment astray. He is too trusting. He lets his compassion and desire for kinship cloud his judgment. In the 11th century this was made very clear to me. Tariq wants to save others from harm, but in the face of danger he hesitates and doesn't realize that it is Allah who saves others from harm, not people. It is Allah who is compassionate, not humankind. A linguist who cannot separate his own desires and compassion from the will of God is not fit to create our message."

"Of course, Yusef. I understand. In submission to the will and the words of God alone, I have no doubt that He will lead us to our Clepsydra and inspire us with the final message. Is he not the Maker? The Benevolent One? The Way?"

"The names of God are not easy to proclaim, Ibrahim. But when the seeker finds oneness with His cause, as you and I have done, and as Amara will return to do, then all of His words shall become one and the same."

Just then, Yusef's phone beeped. He pulled it out and read the message. His face went pale.

"What is it?"

"There has been another attack." Yusef's lips went stiff. He could hardly pronounce the words.

"What kind of attack? Where?"

Ibrahim's own phone beeped, but he waited for the imam to respond.

"Toxic gas. In Madrid."

"What was the target?"

The imam wiped his face.

"It was the Almudena Cathedral. They infiltrated the crypt beneath the cathedral and pumped toxic gas into the ventilators. More than sixty people are dead and counting, probably all Christians, apart from tourists."

"Was it the Islamic State? Those devils!"

"That has been confirmed. They went in with gas masks and barricaded themselves inside the Almudena. They announced their presence with a megaphone."

"We must move our army quickly, Yusef! This may be our only chance to destroy the terrorists all at once. Maybe these crocodiles will have some bite in them after all!"

"Dear friend, have you gone mad? Have you forgotten why the Watcher chose this army for us? There will be no bloodshed unless it is my own. Continue to have patience and you will see."

"Of course. But it seems strange to me, Yusef, that the terrorists would have chosen a 19th-century cathedral to take by force rather than one of the Moors' original mosques."

"There must be a reason," Yusef surmised.

"But what reason? If the extremists want to kill and reclaim Al-Andalus, why are they not starting in Seville or Toledo, someplace with a deeper Muslim past? Why choose a modern cathedral in Madrid?"

The imam looked upon his attendant and fell into a state of humility he had not experienced since the beginning. He was humbled, but not by the terrorist acts of the religious extremists; what humbled Yusef was God's very act of bringing terrorists into the world with the power to destroy. It was an impossible contradiction! *Aren't the terrorists also born of mothers and fathers? Isn't life also poured into them? Do they not also weave their way into the grand tapestry of Allah's creation?*

However, this contradiction did not discourage the imam. In fact, it intensified his surrender to God's superior wisdom. Yusef realized that nothing—no action of woman or man—could remove the true essence of what God had created, not by gunfire, not by bombings, or by poison in the air. Yusef realized that there was a greater truth: in spite of every unfortunate death, life itself was endless. Life, in its continual birth and rebirth, remained invincible! Acts of terror could destroy and even decimate a community—like lighting fire to grass—but, once enough time had passed and the air was cleared, the roots would split the earth again and bear new stems. Humankind would keep returning. Not even terrorism could stop life from coming back! After all was won and lost, these attacks would become like futile puffs of violent wind blowing against a soaring rocket. They would become like mere words cast into the air. Try as they might to shred the tapestry of life to pieces, God would always mend it. This was the nature of God, of eternity, of the ultimate reality.

As the imam contemplated this truth, he answered:

"Your questions are the right ones. And we must continue to ask them if we are to make peace." He folded his hands and squeezed them together. His brow grew firm with resolve. "Let us go to Madrid."

Chapter 27

The zoologist's heart raced. She mounted her mystical crocodile companion, whose tail made for a powerful rudder, and set off on her raft. Sweat mingled with salty waves as she pounded her makeshift oar into the aqueous face of the Nile. There was no turning back.

"Seogo," she said to the Mystic, "in case we don't make it across the Nile alive, I want you to know something."

What is it, my child?

"I've been lost for many years. And I don't mean in the desert."

Then what do you mean?

"I'm forty years old, and what have I done with my life? I dropped out of graduate school, can't seem to shake my vices, and I only get a rush out of life when I'm gambling with it."

I see.

"I feel like I've closed myself off from everyone. I never married, never stayed on good terms with my parents. My closest friends have moved on, and it's been years since I reached out to them. I can't even remember the last time I had someone to hold me in their arms and tell me it's all going to be okay."

Above them, birds of prey flew in ominous circles. Fear and hunger still enslaved the zoologist's weary mind. In every wave's dark underside she imagined the head of the Great Nile Crocodile getting ready to leap out and devour her. The raft rattled precariously as they crossed the Nile.

Keep paddling. Have faith, my child.

"And now, for the first time, I feel like my life will actually end. I'm terrified, Seogo! All those loose ends and dreams that

I never got to finish will just drown in this unforgiving river."

The zoologist hugged Seogo's back with her knees and kept paddling. Left and right, right and left—every stroke was a motion toward her destiny. And yet, the farther she paddled, the more the Nile seemed impassable. It was an infinite river that dwarfed her knowledge of how to survive. This river required no words, only actions; no need for religion, only faith. She could feel God watching over her, and yet there was no need to name Him or discuss His nature. All she could do was to keep moving and know she was not alone.

In the background was the faint calling of a heron. It grew louder and louder, sounding of distress. Just then, the bird landed directly upon her, clutching her curly hair and thrashing about.

"Ah! Get off me!" she cried. She waved her oar at the heron and scared it away; however, in doing so she dropped the oar into the ravenous Nile. The raft slid downstream and spun around in several circles before she could regain her balance. Then, it stopped. It had hit something solid.

The zoologist turned to look. It was a hippopotamus. Then she noticed it was standing in shallow waters.

"We made it!"

The hippopotamus grunted and ruffled its rump. The Nile was still flowing fast around them, but the hefty animal sheltered them for the time being. Only a few yards of marsh separated them from dry land.

"Seogo, how do we get through without an oar?"

Close your eyes.

The zoologist closed her eyes. The raft bobbed up and down like the swift ticking of a clock. A vine floated toward her and hit her leg. She retrieved it.

"What do I do with this?"

Tie it to the hippo's leg.

"What?"

Ask him to pull us ashore.

She did as Seogo advised and tied the vine around the leg

of the behemoth.

"But this beast won't move."

She tugged the vine, but the hippopotamus did not respond.

"Move!"

Be gentle.

She let go of the vine and then reapplied her tension gradually. The hippopotamus shifted its feet in the water.

"That's it," she said gently. "Now, *please* pull us to the shore."

She tugged the hippo's leg one last time, but the beast became frightened.

"Don't be afraid. I'm not going to hurt you."

As she tamed the beast, she looked back at Seogo, who winked at her. *You're such a good friend, Seogo. As soon as we escape this hell, I promise I will return you to your home!*

But a sudden, loud growling suggested that it was not the tugging that frightened the hippo—it was the presence of a larger beast. Seogo, too, sensed its presence and let out a deafening bellow.

"What's the matter?"

Before she could react, a forceful wave tossed the zoologist into the water, and the Great Nile Crocodile snatched Seogo from the raft.

"Seogo!" Naomi cried as she leapt back onto the raft to save her life.

But both crocodiles had disappeared into the Nile, leaving nothing but waves in all directions. The hippopotamus strutted frantically toward the shore, pulling the raft behind it. The zoologist wanted to swim after and save her companion, but she knew there was no point. Seogo was helpless against the mighty king of the Nile. She held onto the raft and surrendered. The salty tears of her fatigue and sorrow poured into the tempestuous Nile.

"Seogo, my friend!" she wept. "I will come back for you!"

When the raft hit the shore, Naomi fell unconscious. Exhaustion set in again, and the salt water left her dehydrated. Evaporation cooled her weary forehead and neck. Her body no longer knew whether it was in the desert or on a river; and in a way, it no longer mattered. Water, sand, wind, and sun were an endless burden from which she was about to be released. Nature, which was by all appearances no friend to the poor zoologist, was about to grant her one more day of life.

"Get up!" shouted a voice in English.

The zoologist gasped and wiped her eyes. She coughed to clear the Nile from her throat. When she opened her eyes, she saw two pairs of sturdy waterproof boots wading into the river to grab her. The boots were worn by two men with guns.

"Who are you?" they barked at her. "How did you find us?"

"I don't know. Where am I?"

The men whispered to each other in Arabic and then nodded in unison.

"Shut up and do as I say."

One of them struck the zoologist across the face, sending her thumping upon the marsh grasses.

"You'll answer for your crimes in jail. But we are warning you: the Islamic State doesn't let liars live long."

The other man fired his gun into the zoologist's thigh.

"Ugh," Naomi whimpered, unable to feel the full extent of the wound.

Then, with force, the men tied a blindfold around her head and dragged her off, leaving a trail of blood.

Chapter 28

Amara gripped the orange firmly in her right hand and gazed up at the Tower of Gold. The night sky bore the faint sliver of a white moon.

Abraham marveled at this same moon, she reflected. *But it was Allah, not the moon, in which Abraham beheld the beauty of the night. The beauty is in the Creator, not His creations.*

A tiny gnat tickled her thumb. She lifted her other hand to swat it—but before she could do so, the stillness of the gnat drew her attention. She lent her eyes to the gnat's intricate anatomy. She observed the opaqueness of its dainty wings and the way it knelt forward in prostration with its tiny, valiant legs.

A gnat is such a humble, vulnerable creature. And yet it is written that for those who believe, Allah may reveal Himself in such a lowly creature as this.

The gnat twitched its infinitesimal face and then leapt from her hand like a fugitive from a watchman. Amara followed its path with her eyes, squinting to see in the darkness. She lost the gnat, then rediscovered it seconds later. Soon, a trio of gnats swarmed into view, only to vanish again into the sky's indistinguishable soup of stars and galaxies.

Still gazing, she heard a buzzing whisper: *Go with them.* It spoke to her like the sound of rain upon the shore. She knew it was her intuition speaking to her. *Go with them.*

Amara looked deep into the darkness where she last saw the gnats. *Where are you going?* she called to them. *Can I join you?* Then she inhaled, closed her eyes and imagined being taken into the air. And in that moment, filled with the grace of her intuition and the wonder of the moonlit night, she realized she was instantaneously transformed! Her body was nearly weightless. Her form was slender and efficient like that of an insect. Indeed, she could feel herself twitching two identical opaque wings, kneeling upon the earth with the reverence of a tiny creature. She had become the gnat. Realizing this, she leapt into the sky.

Spiraling upward, her wings shuddered and trembled. For the first few moments, she spun in circles like a moth escaping the dust, unable to fix her course. Then her intuition's voice spoke again loudly: *Go with them.*

She could see the other gnats ascending swiftly ahead of her. Beyond them was the crescent moon, shimmering like a polished tusk of ivory. But the higher she flew, the more distant the waning moon appeared.

"How can I reach you?" she questioned.

There was no response. She vibrated her wings harder.

"Where are you?"

But the shiny sliver of the moon was fading fast. It was almost completely gone, and the gnats were no longer in sight.

"Magnificent One, reveal yourself to me!"

Amara hovered in silence, awaiting a response from God. No answer came. All that resounded was the droning of her own wings, which, she noticed, were drowning out the sounds around her.

I have to stop making noise. Then, I will hear God's voice.

She experimented with her wings, flapping them faster and slower, letting herself rise and sink like a buoy bobbing in water. Adjusting the speed of her wings, however, didn't make much of a difference in noise. To silence herself, she would have to stop them altogether.

But if I stop my wings, I'll fall...

The stars glittered in the night like speckled reflections of light upon a river's waves. Gradually, she let her wings slow down to a minimum, then became still. For a brief instant she was weightless, suspended in the air, but soon gravity pulled her swiftly down toward the earth. To pacify herself, she fixed her multitude of eyes onto a star to admire the Magnificent One's creation.

God's beauty outshines even the most brilliant star.

Amara waited in the freefall for the sky to catch her somehow, like the arms of a father, offering a resting place. But it didn't. The darkness of the sky, like her folded wings, was powerless to stop her fall. Tumbling down, Amara surrendered and did not resist.

Dear One, let me be low to You. Let me submit to Your will and land upon Your divine mystery.

Through her many eyes, she watched the face of the earth draw nearer. Falling was terrifying, and yet she wanted to take this fall. She longed to be struck by the earth's hard surface and released from the worldly form that held her.

This is the end. All that remains is the experience of death and judgment, the Last Day.

Then, as she surrendered her last shred of hope, a web of milky, flowing strings caught her. She instantly realized their shape: they were Arabic words, spun like threads from the Holy Quran. The *suras*, the verses, and the prayers that had given her family faith for a thousand years supported her. They were words of truth; they were proof of the mercy and compassion of the One Most Holy.

Like spider webs, the shimmering Arabic words clung to every curvature of her body. They fixed her in a state of pure conscious awareness. She no longer contained the need to fall or rise. She knew the truth was close by, ready for her to discover. She felt the truth welling up within her, asking to pronounce her heart and bones and flesh as a prayer to Him.

Above her, the crescent moon released its last ray of light. The sky went dark. Not even the stars were visible.

Allah, where are You?

As she looked up toward the invisible moon, the milky web of Holy Words melted and dripped off of her like sweet water after an ablution. With the disappearing of the Words she felt liberated, free to ascend higher than any religion or doctrine had been able to carry her. There, higher than words, she was equal with the stars, equal with the nebulae and with every shiny atom of the golden cosmos. And yet, she still could not glimpse the infinite glory of God. The dark moon was in the way. Everything she sought was still unreachable behind the darkness of the new moon.

How do I get through to You?

She decided the form of a gnat would no longer do. She needed something else—some kind of tool.

If I were a wasp, I could use my stinger to pierce through the moon.

Instantly the thought manifested into reality. She was no longer a gnat; she was a wasp with a deadly stinger. She felt an overwhelming urge to wield her great new force. *What a frightening power I have now! But how shall I use it?* She looked up at the moon and its dark surface. At first she felt her baser instincts compelling her to force her stinger into the moon's surface. But then, she thought of the Mystic's words: *Make your message in partnership, not by force. That is the true victory.* She looked up into the darkness and flew toward the moon. As she neared the moon's surface, she realized that it was not merely made of rock. The moon was alive! And furthermore, it was shifting. As if greeting her, the giant moon bulged and convulsed, opening a deep, rocky crevice.

Hello, dear moon of Abraham. Hello, my partner.

The wasp flew into the dark crevice and landed gracefully upon the lowest surface she could find. The moon gave a soft vibration. She could tell it was inviting her further inside. She felt around with her many legs and discovered a deeper crack. However, it was peculiar. Its shape was perfectly tailored to fit her.

Are you opening your heart to me? Let me do the same to you.

Amara probed carefully into the crack with her tongue, then she drew back her tongue and paused. She could taste the moon's intimate friendship. She could feel its partnership.

She knew it was ready for her.

I am here, my Dear One. Experience me.

Slowly and affectionately, Amara slid her stinger into the crevice. Her entire being quivered as she felt her closeness with the moon. She was close, so close that she was no longer able to hear, think, or feel. All was infinitely cold to her senses, yet also infinitely warm. God's light welled up within her heart like steam in a cooking pot. All she had to do was let it pour out of her and into the shadows, and the sweetness of Allah was hers.

Then, the moon gave a massive rumble. Amara knew exactly what was happening. It was just as the Quran had prophesied: the moon was splitting apart! But it split slowly, like the shifting of the tectonic plates beneath the earth. Each half of the moon went its way, and as ages went by the wasp was released from inside. Yet the path of the moon's destruction was so precise, so ordained by the laws of nature, that Amara could feel all of eternity passing by in a singular moment. Just as all was ordained to come together, all was predestined to split apart. This was the Last Day.

Once the moon's crack was wide enough, she could see the stars again. At first, the stars were perfect spheres, whose light was pure and undistorted by the retinas of human eyes. Then, one by one, as waves rippled throughout the galaxy, all the stars began to vibrate. Even invisible suns too far away to see were vibrating. The stars of the galaxy were fluttering like a swarm of still hummingbirds—pulsating, fleeting, and keeping infinite time.

As Amara regained her human consciousness, a verse of poetry flashed before her face in Arabic, producing a conclusion to her wondrous mystical vision.

Each star is a creature, a soul, a heart,
Witnessed by God in its towering light
That light is received by all
That star is watched over by all
Each one is a precious visitor in the night

Derek Olsen

Chapter 29

Tariq pulled his head back and gasped for air. Water ran down his face and neck. The nuns sat him down on a chair and dried his hair with a towel.

"Was that it? Did I go?" He looked at his watch. The entire baptism was instantaneous. "But nothing happened!"

"Search your memories, Tariq. Then you will see where you have been."

Tariq closed his eyes and tried to recall. He traced his memories of Yusef and Amara. He replayed the event of nearly spilling their secret at the Tower of Gold. He thought of the Quoquamish village and the Waymaker and the Silent One. He recalled the Windstepper and Gray Fin leading him through the Nanaimo mall. *All this I remember exactly as it happened.* But then his mind went back farther, much farther.

"Yes! Now I can see it!"

"What do you remember, Tariq?"

Like a movie in fast-forward, the entire memory flooded his mind, and he recounted it to nuns of the Order of the Libraries.

∽

I was in bed, groggy from the desert heat. Grandfather was standing near me.

"Wake up Tariq," he said.

I rubbed my eyes. I figure I must have been a young child, since my hands were so small and tender.

"You had quite a dizzy spell, my boy!"

"What happened?"

"Don't feel bad. Pilgrims fall down all the time. The *Kaaba* makes us fall at its feet if we are humble."

I remember listening to Grandfather, picturing the vision I had had of the bluish-white hand and the face in the sky. It must have just happened that day, since it was more vivid than I had ever recalled it before.

"You've had quite an adventure, Tariq."

I closed my eyes again and feigned sleep. Grandfather rubbed my hair and kissed my forehead.

"I tell you what, my boy. You've been strong. You made it to Mecca, and that is enough."

And then he said it. He made me the offer.

"Tomorrow morning, first thing in the morning, you can go home."

When he said this, my little brain rejoiced. But somewhere inside me, a voice was whispering. It was me! I mean, it was the me that I am now, whispering to me as a little boy.

It said: *No! Stay here. You're not done yet.*

And I remember clenching my tiny fists, anxiously thinking, *why is Grandfather saying this? I know we're not done with the* hajj. *I'm not stupid.*

"Just get some rest, Tariq. You'll be in your own bed by tomorrow evening."

Grandfather stood up and walked away. And I just lay there, still, with my eyelids shut even though I was wide awake. I thought about telling him "No." I wanted to act on my intuition and tell him I could still be strong and finish the *hajj*. But I couldn't. I wanted badly to go home.

Then I heard the whisper again. Only now it was louder. And I felt like I was also making the whisper out loud to myself, reciting it over and over: *stay here, stay here, stay here.*

Saliva was dripping from my mouth, and I wiped it off. Then my lips started to join in the chant: *stay here, stay here, stay here.*

I rubbed my eyes again and flexed my backbone. The lights were off. I thought, maybe, Grandfather was still standing beside me, watching.

But when I opened my eyes, he wasn't. And so I spoke it out loud. "Stay here. Stay here. Stay here."

I looked around to see if anyone had heard me. I didn't think so. And so I said it again, this time louder. And again, louder still.

Until finally, I was so convinced I had to stay, that I got out of bed and screamed it.

"STAY HERE! STAY HERE! STAY HERE!"

Grandfather rushed into the room.

"What's this about? Are you mad?"

"No! I'm strong! I want to stay here."

"What do you mean, you want to stay here?"

I didn't know how to explain. I didn't even really comprehend why I was saying what I was saying. But I said it.

"I want to stay here. On the *hajj*. With you."

Grandfather's eyes welled up with joy. He looked right into me, like he could see straight into my soul. He spoke a phrase in Urdu that I don't remember, but I remember its meaning. It meant that I was a true believer, a true pilgrim. It meant that I had won the struggle within me that made me fight against my destiny.

I don't remember much more of what happened that night. But we didn't leave the next morning. We completed the *hajj*. And I have been a believer in Islam ever since.

Stay here.

Just like that, I declared my destiny.

Those two words changed my life.

"I don't remember anymore," Tariq finished. He opened his chest and stood tall. "But I understand now what I have to do."

"You do?" asked the Sisters.

"I have to find the Clepsydra. I have to write the message and deliver it before the Last Day."

The Sisters looked at him in terror.

"Be patient, Tariq. You have not yet fully understood your sin!"

"My sin, if there is such a thing as 'sin,' was to deny my true nature as a Muslim. It was to deny my duty to Allah! Even into my adulthood, there were times I forsook my intuition and took the way of ease and convenience instead of doing what was right. But Allah knows the path—He has made me from water and poured into me a soul. And whatever you believe the soul to be, there is one thing that is undeniable: *the soul knows the way, if only you will listen to it*."

"Slow down, Tariq! Think about what you are saying!"

"I don't have to think about it. I've known since the day I was born. The message is inside of me! I only have to open up and let it out."

"What message?"

"*Innaa fatahnaa laka Fath-am mubeenaa…*"

"What is he saying?" whispered Sister Clarinda nervously to the others.

"It's the message that could have saved the Silent One and saved Mayra—"

The linguist became still.

"What is it?"

"I know where the Clepsydra is. I have to go."

"But it's after midnight!" Sister Martirio pleaded. "Stay with us. Don't leave in haste!"

"Rest here for a while longer," invited Sister Belén.

But Tariq passed up their offer and wound down the tower's stone staircase. The candlelit sanctuary glowed like an altar to the dead. But even thoughts of death did not stop the linguist this time. With the strength of a firm believer, he drew nigh toward his destiny.

"Tariq!" the Sisters called. He didn't listen.

He made his way over fallen piles of books and proceeded to open the locks on the front gate. The first one was a large wooden plank, which he removed with ease. The second was a crank, which he turned to unlocked a massive deadbolt.

"Be careful! Do not seek the Clepsydra! Yusef doesn't understand!"

However, the third lock required an electronic passcode.

"Tell me how to open it," he commanded.

"Stay here in our chapel instead," urged Sister Clarinda. "We will make a room with a bed for you."

"You'll spend the night here with us," insisted Sister Martirio.

"No need to rush out into a dangerous world!" implored Sister Belén.

The three protesting nuns turned to Sister Sabina, waiting for her to break her silence.

"The passcode is A-M-O-R."

Tariq entered the code while the nuns gasped at their fellow Sister.

"Sister Sabina, why did you let him unlock the door?"

"Now he will leave, and the Clepsydra will syphon from us the rest of our days!"

But Sister Sabina stood calmly, motionless, and watched him open the gate. The hinges squeaked and the knockers clanged, and the cold air wafted into the sanctuary. She cast her eyes down onto the chapel's granite floor.

To Tariq's surprise, a woman was standing outside. It was Amara! He could hardly believe his eyes. The robed one stepped into his presence and drew her face close to his.

"I need to tell you something," she whispered.

"So do I," Tariq answered. "Come in."

Tariq led her over to a pew in the front of the main sanctuary, behind which the four Sisters stood quietly, listening.

"Tariq," she began. She looked into his honest eyes and then grabbed his hand. "What was your reason for joining us? I mean, why did you come here?"

"Well," he started, "I didn't exactly search you out. It just happened. Yusef's message appeared on my page in green, glowing letters, and I answered. I didn't put much thought into it."

"You were chosen. Do you believe this?"

"Yes, I suppose so. Wasn't it the Watcher who orchestrated your plan to build the army? Wasn't it Yusef who recruited me?"

"You call it 'orchestration' and 'recruiting'—I am only now realizing the significance of our being here."

"What are you saying?"

"The Watcher! Do you know who he is?"

Tariq stared back blankly.

"He is God!" she exclaimed.

"What?"

"The Watcher is not a man. He is Allah!"

"That's impossible!"

"It's true, Tariq. The Watcher is the Lord of Lords, the Protector, the Magnificent One, the Giver of Life Himself! He is all these names summed up into one, the Watcher of every soul in the cosmos!"

"But it can't be! I saw the Watcher in my vision. At least I thought I saw him. He was an old man with a beard, and he stared at me with wise, old eyes."

Amara's faith did not waver.

"What you saw, Tariq, was the face of your own intuition. Allah cannot be represented in human form. He is beyond form! But when you experience a vision sent from God, your intuition becomes clear."

"Well," the linguist accepted, "if you are right, I suppose it explains why Yusef didn't want us to meet the Watcher. Only an imam is allowed to translate the will of God directly."

"But that is the rule in Islam," she acknowledged. "Yusef was doing his duty as an imam to keep his connection with Allah sacred."

Finally, Tariq began to digest this revelation. "We really are here for a reason, aren't we?"

Amara squeezed his hand and nodded. She couldn't explain it, but he seemed different, more at peace with himself.

"But didn't you also want to tell me something?"

"Yes, and you might like to hear it."

"I'm listening."

"I know where to find the Clepsydra."

She cupped her hands in her lap and sat still with her eyes downcast, tracing the colorful loops and spirals on her robe. This was not at all the reaction Tariq had anticipated.

"What's wrong?" he asked.

"Everything is fine. Everything is *santo y bueno*."

"Aren't you surprised?"

"After experiencing God as I have done, how can there be any surprises? Yes, of course you know where the Clepsydra is. For it to be His plan, you *must* know. How can the universe hide anything from us when our eyes have reached their moment of revelation?"

Amara closed her eyes. In the profile of her face she bore a striking resemblance to her brother. She shared his dimples, his narrow nose, and hanging earlobes. And yet now her penetrating aura of knowledge, which came from her direct experience with the Divine, even surpassed the imam's. Tariq bowed his head in admiration.

"But yes, tell me how you found the Clepsydra."

"It was in the image of the little girl—my sister—from the eleventh century. Her name was Mayra. She was taken from me and I couldn't stop it from happening."

"Oh, Tariq, that must have been awful to go through."

"Horrendous. That is why she has remained on my mind ever since, tormenting me with shame and regret."

"How did you overcome it?"

The linguist smiled. "Everything is connected. We are all 'chosen,' as you say, including Mayra."

"How is Mayra connected to us?"

"Mayra's name, in Arabic, means *water channel*. The word '*mayra*,' when added to the suffix '*-it*,' meaning *place*, gives us the word *mayrit*, meaning *place of the water channel*, which is the etymology of—"

"Madrid!" the robed one exclaimed. "The city's name is a dead giveaway! How did I not realize it sooner?"

"The Clepsydra is in Madrid," he concluded.

"Then, it must be at the site of the Almudena," she deduced. The nuns whispered in reaction to her mention of it.

"The Almudena? What makes you say that?"

"What other site in Madrid could represent Spain's central importance in the history of the world? The Almudena is the cathedral right next to Madrid's royal palace. It was built on top of a medieval mosque that was destroyed in the late eleventh-century. Not many people know that! That mosque was seated beside a fortified wall on the outskirts of old *Mayrit*, which means there would have been a canal system and to bring water out to it."

"A canal system, but not necessarily a water clock."

"Water was a precious resource to the Moors; they wouldn't just pump it through their irrigation channels without metering it by the hour. This canal, if it still exists, will contain our Clepsydra."

The four nuns shuffled anxiously behind them.

"But how could it still exist? Didn't you say the mosque was destroyed a thousand years ago?"

"Part of the wall remains. In fact, it is the oldest standing structure in Madrid, and I think that is not a coincidence! The Clepsydra will be near that wall. I am certain of it."

"Stop!" exclaimed Sister Sabina. Terror lit her aged face. "Haven't you paid attention to what has happened earlier today? Terrorists have struck the Almudena with poisoned gas, and they have locked themselves inside! Who knows what they will do next? This is no mere ideological war; the threat is real!"

Tariq and Amara looked at each other. *The Watcher surely has a plan for inviting us to that exact location.*

"All your talk of coincidences and being chosen," the nun continued, "is the road to peril! Don't you see? The choice is yours—but! If you take the time to sit and reflect, you will observe that none of it really matters. It is only the superstition of your mind! You may pursue this mission, or war, or whatever it is, but nothing new will come of it. The Clepsydra is better left buried in the earth. Peace may evade us, but that is no reason to think the world as it is will really end. It can't just end! We're not—"

"You're not ready?" Amara challenged, keeping her cool. "Who is ready for the Last Day? You? Me? And yet it happens, it comes. It rolls out before you like a royal carpet, calling you forth—you alone—to take the first step. You cannot hide away from judgment; you cannot avoid walking life's path."

"Amara is right," Tariq confidently agreed. "Surely, there is a time for inaction, for prayer, in your sense of the word. Slowing down is one of the many activities under the sun for which there is a time. But that means there is also a time for haste, a time to step forward and bravely take your stance in the course of history."

"Let's go, Tariq. And bring your message with you!"

Amara led the way to the front gate and pulled it open. Tariq grinned incredulously at how imminently his message would be needed.

"You should come too," Amara said to the Sisters. "This event concerns the Order of the Libraries as much as it does us. Will you join us?"

Sister Sabina looked at the other nuns. Their faces wore a congealed panic that did not improve with Amara's words. Not one of them managed to respond.

"Fine. Let's go."

The imam's sister opened the gates and strode out. Tariq turned around one last time to look Sister Sabina in the eyes.

"Thank you, Sister," he spoke. "The Lord be with you."

Sister Sabina rubbed her wooden necklace as she watched the two of them leave. The gates shut decisively behind them. Then, when the last of the cold air dissipated into the inner warmth of the chapel, the nun whispered a soft response.

"And also with you."

Chapter 30

After hours of driving, the van came to a halt. The zoologist could hardly see anything as she lay captive inside. She held a cloth around her wounded thigh to stop the bleeding. Her entire leg was throbbing like the beating of a giant heart. The bullet was still inside; she pressed on it to remind herself she was still alive.

The doors opened, and the sack covering her head was removed. The light scorched her retinas. The straps around her wrists were removed as well. She rubbed her eyes and then realized that she was in some kind of interrogation room. All she could think about was Seogo.

Seogo, forgive me for losing you.

She could feel the air cool down as night set in, and a guard came in to tend to her wound by pouring a glass of water on it.

"Ahhhh!"

"Relax. It's only water."

"Yes, ah, thank you."

"Here's a new cloth for you. That one looks a bit old."

The guard took her bloody cloth and tied the new one around her leg.

"Will you take me to a hospital?"

"That all depends on how you answer our questions. And what we may need you for."

"Seogo!" she cried into her hands.

"What?"

"He's gone!"

The guard pulled her hands from her face to see if her tears were genuine.

"Who is he?"

"He's my partner. My only friend. I have no one else."

"No family?"

"I'm an orphan."

"From what country?"

"Spain."

He smiled a seditious grin.

"Today is a beautiful day for Spain."

"Why? Where are we?"

"First, tell me your name."

"Naomi Rivera."

"Your province?"

"Salamanca."

"Your birth date?"

"Aren't you going to restrain me?"

The guard stepped back.

"Do you need restraints?"

"I need more water. Let me drink."

"Very well."

He left and locked the door behind him. The cell walls were clay and dirt went from floor to ceiling, and the only light in the room came from a dim fluorescent bulb at the end of a stick. *I'm a prisoner of the Islamic State*, she thought. *I'm as good as dead.*

The lock squeaked and the door slid open. The guard handed her a rubber dish that she drank from readily. She thanked him, this time noticing his fair skin and gray eyes. She also noticed he was carrying a bullwhip in his other hand.

"Why have you come here?"

"I was transporting crocodiles."

"Where to?"

"To Seville."

"How many were there?"

"Twenty-five. But one escaped."

"You're a zookeeper?"

"I'm a scientist."

"A scientist should fear God."

"I fear nothing else."

"You said one crocodile escaped. Where is it?"

The zoologist glanced around for a way out of the cell.

"Look at me!" the guard ordered. He snapped his whip and lashed her shoulder.

"What do you want?" she shouted angrily.

He stared at her and lowered his voice.

"Who else helped you transport the crocodiles?"

"No one," she lied. "I work alone."

"Don't lie to me!" He whipped her again.

"Eeeeh!"

"Don't you know I can tell truth from lies?"

"You're a pig!"

"Do you want to die alone?"

"You're a bastard!"

"Tell me! What are you hiding?" His voice had reached full volume.

"You're a Nazi!" she screamed.

The clay walls absorbed her shrill retorts without so much as an echo. The guard threw down the bullwhip and pulled on his own hair. Slowly, holding back a tremble, he sat down.

"Why did you say that?" he asked.

The zoologist stayed silent.

"No, really. Tell me why you said that."

"My grandparents were tortured by the Nazis," Naomi explained. "When they fled to Spain, they thought the war would be over, but it was only just beginning."

"My grandparents were also in that war."

"Were they Jewish?"

"No."

"Were they Germans?"

"They were Nazis."

Before the words had even finished leaving his lips, she lunged toward him with her fists. Anger and screams poured out from the depths of her suffering soul. She could hardly control herself. But the guard sat her down without fighting back.

"No, it's not like that," the guard explained. "They were coerced. They fled Germany before the war was over because they couldn't stand the Nazis."

The zoologist gritted her teeth and stabilized her breathing.

"They couldn't stand the Nazis?"

"That's right. They had to go along with what the Nazis were doing because they would have been killed otherwise. Isn't that another form of torture?"

"Then why do you torture me? Huh? You're a hypocrite!"

"Because it is for my cause."

"Your cause is torture?"

"My cause is redemption."

The zoologist wiped her eyes and took a deep breath. She imagined Seogo's face before her—that saintly, reptilian look he gave that had taught her serenity in the earth's most unforgiving desert. *My cause is redemption.* Her heartrate slowed down.

"Are you afraid?" she asked him.

"Of what?"

"Of being on the wrong side."

"I'm not on the wrong side."

"But my question is, if you weren't sure which side was right, would you be afraid?"

"Well, wouldn't you?"

She picked up the rubber dish again and squeezed it.

"Sometimes, when I cage reptiles, I wonder if I am on the wrong side of the bars. I mean, when you look at all the violence and destruction people can make, what would you make of humankind if you were a reptile?"

"But that's what we are."

"No. That's what we *fear.*" The set down the rubber dish. "Why do you think we lock up crocodiles? Because we know ourselves capable of the inhumanity we see in them, and we fear ourselves for it."

"Wouldn't you lock up a crocodile if it were coming at you from the wild?"

"Before this job, I might have agreed. But in the Sub-Saharan desert I met crocodiles more pleasant and docile than any human being I've ever known."

"So, what are you saying? We should be the ones in cages? Is the human race nothing more than a zoo?"

"I believe the real zoo is what takes place within your heart. If you fear your own nature, then in yourself you'll breed more fear every time someone or something reflects that part of your nature back to you."

"But how can you say we fear ourselves when it is clearly the crocodiles who are dangerous?"

"That's a logical point. Or, at least, it seems logical. But what if it isn't? What if it's the fear itself that creates danger in the beast? Have you ever considered that your innermost logical convictions are flawed? That your ability to think and reason is no better than any animal on earth, including the crocodile?"

"What are you getting at?"

"I think our greatest fear is that we are, in our very nature, irrational beasts. And fear exposes our irrationality when we close off our hearts and make cages for those who don't conform to our views. You might say it is inevitable that a certain type of person or animal will attack you, but consider this: in the state of fear, you ignore the greatest possibility of all—that the fiercest beast on earth is no more ignorant of God's love than you are. You may lock me and others like me in a cell, but in the end it is you who are chained up in presumptions and imprisoned in a cage of distrust. Will you ever set yourself free?"

"But what if setting them free leads to your own death?"

"That's just a risk you have to take. And who knows? Maybe they'll join you in taking it."

The guard closed his eyes in memory of his grandparents. The zoologist held the cloth tightly around her thigh, feeling healthy blood course through her veins.

"There's a van coming in about an hour that can take you to a hospital. I'll tell them you're not a threat."

"So I am free to go?"

"Sure." He pulled out a pack of cigarettes and a lighter. "Unless you want to join me for a smoke."

Chapter 31

The Quoquamish elders stood near a barricade outside the Almudena. Police officers closed off the entire area in the wake of the Islamic State's occupation of the cathedral. It was the middle of the night, and yet sleepless crowds spilled into the streets trying to catch glimpses of the terrorists' plot.

"I don't understand it," complained the Windstepper. She scratched her head with all ten fingers. "This crowd contradicts the laws of Nature, don't you think, Gray Fin?"

"How so?"

"Normally, the one who is attacked draws backward; but here the people of Madrid are actually clawing their way into the seat of the violence."

"Maybe they have given up against what they cannot defeat," he surmised.

"Like wind," she observed, waving her arms in the air and ignoring his suggestion, "they're all rushing in to fill the space!"

"Maybe," Gray Fin tried again, "it is their nature to swim upstream."

"Or," she continued, "they have taken the side of the terrorists and are going against us!"

"O, please!" he retorted. "You know very well that not everything is as black-and-white as it seems."

"Shush!" she whispered. She closed her eyes and took two small dramatic steps backward. "I think Tariq is nearby."

"So what, eh?" the old man grumbled. "He chose not to be our hero."

"But maybe he still can help us!" encouraged his companion.

"How can he help us if he's not a hero?" Gray Fin retorted.

"Well, he is certainly not a villain," the Windstepper answered, crossing her arms.

"And yet he has led us to the villains right here before us!"

"Then maybe he will also lead us to the real hero!"

"Or maybe," the Waymaker interjected, as a light dawned on her smile, "there are no heroes at all, unless there are also villains. Each one defines the other."

Through the windows of the Almudena the three elders could see silhouettes of large machine guns in the hands of the terrorists hiding inside the building.

"But," countered an anxious Gray Fin, "if there were no heroes, then how could there be villains in the first place?"

The Waymaker's smile grew brighter:

"Because we are all complex people with many sides. We are like mountains in the distance, plain as day before each other's eyes and yet unable to be seen from every angle at once."

A trumpet rang out and a deep, raspy voice began to sound from a loudspeaker:

"IN THE NAME OF ALLAH, THE MERCIFUL, THE COMPASSIONATE."

The voice was coming from within Almudena. The crowd simmered down and paid attention.

"YOU WILL LISTEN TO US AND DO AS WE ASK. WE HAVE PRISONERS, AND WE WILL KILL THEM IF YOU TRY TO ENTER. WE HAVE WEAPONS, AND WE ARE NOT AFRAID TO USE THEM IF YOU DO NOT FULFILL THE WISHES OF THE ISLAMIC STATE."

The people turned to each other in outrage and cursed at the terrorists. *Why are they here? What do they want?*

"IN THE NAME OF ALLAH, THE MERCIFUL, THE COMPASSIONATE. ALL WHO LIVE HERE IN AL-ANDALUS SHALL BOW DOWN BEFORE ALLAH. YOU

WILL SHOW SUBMISSION TO HIS WILL."

The masses stood bewildered for a few moments, until their panic was silenced by an unspeakable act of aggression. From the highest window of the Almudena, a prisoner was tossed out the window and sent to his gruesome death upon the street below.

"EVERYONE WILL BOW BEFORE GOD!"

Screams burst forth. Shots were fired into the air, and slowly the people began to kneel and lower their heads.

Let's get out of here, decided the Quoquamish elders. But as they turned around, the crowd cleared and an imam with an army of crocodiles made his way through.

"Be at peace!" shouted the imam. The crowd didn't dare look up to see who was heralding their rescue.

"IN THE NAME OF ALLAH, THE MERCIFUL, THE COMPASSIONATE," sounded the loudspeaker.

"Show us *your* mercy and compassion," exclaimed Yusef, "let us speak together like citizens of His nation."

"HIS NATION WAS DESTROYED LONG AGO. AND ALL OF YOU ARE COMPLICIT IN ITS UNGOD-LY DESTRUCTION."

"And so, what? Will you kill all of these people to prove it?"

The terrorist on the loudspeaker paused to address the imam personally.

"WHAT IS YOUR NAME?"

"I am the imam Yusef Tejedor. I am a believer in God's will above the will of aggression, God's will above the will of vengeance, God's will above—"

"YOU ARE AT WAR WITH GOD, YUSEF. AND YOU ARE EXPENDABLE."

A gunshot blast came from the cathedral, and Yusef collapsed. The crowd screamed, though they did not turn their faces from the ground.

"IN THE NAME OF ALLAH, THE MERCIFUL, THE COMPASSIONATE, YOU ARE LIVING IN THE

ISLAMIC STATE OF AL-ANDALUS."

But Yusef wasn't conquered. The bullet had missed! And as he pretended to fall, he skillfully slid onto the back of one of the crocodiles, who continued its march through the gates of the barricade and up through the plaza of the Almudena.

The crowd shivered in terror.

Amara drove herself and Tariq into the heart of Madrid's historic downtown.

"Why is there so much traffic?" he asked. "Isn't everyone asleep by now?"

"Who in Madrid can rest when such an attack is made against us?"

She pulled into a small park behind the Almudena, the site of the ruins of the old *Mayrit* city wall.

"We're lucky this site wasn't barricaded off like the rest of the block."

"It's not luck, Tariq. Do you forget who is really in charge here?"

"Of course not."

"Get out."

Amara leapt out of the vehicle and hastened toward the wall. Tariq admired her swift footsteps as she treaded upon the ground of her ancestors.

Above, he could hear the muffled voice of a loudspeaker giving instructions. But a different command stole his attention. It came from within. Again it was saying, "Stay here."

"Tariq, get out here!"

He ignored Amara's plea. His intuition was beckoning him to take notice again. He widened his attention and listened for the message. And indeed it came to him, just as it had come to him earlier that night—it was the Quranic verse he had recited in Arabic to the Order of the Libraries:

Innaa fatahnaa laka
Fath-am mubeenaa...

As these holy words left his lips, Tariq realized their double meaning: the Arabic root *'fath'* was often translated as 'victory,' referring to the victory of Islam over other religions. But this word had another interpretation: *an opening. Fath* meant the opening of a clear path before the seeker; it meant the opening through which spiritual wisdom could enter the heart and win it over. Indeed, *fath* was the act of opening the heart so it might receive love and guidance from the One Power and One Presence known as God, who pours His glory into all life throughout space and time. Through this opening—this sacred victory of the heart—was how the message of peace would be received. He recited the whole verse out loud:

Indeed we have given you
A manifest Opening,
That Allah might perfect
His grace to you
And guide your way clearly

He is the One Who sent down
The spirit of tranquility
Into the hearts of the believers,
That they might have
An increase of faith
Along with their faith

For Allah's are the armies
Of the heavens and the earth

For the Watcher's army, *fath* did not need to come through war or through conversion. The true victory of religion was in its charming of the heart so that all people—regardless of their particular ideologies—might act according to the courageous path of peace.

Tariq let this verse flow into his being like water through the cosmic clock, opening within him the ingenious channel that connects all human consciousness. Its words, like a river, were following their natural path of expression; they were emerging from their channel to be broadcast to the people by water—the very water that bore life to all, sustained all, and became all, streaming itself through and within every being on earth. The verse was water, and the Clepsydra was its opening. Water itself, he realized, was the message! Water was the perfect expression of Nature's divine essence; water was the perfect medium for the heart to make its cosmic communion with all things divine.

Without analyzing any further, the linguist hopped into the driver's seat and started the car. Amara raced toward him.

"What are you doing?"

"Get out of the way!"

Tariq accelerated the car as fast as he could and sped right into the ancient *Mayrit* wall. Sparks ignited. The airbag inflated. And from the humble crack in Madrid's oldest standing edifice, new water sprang forth. It gushed out vigorously at first, but as the wall crumbled it slowed to a more harmonious tempo. Despite the trauma of the impact, Tariq could see into the wall's crack, into the source of the water deep below the ground.

A chamber longer and more intricate than he had ever seen appeared within the crack. Thousands of rusted pipes and canals wound their way around the periphery like tubes leading out of a massive steam engine. At the center was a large, spherical buoy as wide in diameter as a galleon, lying half-submerged in a circular lake of rippling water. Seven iron rods anchored the buoy as it bobbed decisively in the water, pulsating like an immense mechanical heart.

Tariq gazed farther down into the dark lair of the Clepsydra, unable to see completely with his natural eyes. Even what he filled in with his imagination paled in comparison with the true image below. Nevertheless, the Clepsydra's imperceptible contours dazzled the seer with the feeling of being present to the most ancient spiritual relic on earth. And at the same time, its mechanistic valves and arteries sang of impossibly futuristic times.

Water settled and ran in every direction through the Clepsydra. Some streams jetted out like geysers, spewing mist upon the seer's face. Others poured through like viscous lava. In the lowest pools, water was carving out new channels like a glacier, in slow motion, causing the majestic timepiece to claw its way down into the earth.

Indeed the entire machine was a tectonic marvel. It shifted its own foundation in precise and powerful intervals as the centuries ticked by. At its deepest point, the Clepsydra penetrated the earth so profoundly that it appeared inseparable from it; as the earth quaked, so did the Clepsydra. As the earth sang and cried and gasped for peace, so did the Clepsydra. The timepiece was itself timeless, proffering its peaceful, immaculate beat forward and backward, fast and slow throughout all eternity, keeping the right and perfect time for each activity under the sun.

As Tariq beheld Umar Al-Hayek's inspired invention, he could no longer tell whether it was made by God or by human hands. And yet no distinction between the two was needed. All originated from the same divine intelligence, the formless eternity that begat all of time and compelled all hearts to the task of keeping its rhythm. *Each heart lovingly holds onto life for what precious little time it can, until the water of life—the soul—is drained completely and returned to its source.* So vast and intricate was the mechanism for filling and emptying these billions of hearts that Tariq could not sense anymore whether he was himself or some other person. He lost awareness of whether he was living now or in some distant period of the past or future. Time, consciousness, and peace were an infinite reservoir that could be tapped at any moment.

Then, a vision came. The Clepsydra was weaving an image in his mind, like a psychedelic tapestry cloaking his field of view, drawing him into its hidden world of meaning. Colors spiraled outwardly from a dense, geometrical nexus. They curved round and intersected with each other not in an abrupt or diametrical way but in a compassionate, conjoining fashion. Lines and curves meshed and locked together like distant friends reuniting in celebration. Squares and trines and ovals interlaced dynamically before his eyes to create a perfect map of the human psyche. The map, he was certain, could reveal and redefine any element of knowledge that could be thought or imagined.

Watching this tapestry emerge from the Clepsydra, he concentrated his eyes on the image he felt growing inside him. The image of Yusef's face emerged, and yet it was not wholly Yusef. The face was of all true believers who strive to do well by Allah, to keep to the straight path, the steep path. He studied this face, identified with it, knew it. Yusef's smile was the same smile revealed in every Muslim who delights in charity, whether having much or little to spare. Yusef's brow was the sad-turning furrow of hunger during Ramadan's holy fast, and it was the awe-turning crest of power that came on its final night. Yusef's jaw was the jaw of a devotee bent over in prayer, bowing and returning upright in accordance with the *salat*. Yusef's eyes were the eyes of a pilgrim in single-hearted devotion to the one and only Watcher of all, the Guardian of every soul.

As Tariq listened to the Clepsydra's pouring waters, the face transformed into Sister Sabina's. Hers was a face of wisdom and piety and order. In her wrinkled forehead he could read the books of the holy gospels, translated from God's lips to human ears. From her mouth he could draw in holy breaths of the spirit. He could taste the sweet ambrosia of his soul's salvation through wisest of all teachers, the master of prophets whose name was inscribed on the cross—the Lord who had let his heart be born anew. And yet the name and the face of Christ were different in every language, in every religion, each one leaving footpaths from the same knowledgeable source.

Just as the face was changing before his eyes, the names of God were also transposing themselves one after another in brilliant new octaves, each one more resonant than the last.

The sound of water continued, and the face continued to shift. Next it became the image of a smiling crocodile. An expression that radiated an inexplicable peace—an impossible comingling of joy and fear, of toughness and sensitivity, of predation and redemption. Tariq watched as the crocodile's skull sank into a bed of sand and become a fossil. And yet, its mystic heart was still beating! The heart of a hundred million suns rising, spawning, evolving, and sinking into darkness beneath the earth. It was the heart of his ancestors and his lineage, recapitulating every trait and teaching he had inherited and was able to pass on. The heart was the heart of Babel, able to decode every wish, warning, and whisper ever uttered between creatures.

From the sand that covered the crocodile fossil rose one final face: the face of the Silent One. In his wrinkled eyes, Tariq could see traces of war and the imprint of unforgivable violence directed at the native people. He could taste the bitter tears of the First Nations tribes whose villages were destroyed and wiped clean from the land they tended. He could feel the call to take action, to counter terror with words of power, and to give himself up completely to the fight for reconciliation. Indeed, it was *fath*, the opening of the heart, that was the true victory. The Silent One's eyes had already opened to reveal their tears. All that remained to be seen was *fath*, the heart's victory in receiving them.

Upon closer inspection, Tariq realized that the Silent One was not suffering or even lamenting his own death. Instead, he was rolling out a hearty, booming laugh. The Silent One was laughing loudly and deeply, though not at anything particular. He was just laughing! The laughter vibrated through Tariq's skull like sound waves through a tuning fork. It attuned his awareness to the space between words and meanings, to the ultimate reality woven into every message: the reality of water. Water flowed through all things and through all creatures. It became all beings in death and in rebirth. Water was the unifying, immortal connecting threaded through all earthly forms. And now it was no longer a secret, no longer a mysterious language to be decoded. It was all one. Like rain professing itself upon the ocean, the Clepsydra's waters filled the earth with its cosmic message, and everyone listened.

The Clepsydra had opened.

"IN THE NAME OF ALLAH, THE MERCIFUL, THE COMPASSIONATE, LET IT BE KNOWN THAT ALL IS FORGIVEN BY US. EACH MUST FACE HIS OWN SINS ON THE LAST DAY. THIS IS WHY YOU MUST MAKE AMENDS TO GOD, SUBMIT TO HIM, LIVE IN PEACE IN OUR ISLAMIC STATE OR MOVE OUT. THERE WILL BE AN INQUISITION."

At the end of this decree, a loud crash of thunder deafened the streets. Instantly, torrents of rain poured from the pitch-black sky.

"HEAR NOW, IT IS THE WILL OF GOD THAT YOU SURRENDER. IN THE NAME OF ALLAH, THE MERCIFUL, THE COMPASSIONATE."

The crocodiles held their ground as the plaza flooded. Yusef opened his eyes to see what was going on, careful not to give away that he was still alive. But the water, he noticed, was not only coming from the sky. It was also leaking from the Almudena. The entire building was being filled with water.

"The Clepsydra!" the imam exclaimed. "It is beneath the Almudena!"

The sound of the rain became so loud that no one could hear the loudspeaker. One by one, the people stood up and gazed at the cathedral. Water poured from its rooftops and streamed through its windows. No one could look away! To Madrid, the city of the Clepsydra, the sight of water being channeled from its source was a sure sign that God was watching. Their hearts opened.

"TURN OFF THE WATER! IF YOU KILL US, YOUR PRISONERS WILL ALSO DIE! IS THAT WHAT YOU WANT?"

Unable to sustain the pressure of the water, the gates of the Almudena burst open, releasing a river of commingled captors and prisoners to fill the plaza. The crocodiles swam to their rescue, not discriminating one from the other, but taking each one to dry land. The imam smiled inwardly.

Soon, the rain stopped, and the clouds cleared. The Clepsydra's water slowed to a gentle stream. It was nearly morning. The imam stood up and greeted the dawn.

Pulled helplessly by the waves, the leader of the attack surfaced at the imam's feet. He lifted himself up and pulled out an ignition device, which was linked to an explosive pack around his chest. The crowd's hearts skipped a beat.

But Yusef did not tremble. He drew the man in by his cold, shivering neck and embraced him.

"Allahu Akbar," muttered the man as he pressed the button. Yusef didn't flinch. All that exploded from the pack was a single, desperate bubble of water.

"Be at peace," the imam commanded gently. "For it is written that Allah created every living creature from water pouring forth."

"I know what the Quran says," argued the man who persisted in being a terrorist. "It says—"

"But now, you must feel it. Live it. See that your heart is also created anew from this water."

The man put his hand to his own chest. His body fell limp. He could not speak.

"Brother," invited the imam, "let us make peace with Allah. Let us put aside our differences and our preconceptions and understand one another. There is much to do to bring about peace on the Last Day. Will you join us?"

EPILOGUE

"She's late."

Amara looked up and down the grainy walkways of *El Retiro*, expecting someone.

"Not everyone is as punctual as you are, Amara."

"I haven't seen her since she left the hospital and went to Africa to return the crocodiles. And after all this time, I still cannot shake the guilt from my heart. We were stranded together in the Sahara. I left her there to die, Tariq!"

"Then we can be grateful the Magnificent One did not delay in restoring her fully to life," Tariq said lovingly, planting a kiss on the robed one's lips.

"On second thought," decided Amara, "let her be late. I could take Sister Sabina's advice and wait a little longer in this moment with you."

"Would you wait a thousand years to see me?"

"Have you forgotten?" she answered. "I already have."

The sound of water rang throughout the park, and was heard in every footstep and every voice. Ever since the attack on the Almudena, followed by an imam's inspiring show of compassion toward the attackers, all the hearts of Spain overflowed with tranquility. Madrid had taken its place in the world as a beacon of profound tolerance, a sacred refuge for all.

"Amara!"

"Naomi!"

The zoologist hobbled over and embraced the robed one, letting her crutches fall to the ground. Tariq retrieved them for her.

"I'm so relieved you made it back. Returning to Africa must have brought back insufferable memories for you. I still feel guilty and indebted to you for what I put you through."

"I already told you I forgave you. It was a journey I wouldn't have chosen for myself, but it was meant to be, and I am closer to God for it. And I do appreciate you being by my side at the hospital. At first I couldn't believe you had a soft side!"

"Doesn't everybody?" She blushed.

"So, this is Tariq the hero, eh?"

They greeted.

"I'm not a hero," Tariq responded humbly. "In fact, I'm not sure anyone is a hero."

"What do you mean?" asked the surprised zoologist.

"I mean that many people fight to try and change the world through their words and actions, but what they are really fighting against are the weaknesses within themselves. That is what you meant by *jihad*, right, Amara? It is the inner struggle of keeping one's bearings in life despite its challenges, like a pilgrim moves across sand and trenches in order to reach the Mecca of his or her faith. I think pilgrimage is a much better metaphor than heroism. I'd rather describe us all as pilgrims, all struggling toward our own destiny, which is a cause greater than ourselves. To me that is good enough."

"Well said," commended the zoologist as she turned to Amara. "He's a keeper!"

"Naomi is the reason the crocodiles stayed fit for our adventure," Amara interrupted, explaining to Tariq. Then she turned to the zoologist. "Tell me. What was the Mossi people's reaction when you returned the crocodiles?"

Naomi leaned in.

"You won't believe me. Not more than a few hours after Ibrahim and I arrived with the whole troupe, Seogo simply appeared out of the desert! And in the same instant, it began to rain. Streams rushed in and the ponds filled higher than they had ever filled before, according to my hired guide."

The Mystic lives on among them, Amara thought to herself.

"That's amusing," Tariq chimed in. "In the Mossi language the word *seogo* means *rainy season*."

The two women laughed.

"I'm truly glad we've gotten to become friends," Amara commented.

"Me too." Naomi held her crutches to balance and relaxed into them. "So what is next for you, Amara? Is your heart still set on becoming the next great imam?"

She smiled inwardly, recalling the Mystic's lesson on the Tower of Babel.

"Religion is not for everyone. And yet I want to reach everyone. That is why I will continue as an Arabic teacher. By teaching language I will guide people to construct towers of understanding, towers that may, if the learner is so inclined, build up high to the knowledge of God. There are as many ways to reach Him as there are languages in the world."

"If only you could convince Yusef," Tariq wished.

"My brother and I may never see eye to eye on Islam, but we have accepted it and remain loving of each other. How could we not reconcile? Aren't we part of one family?"

"Coming from someone estranged from her family, I say that's exactly the message I think everybody needs," commended the zoologist. "Bringing kindness to a divided world—in my religion we call that *tikkun olam*."

"Tariq, do you know that expression? It comes from the *Kabbala*."

"I know it now."

The three of them made their way to one of *El Retiro's* lavish fountain ponds. Water poured from a sculpture in the center of the pond, while a listening breeze caressed their faces.

There, they exchanged the many tales of their adventures: Amara's meeting with the Mystic and her encounter with Christian the beggar; the zoologist's harrowing trek through the desert and her raft across the Nile; Tariq's exchange with the Quoquamish people and his unofficial baptism at the chapel. Each narrative's breath, whether summoned by fondness or pain, wove together the image of a beautiful life. Their words were genuine and yet also spared the listeners from the secret details too rich and too personal to tell.

After a time, the zoologist bid them farewell. Tariq and Amara stood in front of the pond admiring the water. The hasty Amara broke the silence.

"So, Tariq. Do you have any new words of insight to share?"

Tariq smiled at her and leaned in.

"In fact," he began, "I've been thinking about the Way-maker."

"Go on."

"On the day I met her, she showed me a waterfall that ran like a natural clock."

"What do you mean?"

"I mean, the waves ran through in precise intervals, exactly like a water clock."

"How is that possible?"

"It was the algae! They moved water through time so that it never dried up or overflowed. If you look carefully, the earth does this too. All water in nature is recycled and conserved; it passes through rivers and seas, appears as the morning mist and evaporates just as easily. Just look at how the oceans rise and fall as the moon revolves around the earth. The whole planet itself is a kind of water clock, don't you think? A clepsydra?"

Amara's eyes opened wide. "When I was hovering in space, looking up at the stars, I could see the earth too. And it was exactly as you describe: a cosmic clock! A clepsydra ticking time away with its ever-flowing tides!"

"I think also, maybe," Tariq surmised, "the way to reconcile two opposing worlds is to see that they are really two sides of the same world. Only our terminology makes us think they are different. What the Quoquamish call *Nature* is not merely the earth and trees as we think of it. To them, *Nature* refers to the sacred force that is within the earth and trees and also beyond them. The meaning of the word Nature *includes* the notion of God! To try and tease apart different aspects of spirituality and the forms it takes in the natural world really misses the point of what God and Nature are."

"Good point. There are many names for God. They are names for what is too great for our understanding. They are names for what feeds us, what watches over us and guides us in following our truest path. Isn't *Nature* simply one of these names?"

From the core of Tariq's belly grew a deep inner laughter. *Can it be so simple? Can God and Nature be reconciled simply by expanding the notion of one to include the other? It seems as clear as day!* Tariq pictured the Silent One's face again, and again it laughed back at him. But this time the linguist shared in the laughter and smiled, relieved. *It's so simple! It's utterly laughable how people of different faiths quibble over names and definitions! What word or name could ever hope to represent God's nature without leaving something out? None of them! These names exist to connect us back to the source—a source that needs no words or concepts to express what is most sacred.* The linguist beamed his smile upon Amara's expecting face.

"Don't you agree?" she asked, drawing Tariq out of the silence of his revelation.

"Perhaps," the linguist answered, keeping his silent laughter to himself. "But none of us knows the true name of God. We can only expand our notion of God by adding to it each time we learn a new name or concept related to God, even if it doesn't fit in our current framework."

"That's a fine conclusion for you and me, Tariq, but many people might get lost in what you say. They are only your words, after all."

"That is indeed a paradox," the linguist conceded. "At a fundamental level, all language may be meaningless."

"But language is necessary!" Amara countered. "Especially when you want to share the experience of God with others."

"How do we get from mere words to experience then?"

"Speak from your heart, *Mahatma*," she urged playfully.

"What would the Waymaker say?"

Tariq opened his heart and without thinking gave his response:

> The names of God are like the desert sands,
> Pronounceable when counted grain by grain
> Yet unspeakable when poured from the fist.

The End

Derek Olsen has been enamored by the study of world religions since reading the Bhagavad Gita at age 16. Since then he has traveled to many countries and engaged with diverse spiritual traditions searching for their unifying truths. He has given occasional talks in association with the Unity Church and is grateful for the opportunity to share ideas that have inspired peace, understanding, and coexistence among spiritual seekers everywhere. Derek lives in Tacoma, WA, and teaches middle school Spanish and drama. *Photo: El Retiro Park in Madrid.*

CPSIA information can be obtained
at www.ICGtesting.com
Printed in the USA
BVHW061340180319
542960BV00007B/247/P